ENTER

a world of dreams that music makes real, as real
as the world you know already, and more ecstatic
than anything you can imagine.

EXPLORE

a future that is free of pollution and sickness and
war, a future all yours to shape as you wish, except
for one small price—a price you may not be willing
to pay.

TINTAGEL

The ultimate trip.

TINTAGEL

PAUL H. COOK

A Romance of the Future

BERKLEY BOOKS, NEW YORK

TINTAGEL

A Berkley Book / published by arrangement with
the author

PRINTING HISTORY
Berkley edition / September 1981

ISBN: 0-425-05055-6

A BERKLEY BOOK® TM 757,375

PRINTED IN THE UNITED STATES OF AMERICA

AUTHOR'S ACKNOWLEDGMENT

I think it goes without saying that all of the pieces of music mentioned in this novel actually do exist, with the exception of Shostakovich's *Sixteenth Symphony*. Upon his death in 1975, Shostakovich is believed to have left behind drafts of two movements which would have become his 16th symphony had he lived to complete it. That it is in G Minor is a fabrication of my own.

I would also like to mention that in the three years it has taken to write *Tintagel* Roy Harris, Samuel Barber, and Howard Hanson died. We don't have too many left.

On a lighter note, I would like to extend my appreciation to Pete Zorn, Jim Hawks, and my father, Harlin Cook, for the music they've shared with me over the years. Much of *Tintagel*, as a consequence, is due to them. And lastly, I would like to thank Scott Card for his enthusiasm and Corrinne Hales for her friendship during my stay in Salt Lake City. They both made my life with Uncle Fudd a little more endurable.

PAUL H. COOK
Salt Lake City, Utah, 1981

For Paul and Suzy Kinsey
and Mike Williams

Music

What are you playing, boy? Through the gardens it went
like many steps, like whispering commands.
What are you playing, boy? See, your soul
is entangled in the rods of the syrinx.

Why do you lure her? The sound is like a prison
where loitering and languishing she lies;
strong is your life, and yet your song is stronger,
against your longing leaning sobbingly.—

Give her a silence, that the soul may softly
turn home into the flooding and the fullness
in which she lived, growing, wide and wise,
ere you constrained her in your tender playings.

How she already wearier beats her wings:
Thus will you, dreamer, waste her flight away,
no more may carry her across my walls
when I shall call her in to the delights.

—Rainer Maria Rilke

From *Translations From the Poetry of Rainer Maria Rilke*, ed. by M. D. Herter Norton. New York: W. W. Norton & Co., 1938.

From Sound And Symbol *by Victor Zukerkandl*

It has been said that inner and outer world meet in melodies. It would be more to the point to say "penetrate each other"; a "meeting" of inner and outer world occurs in any experience of our senses. The mode of the meeting is different, however, when it occurs between physical things and our eyes or hands, or between tones and the ear. Eye or hand keeps the physical thing that I meet away from me, makes me conscious of distance, reinforces the separating barrier. Tone penetrates into me, overflows the barrier, makes me conscious not of distance but of communication, even of participation. Our current schema "inner-outer world" is derived solely from one type of encounter—that brought about by the eye and the hand. William James warned—and he·had anything rather than music in mind—" 'Inner' and 'outer' are not coefficients with which experiences come to us aboriginally stamped, but are rather results of a later classification performed by us for particular needs." The needs are those of so-called practical life, our active and passive encounter with the physical world. Only in this encounter do "inner" and "outer," I and the world, face each other like two mutually exclusive precincts on either side of an impassable dividing line. But if what we encounter is nonphysical, purely dynamic—as it happens to be the case of musical tones—the quality "out there" is replaced by the quality "from-out-there-toward-me-and-through-me." Instead of setting off two precincts from each other and presenting them as mutually exclusive, this encounter causes them to penetrate each other, participate in each other. . . . To think of the musical view of the universe as a bridge between the scientific and the religious views is not sheer nonsense.

From Victor Zukerkandl, *Sound and Symbol: Music and the External World.* New Jersey: Princeton University Press, 1956.

"We do not compose; *we are composed.*"
—Gustav Mahler, 1904

CHAPTER ONE

Overture

It was all a question of acceptance.

As his patient burro cleared the rise of the sparsely wooded hill, the old Chinaman realized that sooner or later the veil that blocked his memory would lift and everything would be explained. *Everything*. Until then, all he could do was accept his situation, like accepting the lazy breeze that accompanied him on his journey across the taiga, or those beautiful yellow-black finches that darted between the gnarled evergreen pines.

The old man shivered just as his burro reached the top of the dirt road that breached the hill. But his shivering had nothing to do with the growing coolness of the afternoon as the day waned toward dusk.

He was ill, and he knew it. The disease his body harbored, he realized, was slowly dying out, like a beast in its final death-throes, weakly striking out with only a hint of its former desperate energy. But what it was he suffered from, he didn't exactly know. Blood rushed into his brain, his vision momentarily blurred. A chill had settled about his shoulders like a cloak. His nerves suddenly jolted with the machinegun-fire of tiny spurts of uncontrollable electricity, and the muscles along his spine, and on up to his frail shoulders, jumped and shuddered.

Then came the voices, and the music.

How long this had been going on, he really didn't know. But the music seemed to be with him always. And returning to full consciousness from the grip of this partial amnesia of his was like a fog slowly lifting from the countryside. Only a few details at a time came into focus, and still many of those details remained very much in doubt.

The disease not only affected his body, but seemed to reach very deep into his preconscious mind as well. And just what the voices were that queued in as the music faded, he had absolutely no idea: a million yammering voices, in all the known languages, and some unknown. He felt weak, often nauseated. But as he rode upon the sturdy back of his burro from town to town, he tried to search for an answer to a greater curiosity than his own personal illness.

For weeks now, there had been no people in the villages he passed. The provinces were no longer crowded, teeming. The roads were completely empty, and the woods were filled with only the voices of birds and cries of an occasional beast.

China was empty of people.

And this notion led him to believe that he was insane. Especially when the voices badgered him from within, and the peaceful silences of the Shensi forests battered him from without, for he knew that this was simply not the way things were meant to be.

But rather than ask the one thousand questions that his mind demanded, he merely accepted the situation for the time being. He trundled along the deserted roads and highways, hoping for an end to his search.

He shivered again as the music lurked in the darkest recesses of his mind. It was like the wind through silk curtains. Even without thinking—merely feeling the pulses of energy in his tired body—he knew that something was wrong about all of this. Frightfully wrong.

It seemed so strange that the sky over the industrial regions did not sag with chemical waste, that the air did not burn his lungs. It was equally strange to him that the streams he passed ran ferocious and free. There were even no dams for the furlongs of rice paddies; no dams for the megawatts needed to run an ever-vigilant Republic. Moreover, there were no high-tension wires strung up like cat's-cradles across the provinces. The highways were empty of the common flatbed trucks loaded with industrial equipment, or the tractors lumbering like insects off to harvest. There were no steam- or propane-powered automobiles filling the countryside with the interrupted energy of a growing nation. So much was missing.

The old man coughed, and the burro halted, feeling its rider shake in the seizure of his mysterious ailment.

To calm his mind, the old Chinaman closed his eyes and recalled his Buddhist mantra. His nostrils flared as he drew in the refreshing, bitter air. Soon, perhaps tonight, it would snow. And the snow would fall clean and white, and it would cover the province for hundreds of kilometers and the old man knew that no human foot would trample it. In a land of over three billion inhabitants, there were simply no longer any inhabitants. No one.

Slowly, he breathed.

Somehow, intuitively, he knew that as he inhaled a breath of clean air, that his mantra, and his *pranayam*, his breathing, were the key to all of this. He didn't quite know why. But the concentration on the breathing and his mantra—complex and long in its derivative Mandarin—drew out the voices, and then quieted them. And soon, when he was relaxed enough, the music would vanish as well, and everything would be all right. For a while.

But for the moment he let it all pass from his mind. All the questions, in the end, had their answers. Several kilometers down the road from the hillside, he could see a modest, thatched hut that would be his way station for the night. It stood alone in a gentle clearing. The thought of a warm meal and a place to pass the long night pushed everything aside.

And tonight it would snow. That was something he could easily accept, given the circumstances.

"Yes, Fran," came Christy's voice, over the intercom, relieved. "We're all here."

The overhead fluorescent lights blazed on and the door to the workroom opened noiselessly and Christy entered. She was trailed by two medics who had brought with them a collapsible metal stretcher. In a very businesslike manner, the medics laid Randell out and lifted him onto it. Christy glanced down at the large puddle of blood that Francis Lanier's boots and clothing made.

She gasped slightly, but Lanier waved her off until the medics were just about to leave.

"It's OK," he told her calmly. "There was a lot of blood where I found him."

At that moment, Lanier noticed the two men, each carrying a briefcase, who stood solemnly at the door. The medics were wheeling Senator Randell out, and the other two gentlemen stepped aside to let them pass. Outside Lanier's home, a helicopter waited, its blades churning slowly.

Francis Lanier stood before the two men. They walked into the workroom, looking grim, but also relieved. Lanier addressed them. "I think he'll pull through. I wouldn't worry. It's like this with most of them. But as you can tell, it was a nasty one." He gestured to the blood on the floor.

Blood covered his pants, boots, and his hands. None of it, though, belonged to either Senator Albertson Randell or Francis Lanier, for both had returned unharmed.

The first man, tall and thin with a graying mustache, was Senator Verne Roberts from Massachusetts. He smiled, holding out his hand. "You don't know what this means to us, the service you've done. We can't afford to lose a man like Senator Randell to this awful disease in this day and age. I'm sure you understand. We do appreciate your work."

Lanier momentarily thought back to the world, the strange dreamlike fantasy, from which he had rescued Albertson Randell. The two officials before him couldn't possibly know where Randell had gone upon hearing Bartok's *Concerto for Orchestra* at a concert in New York. *A city in an enormous wall that circled the world. And the blood, the fighting* . . .

"Just see to it that his immunization card is updated when he comes out." He didn't smile, but the two men took no immediate offense. Lanier did not know who the other man before him was. An aide to Senator Roberts? Someone from the Pentagon? "Make sure he always has his Baktropol near. If he's as important as you say he is, you should see to it that he takes care of himself."

Christy showed them out to the helicopter that was impatiently swirling up dust and grass from the two acres that served Lanier as a front lawn.

When she came back in and sealed the door, Lanier looked at her, making a face. "What the hell is that smell?"

She wafted by him, rather nonchalantly. "We had another quake while you were under going after Randell," she announced. "That's part propane and part good old L.A. air you smell."

He opaqued the large picture window that opened up to the small ranch he owned in a secluded arroyo in Malibu Canyon. The window faced the rear of his home, and afforded a calming view of scrub oak, pine, and transplanted dwarf maple. The fields of his uncultivated ten acres paled in the harsh summer sunlight, and had just recently become a fire hazard. But when Congress orders a special helicopter for one of its members, the threat of a brush fire from an emergency vehicle's engines becomes somewhat insignificant.

"Damn," Lanier swore as he unbuttoned his shoulder holster that contained his British-made Malachi. "Look at that." He pointed out the window.

It was supposed to be fog. That was one of the principal reasons he took the land option here in Malibu Canyon, expensive as it was. The mountains usually fought back the stifling smog that poured out of the L.A. basin. But lately it was losing the struggle. Today was one of those days.

Christy tossed some papers on Lanier's desk, pushing back her long blond hair from her shoulders. "You got three emergency runs this morning while you were gone. I turned them all down. About that time, we got the shake. It wasn't too bad, considering. Jack Reynolds rushed down here to patch up the propane tank while you were under. But we couldn't find the leak in the filtration system." She smiled at him. "But it's somewhere."

Lanier sat in an oversized Day-Glo beanbag chair on the floor. It gasped as it enfolded him. He coughed and frowned. "Is it safe to breathe in here?" He turned up his nose.

"Of course it is. Think I'd stay here all morning with those boring medics and those two goons of Randell's from Congress? They were here during the tremor. Didn't bat an eye. You were lucky, though."

"What do you mean?"

"Randell's wife flew into L.A. International just to see if you needed any assistance."

"Great." Lanier rolled his eyes. Christy brought over a tumbler of iced tea.

"And the Hollywood freeway and the Ventura are down in a dozen places, so she's still in Los Angeles. Somewhere."

Very tired, he squinted. "How bad was the earthquake? I can't feel things like that when I'm under. Did it make the scale?"

"News says it was centered up the coast about fifty miles or so. It only reached 6.5. The freeways that went down were loose anyway from last year's shake. Then some pipes broke somewhere in Pasadena, and now there's a big fire. It'll be on the news tonight, I'm sure."

He eased off his bloodstained boots. "Doesn't sound like a 6.5 to me. I suppose they're lying to us about the Big One coming up again."

Christy looked indifferent. "They probably wanted to cover up the failures of the Andreas blasting. They never should have tried blasting the fault lines to relieve pressure. The Big One's sure to happen any day now." She dropped the matter, but grinned all the same, as if it were a joke on somebody and only she knew who.

Lanier always did like her oblique sense of humor. Too bad that his best friend, Charlie Gilbert, married her before he could get his foot in the door. But Taoist that he was, he accepted all things before him. Particularly the funny things. And Christy helped with that. The Andreas blasting wasn't funny, but it did make a few bureaucrats look foolish, especially since it was done in an election year. A lot of people in Washington and Sacramento were suddenly out of jobs because of it. You just can't fool Mother Nature, Christy said.

"Did you shut down the transmission?"

"As soon as it played through. How was it? He looked pretty ragged."

Although it was a fifteen-minute flight by helicopter into Thousand Oaks, Lanier knew that he'd have the medical read-out on Albertson Randell by the end of the day regardless of his own judgement of Randell's condition, mental or otherwise.

"Well," he began, "I had done a Bartok only once before."

"Right," she said. "The *Sonata for Two Pianos* last year. It was the mayor of New York, I believe."

"That's the one. But this time it wasn't nearly so strange as the mayor. Then again, I guess it was." He rubbed his eyes. He related to her his mission to retrieve Albertson Randell from the throes of Liu Shan's Syndrome. He told her of the city within a huge wall in which he had found Randell. And the river of blood.

Christy frowned disapprovingly. "Mrs. Randell, on the video, didn't seem at all happy about having you do this in the first place. She said that he could stay put for all she cared. I guess the gossip has gotten to her, too."

Lanier cranked himself up from the bright yellow beanbag chair and walked over to the liquor cabinet. The assorted bottles were only for his visitors, or the families of his patients, since his particular talent involved having a vibrationally attuned body that had to be clear of any drugs. He only allowed himself a light tea that he had imported from Britain every year, which was fine either hot or cold.

He clinked some extra ice into his tumbler.

"Well," he said, "We've gone through the 'hidden' lives of our Congressmen before and it shouldn't come to anyone's surprise that they fool around as much as anyone. It just wasn't important to me since I don't particularly care for his politics. He was just another mission."

He thought for a minute, sipping tea. There were many people in Randell's fabulous world-girdling wall, most of them women. Lanier couldn't recall recognizing anyone familiar. If any were images of Randell's alleged lovers, he had no way of knowing. He set down his drink.

"I was only doing my job. He could've been a street cleaner for all I care."

Lanier's house was extraordinarily quiet. It had to be. Back up in this valley was one of the few places in southern California where he could find a place that didn't vibrate with the incessant shudderings of freeway traffic. The canyon itself still only accommodated one highway and boasted enough side-detours and smaller canyons that one could get away if one tried hard enough.

And Lanier tried and succeeded, now that being a Stalker— one who was immune to the Syndrome—brought him enough money from the government. No longer did he have to live and work in Los Angeles proper to earn his keep as a real estate counselor.

He looked across the room to the indiscreet console of equipment built into the wood-paneled wall to see what the indicators held. Everything was still. No vibrations anywhere that would disturb his meditations.

"Any other damage, other than the ventilation?"

Christy saw him glance toward the delicate instruments. "No, none. The traffic dropped to almost nothing, since most of the interchanges back in town are pretty gummed up. But, no. I checked as soon as the tremor died down."

He walked over to check the gauges. It was essential that his "transmission room" be as quiet as possible when he worked, since the crudest vibrations interfered with his "stalking."

Christy read his expression as he checked.

"It would have been bad if the music stopped in the middle, wouldn't it," she asked.

Lanier merely nodded, taking another swig of tea.

"Well," he began quietly, "I hope the 'copter makes it through all the shit in the air. It probably would have been suicide if they tried to wheel him out of here in an ambulance. What a wreck he was."

"Before or after?"

He looked at her. "Very funny." Christy was no politico either.

But Lanier was still thinking. *If the music being sent from Christy's transmission board into the transceiver in my ear wasn't recorded fully, I wouldn't have gotten to Randell. Or . . .*

He let the thought pass. It hadn't happened to him yet, but the "experts"—if ever there could be said to be any—said that it was just possible to get stuck in the mind of a man lost to Liu Shan's Syndrome and forever wander the world that mind had created for itself. But being a Stalker, immune from the Syndrome's effects, he didn't believe a word of it.

The idea was only unpleasant when Lanier reconsidered the river of human blood inside the wall city. When he had chased the fleeing Randell outside onto the grassy, sloping piedmont, he knew that he could have spent the rest of eternity under that wonderfully blue sky and not minded a thing. Except that he would be there with Albertson Randell and Bartok's *Concerto for Orchestra.* As a Stalker, he could come and go as he pleased, fortunately.

Lanier shivered suddenly. Christy, about to go back into her own office in the rear of the house, caught sight of it. Lanier gently put the glass of iced tea down.

"Again? So soon?" she asked.

"No, I was only thinking back to the place where I found Senator Randell."

"You shouldn't do that. It might bring it on again."

"I know," he smiled. "But not too likely. Not with me, anyway. I wouldn't be paid so much for being able to do what I can if I would slip into the Syndrome as easy as most." He paused, almost as if catching his breath. Christy watched every nuance his face made. "But sometimes..."

"Yes," she said. "I know." They looked at each other momentarily. They both understood. Christy knew all too well what Liu Shan's Syndrome did, and what Fran Lanier always underwent to pull people out of it.

Two years ago, when Lanier moved out to southern California to retain his anonymity as a Stalker, his best friend and lawyer, Charlie Gilbert, called him up as soon as the video was installed. He had a problem.

His girlfriend, Christy, whom Lanier only barely knew at the time, had succumbed to Liu Shan's Syndrome at a modern dance concert at Palo Alto. Everyone in the theater was surprised, since to get into the hall for the performance in the first place, patrons had to have a clean immunization card. Even at the time, Lanier was swamped with government rescue requests that ranged from bishops to princes, to the sons of millionaires. Even farmers and laborers in the Yucca Valley had tried to track him down. A waitress from Jackson Hole, Wyoming, needed him to find her mother. Everyone needed him, it seemed.

For Francis Lanier was one of eighteen hundred of the most sought-after Americans of the century.

Liu Shan's Syndrome fed off the emotional variances of its victims, especially when spurred on by any form of music. And everyone likes music. Lanier was one of a small community of people immune to the disease that manifested itself as Liu Shan's Syndrome. When individuals would succumb to its effects and literally vanish from sight, he would meditate on the music and "go under" to return as many people as he could to the real world. In times like these, this usually meant scientists and politicians first, and special cases second.

Yet the Syndrome was relatively new to the west coast of the United States when Christy went under. In his sudden shock, Charlie Gilbert himself nearly vanished where he sat next to her in the theater, enjoying the rare performance of the ballet company, taking in the fragrance of the perfume he had only that day bought for her: the dance company had come out in semi-shadows, and the small touring orchestra unfolded the fragile melodies of a nearly forgotten work. The work was not originally meant for the dance theater, but it had become the strategy recently—almost by governmental decree—to combine music with some other medium in order to provide some kind of distraction and retain more control over the emotional states of the audience.

In the beautiful, lilting second movement, one of the male dancers, symbolizing Autumn, reached sweepingly over the sleeping form of a frail young woman. He lifted her on balmy winds. He carried her through dreams of the passing seasons.

And Christy Cooper sighed, then vanished with a sudden *pop!* as air rushed in to fill the space she occupied next to Charlie.

The audience went wild with fright. The orchestra stopped and the house lights showered everyone with a bold, vivid luminescence. The dancer in the arms of Autumn swooned.

At that time, vanishings were quite uncommon, at least insofar as the general public was concerned. This sort of thing only happened to "other people," but not here. Not in healthy Palo Alto. The disease only struck those more emotionally unbalanced than the rest of the citizenry. The crazed and the troubled in mental institutions were the first to go. But no one paid any attention to them. They just weren't in their beds when morning came, their radios having played all night.

But then the bacterium that caused the Syndrome began working its way up the ladder of emotional instability as the disease mutated or spread.

And Charlie Gilbert wandered the streets for the best part of the night, confused. Then, embarrassed and apologetic, he rushed to the nearest video to summon the aid of Lanier, whom he knew to be immune to the disease. He knew that Lanier could succumb and not succumb at the same time. Lanier, like everyone else, suffered from the disease, but could prevent himself from vanishing. Or he could succumb—vanish from the very earth—and return at will. And no one but a Stalker could do this.

Francis Lanier had, just moments before Charlie Gilbert's call, returned from fighting Seminoles in central Florida ca. 1870 in an odd phasing of Rachmaninoff's *Prelude in G*, rescuing a bitter industrialist bent on self-destruction. After a chase through steaming everglades and a decent burst from his Malachi machine pistol that fired rounds of anesthetic needles, the man returned to Lanier's workroom quite unconscious, but safe. But this was not until the man, in his flight of manic despair, had managed to secure sixteen blood-matted Indian scalps. The Defense Department expressed its gratitude to Lanier in an eloquent communiqué which he summarily trashed. Killing Indians to the tune of Rachmaninoff was not Lanier's idea of a good time.

Tired as he was, and soaking wet from the Florida swamps, the plight of Christy Cooper seemed to rally his interest and strength.

By the time Charlie had found his way to Lanier's Bel Air home, he had calmed down somewhat. Lanier left him nursing a quart of the best Scotch he owned, and assured his friend that the best would be done. He only hoped that it wouldn't have anything to do with angry Seminole Indians.

Ben-Haim. *Orchestral Suite: From Israel*. Second movement. It was an unusual work, quite nationalistic, very beautiful, and nearly forgotten. It was from the middle of the last century and was just the thing that one could easily lose oneself in, if one were in the proper mood, romantically speaking. Lanier grinned to himself as he entered the workroom alone: only a person in love—*deeply* in love—could lose herself so well in such a piece of music.

Lanier dimmed the lights. He sat on the floor in a half-lotus position at the center of a circled area that was tiled in the form of a Tibetian mandala—lines, circles, and stars, pointing to an illuminated center that itself was a five-pointed star. Lanier began his inward concentration.

In the other room, Charlie Gilbert drank himself silly, as the console silently transmitted the crystalline sonic-wafer of Paul Ben-Haim's work into the transceiver implanted in Lanier's right earlobe. Lanier didn't want Charlie himself to succumb to the Syndrome, knowing full well what grief, anxiety, and twelve-year-old Scotch could do. So he played the piece silently. He concentrated on emptying his mind of all thoughts, all images, letting it fill with the muted tones of the second movement of the orchestral suite.

Even through the soundproofed walls, Charlie felt the sudden collapse of air as Francis Lanier vanished. He swallowed a double shot in one easy motion, thinking of Christy—wherever she was.

What experts there were at the time said that Liu Shan's Syndrome was many things, but no one had a firm grasp on what it actually did to the nervous system. For it seemed that the Syndrome affected more than just the body.

The eighteen hundred known Stalkers privately insisted to the government authorities that the answer would lie in a total rethinking of Western man's attitude toward science.

Even though for thousands of years sages and wise men of the East had been saying it, it wasn't until the Unified Field Theory, once begun by Einstein himself, was validated in the previous century that a simple fact had become known. Reality was nothing more than a certain series of vibrations to which every person on the planet was attuned. Everything is energy, there is no such thing as matter: it all reveals itself in frequencies of vibrations only the most sensitive can see or feel.

And the mystics—the *walis*, the *sadgurus*—say our world is literally crisscrossed with other worlds beyond our normal perceptions, some of which we enter when we sleep, some of which we enter when we die. There are higher worlds of higher beings, lower worlds of lower beings. Only the saints of the world religions have had access to them.

Until now. Until one day in the highlands of China, a man named Liu Shan, a renegade popularly associated with the People's Democratic Revolutionary Front, developed an airborne bacterium that had a lifespan of twenty days, which would merely heighten the neurosis of anyone who inhaled or ingested any of the culture. He and some colleagues of his, it is said, in an attempt to undermine the government of Peking, turned the bacterium loose, to blow first over southeastern Asia, then to Japan, home of the world's largest suicide rate. Then on to America, and eventually Europe. It would die down before reaching the western stretches of the Gobi Desert. The People's Democratic Revolutionary Front would survive, unaffected, to create a new China, and a new world. Or so it is said.

Everyone—including Lanier, Charlie Gilbert, and Christy Cooper—became quite familiar with Liu Shan's infamous disease. And they soon realized its implications when they tried to recall a classic blues song, or an old Bob Wills and His Texas Playboys favorite. These were now outlawed because old-style country western and blues appealed to the strongest, deepest emotions. The Syndrome fed off those pits of despair. For what happened came as much as a surprise to the revolutionary Chinese as it did to the health authorities world over: the bacterium mutated horribly into a more powerful strain when it mixed and breeded rather plentifully with the industrial air-pollutants over southern Japan. No one could foresee the consequences of such an accident.

In Kyoto, only a few days after the disease was flown into the upper troposphere in Chinese "weather" balloons, the Syndrome manifested itself as thousands of individuals, watching a particularly sad and musical show of local historic significance on their television sets, simply vanished from the face of the earth.

The experts testify that the disease brings on a slight giddy feeling; nervousness that produces a blurring or unfocusing of the eyes. Next comes a humming in the brain. But most importantly, when one is listening to music, the sadness or despair one is feeling—if it is the kind of music that calls for melancholy—wells into a great pit of unhappiness. The mind drifts. It begins to let the music create fantasies. And the disease, coupled with the vibrations of the music and the elements of emotional strain, thrusts the listener literally out of this world and into whatever individual heaven or hell of romantic despair the mind devises.

And in Kyoto, Japan, this meant *thousands*. Vanished.

Yet, not everyone succumbed immediately. Those who were more stabilized never did. But the disease fed off emotional states, even heightened them whenever music was listened to. And all minds are full of simple fantasies. Some of them tell of sadness. Others of love. There are those of hatred and revenge, and those of patient heroism and sacrifice.

All of this was made more terrifying in the fact that these "worlds" were just as real as anything the Syndrome's victims left behind. They were full of people or demons, and anyone could kill or be killed in them and no one in the real world would know the difference.

So when Charlie came to Lanier for help, all of these things were present in his mind. Lanier, because he was a Stalker, a *rescuer*, knew them to a greater degree than Charlie.

Thinking of Christy Cooper and listening to Ben-Haim's *Orchestral Suite: From Israel*, Francis Lanier left the real world and found himself suddenly beside a large pond in a garden of incredible proportions. He focused on the music itself.

To a Stalker, the minds of individuals who have succumbed to the disease cast out slight vibrations, mostly of terror or confusion, and as such act like beacons which can be traced. The longer a person stayed in a world of his or her creation, the less the vibrations were pronounced—the harder they were to locate.

But Christy's despair was quite strong. She was somewhere very near.

Lanier looked around. Nowhere on the earth could there ever have existed such profound beauty. Plants and flowers of all colors and descriptions surrounded him with a pleasant freshness that a field or a meadow in the springtime might bring. Rhododendrons, leafy ferns, snapdragons, lupine, phlox, daisies. But above him was the most startling feature of them all. Instead of clouds, there floated in the sky large, flat pieces of earth! Each one of them contained a hanging garden, like the one on which Lanier had traced Christy.

Lanier walked over to a slight rise in the earth just beyond the pond beside which he had just appeared. Francis Lanier always disguised himself as a priest, wearing a long coat, feeling that the sight of a priest would be inoffensive or, at best, innocuous, to the eyes of a lost and wandering victim of Liu Shan's Syndrome. He hoped now that Christy, in her misery, would not be distraught at his presence.

He listened to the beautiful music that penetrated everything around him. She was near.

He walked through some small bushes and leaped back abruptly. the garden ended and Lanier faced empty space. This garden was just one of many floating inexplicibly in the sky, almost like clouds. And beneath the hovering cup of the garden was nothing. There was only an infinity of blue sky, above and beneath him, and everywhere he could look were the drifting gardens.

He pulled back with a sudden rush of vertigo. He listened to the music, feeling out the vibrations that had coalesced into this unbelievable universe. The pond was about thirty meters across, and at the farthest end was a small waterfall. It was beside the waterfall, clouded in a slight mist, where he found Christy, weeping.

Lanier knew that Christy's mother had just recently died, and the tenor of the music suggested that her grief was also part of her despair. He had to be careful. The bench on which she sat was also very close to the edge of the garden, and the music was sadly beautiful.

She looked up tearfully at him as he approached, seeing only a priest. Not recognizing Lanier—so deep in her melancholy was she—she could only speak of her sadness to him. The disease had distorted her perceptions. To her, it was all like a dream.

Cherry blossoms drifted about them in the breeze like a gentle, crimson snowfall. The sun canted thin shafts of light through the feathered edges of stately bamboo above them. Lanier could feel her unhappiness. The vibrations of the music, its sonorities, gave everything about them an uncanny sense of reality, like those dreams when one is utterly convinced that one isn't dreaming. . . .

The cherry blossoms gave off the right fragrance, the right colors. This *was* real. He caught a petal between his fingers as they fell about the two of them. It was as soft as a moth's wing and cool to the touch.

He gently lifted her up off the marble bench where he had found her and spoke softly to her. She seemed as delicate and as sad as the flower blossoms that dangled in her hair.

He urged her to drink from the small vial of light-colored liquid he had pulled from his medicine pouch on his belt. She didn't resist. Then they walked slowly through the tendrils of lime-green creepers as she relaxed. Lanier imagined the worst possible scenario for this Eden: the music reaches its lowest depths of despair and the lover throws herself off the edge of the floating garden. He had to be careful, always. He could control himself, but his patients often had minds of their own—and hearts of their own.

Suddenly, Christy collapsed beside him. He caught her as the garden began to fade. The tall palms vanished. The cherry orchard drifted away.

The next thing Christy knew was that she was on the floor of Francis Lanier's workroom, in the center of the mandala, and Lanier was slapping her wrists. She came wide awake, no longer suffering from the disease's spell.

When Charlie heard the commotion through the door, he knocked into the doorway—all two hundred and ten pounds of him—his corduroy jacket considerably dribbled with precious Scotch. He was supremely drunk.

Seeing Christy unharmed, he grinned hugely, his red hair surrounding his face like a halo.

"Hi," he giggled, slightly embarrassed. "Where ya been?" And promptly fell flat on his face.

CHAPTER THREE

⟨⊙⟩

The Lament for Beowulf
Howard Hanson

Lighting up the first of the day's endless progression of cigarettes, the President said to her early-bird aide, "Ransom told me last night at Senator Paulson's reception that filter-masks will be required when we hit Chicago for the Women's Caucus." She peered from eyes hardly awake at Ken Collins. "Is that true?"

She inhaled fiercely, illuminated in an aura of smoke. The corners of her quick, brown eyes still flaked with sleep, and the ropey imprint of bedsheets laced her skin where she slept soundly on the single twin bed that was, by her own decree, never made in the morning.

"Yes, Katie," Collins said, looking perhaps too wide awake at that early hour. The sun hadn't even risen, but Katie Babcock perversely admired Ken's sense of efficiency and rudeness. She privately thought he detested being under the country's first female President, but the job called for intelligence and craft, and the shelving of personal obsessions in order that the required dirty work got done. Ken Collins was her best man.

"That's not going to look too good to the environmentalists." She pulled back a stray black-gray lock from her eyes, not really caring how she looked in her open nightgown. At forty-nine, she had yet to lose some of her youth, since she had divorced early and had, as a consequence, never had any vitality burned out of her by fierce lovers and husbands and a generation of nagging children under wing. She had a sister in Michigan, married and with one child, who looked years older than she, but was, in fact, much younger.

She got up, finally, from the ruin of covers and quilts, and lifted the chenille robe from the eighteenth century divan at the foot of her bed. Paraphernalia from last night's reception draped the small couch.

Ken Collins stood at a respectable distance with a mute expression on his face, unable to prevent himself from seeing the open nightgown flutter even further apart just before she wrapped herself in the bathrobe.

Why, God, didn't they keep Janet Walen on to do this? he thought, standing there is his frustration and decency. He lifted his schedule sheet before him.

"Uh, Katie. We've got two . . ."

She waved him off. "I know. The breakfast with the Iraqi ambassador, then the security briefing. What the hell time is it?"

Glancing at his watch, he said, "It's 5:30. You're running a trifle late."

She slippered into the massive and overly elaborate bathroom. Her fuzzy pink house slippers hissed along the carpet like two fussy angoras.

"Be back in a minute," she announced, hardly considering his presence as she vanished into the imperial bathroom.

Outside in the hallway, two other presidential aides stood waiting. Collins slipped out and signaled to them. They were having coffee.

"She's late as usual. It'll be about a half an hour if we're lucky."

Rita Hanks sighed, somewhat relieved. "Well, that's all right. The ambassador is used to it, although we can't resched-ule the briefing if she putters around with him for too long. The Joint Chiefs will be in conference the rest of the day."

They could hear the shower thundering through the open

door. Rita Hanks, Pentagon spokesperson, and Beverly Silva, the President's personal secretary, glanced into the bedroom as the maids scurried about, and understood.

Rita stared at the Press Secretary with a mixed look of envy and ire. "You know what went on last night?" she asked Ken irritably.

"No idea at all. It's none of my business. She just came in late. That's all I know." He wore a constantly naive expression on his face that seemed to tell more of innocence than guile, which gave one the impression that he was not the Wall Street-analyst-turned-Press-Secretary he wanted to appear, but was actually a big pussycat.

"I'll bet," Beverly Silva said cuttingly, though smiling to herself as she drew out a slim cigar from her purse. "And I'll bet the *Post* and the other scandal sheets get wind of it before we do. Who was she with last night?"

Ken smiled conspiratorially at Beverly. He always did like the way she pursed her lips when she was about to smile. There was a grand element of sexuality in her gestures that functioned, to his way of thinking, like the lower part of an iceberg, protruding just the slightest hint of its reality above the surface. And he secretly believed that he was put in their midst as a test, having something vaguely to do with party loyalty or perhaps punishment for crimes committed against womankind in former incarnations.

But Collins knew that to be off-balance, emotionally, in any political situation, meant suicide. And it was rough in the midst of these women. Sometimes Rita Hanks, dark-haired and dark-eyed, would brush too near him in the corridors of the White House, drawing behind her a scent of Catastrophe, that illegal perfume that catalyzed male hormones and adrenaline to dangerous levels, and he often believed that he could burn up on the spot. But all these special women would probably do would be to stick marshmallows on twigs taken from the White House lawn and roast them in the fire of his passion. Catastrophe, like so many good things in life, had been illegal for years, but when filter-masks became part of daily apparel, no one seemed to complain. It was one of life's little pleasures.

But it was Beverly Silva who secretly had his heart ever since she graciously threw up in his lap in the limousine behind the Washington Hilton at the inaugural ball.

These women, he thought, recalling what an old friend of

his had said: God put women on this earth to make Self-realization for man more trouble than it should be. Heaven was a long way away.

Chauvinist that he was, he smiled at Beverly. "I don't know who dropped her off, but Senator Randell picked her up last night. Big thing over at Compton's. Jet set, and the lot." He grinned ridiculously, looking back toward the bathroom. "I decided not to go to this one for a change."

"Randell," Rita muttered. "So he got retrieved OK?"

Collins leafed through a fold of papers, momentarily serious. "Yeah, this time it was Lanier. Francis Lanier from Malibu Canyon, California. He's one of the best, so they chose him." He looked up at the women. "It was expensive all the way around."

"Why is that?" Rita queried.

"They had to fly a psychologist into Fort Meyer after Randell came out. He made Randell confess."

"Confess?" Both Rita and Beverly glowed with interest, almost like Dubuque housewives bent toward the latest neighborhood poop over clotheslines. No one liked Randell and everyone liked Katie.

I don't believe this, Ken thought to himself. But he did enjoy the attention.

"Now that would be telling," he said. But he leaned over as one of the maids breezed by with a tray of coffee and small donuts for the President.

"Smeared with adultery and scandal. Even you-know-who . . ." *Now who's gossiping*, he said to himself.

But the women understood.

Collins frowned. "But don't let any of this out. It isn't quite settled yet. I'll handle the information flow and the scandal sheet questions. But keep a lid on it."

Katie bloomed from the bathroom in a healthy cloud of steam, massaging her short hair with a towel. The maid lowered the tray and Katie grabbed a steaming cup of coffee, lighting up another cigarette.

She caught the expression on Collins' face, and, after looking over to Rita and Beverly, she instinctively knew what the two of them now knew, thanks to Ken Collins.

At least he's up on the news, she thought. "Well, I see word spreads fast these days."

"I think, Ms. President," Rita started rather formally with

an awkward sense of protocol, "that you'd be best advised to keep a low profile as far as Senator Randell is concerned. He's political dynamite and you know it."

Katie Babcock just smiled wickedly.

"What she means, Katie, is," Beverly began, "we don't know what made Randell succumb to the Syndrome. No one seems to. At least, if anyone does know, they aren't talking. But it has to be pretty bad. I'm sure there's more to his going under than the business over his personal finances and his marriage. If what Ken says about that scandal is true..."

Katie waved her cigarette about. "No one knows what Albertson Randell is up to, mentally, except that Stalker, Lanier. But he's no shrink." She looked at Collins standing with his arms folded behind his back, waving his roster. *At parade rest,* she thought. *A good soldier.*

"Ken, make a note," she said to him. "I want to meet Lanier personally. Find the time. It might be revealing. And try to get a meeting with any of the other known Stalkers. If the Syndrome is spreading as much as they tell me it is, then I want to know how they work. Must be fascinating."

"Right, Katie," he said firmly, jotting on the sheet.

"And if you must know," she announced to everyone present in the bedroom, "Albertson says he's cured."

Katie removed her robe quite unselfconsciously, displaying a lithe, tight body in bra and slip. "He's now on an increased dosage of Baktropol, since Baktropol is the only thing that seems to work against this disease." She puffed on her cigarette. "Even if it is only temporarily effective against the Syndrome. As long as he's on it, Lanier says in his report that Randall won't succumb anymore. He may go crazy, but at least he won't disappear like the rest." She paused, thinking for a moment. "And Randell, despite his personal life, is one of the most powerful men in this country. And the country *does* need him."

But Ken wondered just what she meant by "the country." He turned and headed out of the room.

"Oh, yes, Ken," Katie called back to him. "Check the scandal sheets and see how I'm doing. After the luncheon today, I've *got* to see that Greek about the munitions swindle he pulled in Britain."

"I thought you were going to let the CIA deal with him."

"Can't. It's too sticky. I think I can get around both the CIA and the Department of Justice. We can use a mind like his and his connections. Get him."

The President smiled, then busied herself with her morning wardrobe, humming a tune.

Rita cast a quick glance at Ken Collins as he was leaving. Then she looked over at Beverly. Katie Babcock was humming a tune, and she rarely hummed or sang. She was always serious and reserved.

"At least she seems happy," Rita whispered aside to Ken at the door.

"It must be love," he winked, not at all serious. "She probably got laid last night."

"What an awful thing to say," Rita shot back, halfway scolding him.

But the humming concerned them both.

He went on, out of earshot from the President. "They say the more stable you are, the less of a chance you have of going under. I can recommend a checkup, but she shouldn't be singing. She'll have the damn tune running through her head all day long. That could cause some problems. If the pressure gets too rough at the briefing, she could lapse. She isn't immune. Nobody is, these days."

He looked concerned.

Rita glowered at his easy concern, mistaking it for insincerity. "You, the expert. Just watch out for her. If you see the signs, let me know. I can buzz a Stalker just in case. We can't have the President of the United States popping out of sight never to be found again."

"Oh, she'd have to be in the presence of the original piece of music being performed. And whatever it is," Ken said, "it will probably be outlawed sooner or later."

They could hear her humming to herself as she walked in and out of the bathroom preparing herself for the day. Her voice had a rich timbre to it and filled the room pleasantly. She seemed very much at ease with herself.

Ken remarked, "Well, it doesn't sound like the blues. To me, anyway."

Rita looked worried. The President *did* have an ulcer caused by nerves and tension.

Collins patted her affectionately on the shoulder. "Don't worry. The Stalkers are busy, but you're talking about the head honcho in these parts. They'd come running."

"Sure," she said bitterly. "If not for money, then for the attention."

"I don't think they'd do it for the fame. It would put them out of business. They really don't like working with us too much. Most don't like the political mind, and most like to work anonymously." He had a copy of Lanier's report on Albertson Randell. "They say that politicians are sick."

Rita mused. "It's just too bad the blues are illegal now. Just about everything is these days." She coughed. "Even going without a filter-mask on the eastern seaboard."

Outside, they could hear the wind grating against the thick, bulletproof window, as if grains of sand were being tossed around in the air.

Collins frowned, looking out the window. A brown haze concealed any light that the new day was bringing upon Washington. "It's that goddamned aeroplankton again. We're going to get a blow today. I had forgotten the forecast."

He turned. "I *do* have to get a few things done before Katie gets to the ambassador." He waved at the two aides.

Katie swirled into their midst as he clicked down the hall.

"I like that boy," she said to them. "Might make something out of him before it's all over." She wandered over to her makeup table.

Beverly strolled over. "Katie"—she looked down at the bottles of makeup and fingernail polish—"we can get you a professional for this."

"No," she said, struggling to blink a particle of eyeliner out of her eye. "I've been thinking of giving up the whole thing, anyway. I'm not a queen, you know. I don't need someone to wipe my ass when I'm perfectly capable of doing it myself."

Rita and Beverly glanced at each other, surprised, as Katie Babcock blinked before the wide mirror.

"It's just not worth it," she finished, not looking at either of them.

She rose and walked into the wardrobe closet, leaving her two astonished aides behind.

She closed the door silently. *A professional*, she thought, shaking her head. *Just what I'd need to keep me alive. Make things easier. As if a makeup woman would solve all my problems.*

She knew that everyone in the country—everyone with some kind of political muscle—was gunning for her, either literally or politically. She had two more years of her first term to go, and that would provide enough shooting space, enough space for *something* to go wrong. It would be time enough for some typical female weakness to appear. Which, she knew, everyone expected. After all, the first woman President in the history of the Republic had more than just an image of the presidency to maintain. She was still a woman, and sometimes the burden of her success or failure occasionally seemed to overwhelm her. It was enough of a task to simply get the work of the office done, and get Congress on her side when, daily, it seemed to be slipping from her grasp.

She had enough to worry about.

In these first two years of her administration, she had scored three near-assassinations, the most recent one occurring last month during a reception in New York, where she had served initially as a senator. She had barely swung the presidential election without the official blessing of organized labor in the country, a feat no one thought realistically possible, particularly for a headstrong woman. Then there had been two corporate oil scandals that under normal circumstances wouldn't have reached all the way to the White House if her ex-husband hadn't had a finger in the pie. There were rumors. And the country had been getting progressively more dispirited ever since the African War ended a number of years ago, right at a time when everyone was eager to forget the lessons of history and just as eager to taste imperialism's seductive nectar again. Her studies in law and geopolitics—coupled with prudent common sense—showed her just how much of a con game government policy had always been. It was a game, she soon found, for which she had a remarkable skill.

Then came the personal touches to her administration. A divorcée was in the White House. That was scandal enough. In her late forties, Katie Babcock—née Katie Shull—had become one of the youngest Presidents to take office. She still retained her thin figure and much of that stern facial beauty that made her former marriage the modern fairy tale into which it had degenerated. Politics had always contained a certain amount of myth making, and charisma was something that the White House hadn't seen the previous century.

Still, she was honest, and never truly lost her devotees. Her workers, her coterie of like-minded progressives were determined, this time, to make the System work.

Like all the others . . . Katie thought to herself bitterly. You start out wanting to do so much good, then the Lady of the Lake withdraws her offer and things quickly become *real*: a four-year term of shit-catching and shit-flinging. She was the woman in the middle. And she often thought that whoever was on top—for it never seemed to be her—had a very peculiar sense of humor.

Yet she survived her spell in the Senate and her first two years as President with only a small ulcer to show for it. She was tough, the Iron Lady, the warlord of the White House: at press conferences, or any public appearance, she smiled when she chose and spoke to whom she pleased. She never did see the office of the President as a master of ceremonies. She had no jokes to tell; only work to do. And she made enemies very easily.

The Iron Lady bore her stature well her first year, a year of global disaster. The Russian wheat crop failed completely. Diseases that the WHO had declared eradicated from human history had begun appearing in the stagnant Mediterranean area. Worst of all was the Indian experiment in cultivating a genetically altered form of zooplankton which produced tiny, almost microscopic pockets of hydrogen that allowed for the organism to become airborne. Working out of a starving Calcutta, the scientists there thought that the aeroplankton would bolster the world's dwindling food supply. Farmed in the high valleys of the Tibetan Himalayas, the aeroplankton now drifted hundreds of kilometers thick in enormous fronts all over the world due to a jet stream knocked off course by a Chinese nuclear test. Katie had a hard time being friendly to India anyway, with their official starvation policies and suicide lotteries. And thanks to the aeroplankton, everyone now had to own, and wear during the aeroplankton storms, filter-masks conveniently designed to filter out the microorganism and forty-seven varieties of industrial pollutants. And this included, for future use, radioactive wastes in the air.

On her nightstand lay two of the filter-masks, the best American ingenuity could design. With easy-to-replace mouth-pieces, they also had polarized lenses for indoor and outdoor convenience. They also came with adjustable straps. These were custom made.

She hefted one of the masks, the Rockwell "Warrior Blue" model. Its plastic frame was meant to withstand any and all possible corrosive elements that could be carried in the air. It was guaranteed to last a lifetime. Just whose lifetime they meant, she had no idea.

She looked at herself in the mirror with the thing on. The roundness of the mouthpiece stuck out about four centimeters and gave her the appearance of one of the soldiers from the First World War. Wearing it, she was featureless, anonymous. Only her eyes showed.

Death masks, she thought suddenly, and whipped it off.

She tabbed the intercom. "Rita, get me the scoop on the aeroplankton drifts for today. And any projections for the week. We've got Chicago to think about."

"Right," came Rita's firm voice.

Katie leaned back, staring at the clock.

"Damn," she muttered. *Time*, she thought, *there's never enough time....*

She was just barely awake, and three cups of coffee were necessary in the first stages of consciousness. She was now in the second stage. The gathering-of-the-wits-and-clothing stage. From the soft chair before the mirror, she looked into the enormous closet at the various dresses and outfits that hung on the racks. She got up.

As she stood, she rose a little too quickly and took on a sudden rush of blood from her head. Teetering on the brink of blacking out, she thrust forward a hand for support and banged a closet door shut. She dropped back into her chair and waited for the tiny lights behind her eyes to twinkle back into oblivion.

But they didn't.

Light-headed and woozy with the temporary euphoric rush, she suddenly felt a chill at the back of her neck. And suddenly the little tune she had woken up with, and hummed for the first few minutes after her morning encounter with her aides, returned soothingly to her mind. And her mind reeled.

Then came the vibrations, a mellow drifting. One part of her started letting go. The other, in a dispassionate voice, considered the symptoms of what the Surgeon General had mentioned to the nation in his report on Liu Shan's Syndrome. But she didn't listen. The music began to absorb her.

The music was hypnotic. Fascinating. She knew it from a concert she attended years ago, but couldn't identify the piece by name. Something to do with England or Denmark. It had that aura about it.

Fog. Coastline all rocky and brooding. A cry of a lone gull in the nonexistent wind. A crashing of desolate breakers on the shore.

She could hear a chorus of voices, singing, but couldn't move from her chair—didn't *want* to move—for she felt that such beauty in the music would be shattered the instant she did. Her fingers began tingling as if not enough blood was reaching them. A lightness swelled in the center of her forehead and just below the heart. She drifted. Closing her eyes, she could feel the loneliness, the desolation. She could envision the treacherous coastline of England or some other land along the North Sea. A man floating alone came to her mind's eye. But he was not quite alone, for he pulled behind him a line of men, all too exhausted to swim on their own. Their armor clearly sparkled in the dull light of the vision. They each wore expressions of men lost to the world of the living.

The music coalesced upon the man who frantically towed the nearly drowned warriors. She could feel his urgency in the simple yet heroic task. Slowly she began losing her grip on reality. Every inch of her skin vibrated with the tones of the music that rose and swelled with the tides of the North Sea. *Beowulf. Oh!*

"Katie?" the intercom suddenly broke in.

She sagged in her chair, her eyes rolling upward in their sockets as if trying to glimpse a third eye in the center of her forehead. Her breath came in short gasps. Her pulse raced.

Outside there was a commotion and a bustling beyond the door. Rita Hanks and Ken Collins, who had just returned, stumbled in. Beverly Silva was right behind them.

"Sweet Jesus, she's going under!" Beverly screamed.

Katie Babcock's hands twitched freely as she slumped in the chair.

Collins bent over her quickly.

Rita stood pale at the door. "What'll we do?"

Ken grabbed Katie and shook her violently, trying to wake her. "Katie! Katie! Pull out of it!"

The President, with her eyes half-open and her face wan in the luminescence of the wardrobe room's light, rotated her head as if it were barely attached to her body.

"Katie!" He shook her again.

Ken looked back at Rita Hanks, who stood horrified, her hands bunched at her mouth.

"Rita, get the Baktropol from my attaché case. Hurry! I'll administer it. I think we can get her out of it."

Rita spun around and ran into the outer room. Ken pulled Katie up from the chair and carried her to the bed. He could almost feel her skin tingle himself as he bore her in his arms. She still seemed quite tangible to him as he set her onto the rumpled bed.

"Beverly, get Dr. Vucich down here fast!"

He couldn't believe such a thing could happen to anyone, let alone the president of the United States! He tried slapping her wrists.

Rita ran in with a small case, followed by two maids. Collins slipped the tab back and pulled out a bottle of blue pills. He tossed them aside onto the divan. He wanted a liquid formula. Rita gasped when she saw the hypo.

He held it up to the light and drew in a few cubic centimeters. He didn't know how much to use, but decided to gamble on a modest dosage. Katie's arm was outflung beside him. He found a strong vein and, without so much as thinking of sterilizing the skin with alcohol, he plunged the needle in. A long strand of his brown hair dropped down next to his left eye with a small drop of sweat on the tip. Salty, it touched his eye, stinging somewhat. He was suddenly frightened.

He put the hypo aside.

Katie rolled her eyes and moved her head from one side to the other. She tried moving her arms, but found that it was more trouble than it was worth.

"Easy. Easy now, Katie. Take it easy." He rubbed her cheeks.

Looking at Rita, who stood frozen like a column of ice in her horror, he said, "I want some fresh coffee, and all the morning's appointments canceled. And not a word of this to anyone. Even the Joint Chiefs. No one." He turned away.

Katie blinked, feeling the music and voices in her head subside. The vision of Beowulf towing those men back to the shore began to fade away. And with it, the loneliness of the struggle: it was so like *her* struggle. The coldness of the North Sea. The dead of winter. He was about to make it. . . .

She had nearly become that man. Beowulf! A strange interphasing of the man's character and hers nearly overwhelmed her. Those dying men and the forlorn looks to their faces tore her with despair. The music was so compelling, and he, Beowulf, was so strong! He wasn't frightened, not chilled by the terrible gripping cold of the sea. Sea gulls dipped like vultures. She could actually smell the salt, feel the entangling seaweed.

She had almost become Beowulf. *Almost*.

She squirmed, trying to roll over, like one struggling to wrest herself from a nightmare.

"Hold on," came Ken's gentle voice.

He gestured to Rita. "Bring me a cold washrag," he whispered. He gave Katie a tiny slap to her wrists. She blinked.

The last thing to vanish from her mind was the music. The vision of Beowulf faded away, drawing back into the nebulous haunting-grounds of her memory, ready to be evoked at any time in the future. She groaned, feeling a slight pain in the crook of her elbow.

Collins leaned back with relief.

"Where the hell am I?" she breathed faintly. A slight humming remained in her consciousness.

"Right where you're supposed to be," Ken said. Beverly Silva leaned against the back of the chair, her heart wanting to leap from her chest.

Outside poured in the gray light of the early morning sun as it tried to pierce the smog and aeroplankton flurry. It was building up to be another normal day for the President of the United States.

CHAPTER FOUR

✦◈◗❀

Second Essay for Orchestra
Samuel Barber

It was ten o'clock by the time he had showered and break-fasted. Lanier spread himself out luxuriously on his wide couch, enjoying the late morning sunshine that poured lazily through his window. Malibu Canyon had its advantages. Morning came late and evening early. It was an advantage Lanier always enjoyed, because his days often became so much more compressed than those in the Valley, where he used to live. Nights were longer, more relaxing, and he needed that edge.

Christy, in since seven, brought him his tea. With it, she produced three portfolios.

"These," she announced, "seem to be pretty much rush jobs."

Still in his robe, he leaned over the table, drawing the folios out before him.

"What are they?"

Christy folded her arms, smiling coyly. The sunlight haloed through her blond hair. "One is a movie star, I hope you know. The others are technicians the Defense Department says we can't live without. All have been reported missing, and none have returned in two weeks. The Syndrome is suspected in all cases."

Lanier resisted the temptation to consider the movie star's folio first. He knew their lot to be rather consistently neurotic, most of whom easily became lost in their megalomania. The last movie professional he tried to retrieve nearly killed him while they were under Gustav Holst's *Fugal Overture*. He finally managed to elude Lanier's attempts at rescuing him. Lanier had given up and refunded the family money, telling them to hire another Stalker. The rich were easily able to afford the price.

"And these two here?"

"Right." Christy bent over them. "Seth Bryant, working out of Seattle." She gestured slightly to the one folder Lanier held in his hand. "His wife and brother went under a couple of months ago, and his brother returned in a week's time, no worse for wear."

Lanier looked at her, knowingly. "But not his wife."

"Right," she confirmed. "Bryant's in with Lindroth Space and Aviation, working on the moon-mining contract. He has the inside lane on the development of that rail-launcher for the mining team that's up there now. Better than the steam track the Japanese are using. It's supposed to be much more efficient, but they wouldn't tell me any more than that when they contracted you. He has been seconded by the Defense Department and NASA, no less."

Lanier pondered the report on Seth Bryant.

Bryant was middle-aged, far from being handsome, but the photograph showed intelligence and a facial structure that hinted at a fanatical sense of devotion. Eyes wide, harried. The photo revealed a man weighted with more than a man should carry.

Lanier peeled back the pages.

"Says he vanished in his car. Did they explain that?"

"Yes, they did. It was up along a lovers' lane east of the city, believe it or not. He obtained an illegal tape of the Equinox Quintet. We don't know which of the thirteen cuts took him down, but we do have access to the tape. The Quintet never pressed any sonic-wafers in those days, but the Defense Department copied one for us."

"Thirteen cuts. That makes it somewhat difficult." He

thought for a minute, turning the pages of the Bryant folio.

Jazz, he knew, was not his predilection. He had felt for the longest time that those who best grasped the finer details of mature jazz stylings were themselves musicians, or at least had to be. Then there came blues, which he understood but didn't share an empathy with, since by disposition, he was never of the temperament to be satisfied with real hardcore blues. He was rarely despondent. And he never really wanted to be. That desire to be *willfully* down-and-out seemed part of the pleasure of listening to the blues. And as a consequence, he understood the logic behind the government action of outlawing most types of blues: it became too easy to succumb to Liu Shan's Syndrome.

Yet Seth Bryant was an important individual, even though he was just one of a thousand or so a week who were now being reported as victims of the Syndrome.

"Let's send this one up to San Francisco," he decided, handing Christy the portfolio on Bryant. "Harley Albright would be a good try on Bryant. He's a former saxophone player, and one of the best Stalkers for jazz and blues."

"Right." She took the folder.

Still avoiding the portfolio on the movie star, Lanier opened the folio of Perry Eventide. Lanier showed surprised on his face.

Christy watched him. "He's been gone the longest of the three. Almost a month."

Perry Eventide's name was nearly a household word. He was the discoverer of the temporary cure to the disease which caused the Syndrome, Baktropol. It was not an immunization drug, upon which the user could comfortably rely forever, but a stimulant that caused the chemicals within the blood to enervate the brain to a state which allowed for a more intense, vivid state of perception. It was something akin to an amplified amphetamine. It was quite powerful, *and* illegal, unless prescribed by a doctor or psychiatrist. The drug happened to be mildly addictive. The more you took, the less effective it became. It was vital, nonetheless.

Unfortunately, if the Syndrome continued to mutate and worsen, another cure would have to be found. Everyone was looking for a drug that attacked the disease organism directly, rather than a serum that worked on the brain chemistry of human beings.

Lanier closed the portfolio. "A definite." Then he opened it again. "Let's see what made him go under."

Christy walked around through the morning light which poured through the window. "Barber. His *Second Essay for Orchestra*. We just happen to have it on a wafer, in fact."

Lanier craned over the data sheets. "Interesting piece, oddly moody in places, although most of Barber's music would've bored him to death. Barber's pretty much varied in theme and structure. I can imagine someone going under to his *Adagio for Strings*, but not the *Essay*."

Christy brandished the folio of the movie star. "I think that you might want to consider this one, if the Eventide interests you."

Lanier looked up at her from the couch. "Oh, why's that?"

"They're, uh, related." She smiled playfully, stressing the last word.

"Oh, really?" Lanier's interest sparked. He sipped his tea as he sat back with the portfolio, getting comfortable for this one.

"Ellie Estevan." He paused, considering her photograph that was clipped to the report. "So *that's* what happened to her. I thought she was kidnapped for a publicity stunt or went off on one of her binges to Mexico."

Christy had provided a number of newspaper cuttings of Ellie Estevan and her notorious junkets around the world. Jet-set flings, outrageous love affairs, bouts with congressmen, cartel tycoons were all part of her life. It was a wonder that she had time to make films.

"I thought you'd be interested in this." Christy lifted a flimsy photograph cut from one of the nation's more libelous scandal magazines.

Lanier studied it. "Albertson Randell? No kidding." He sat up.

Lanier rarely had time to read the newspaper or the scandal sheets, and usually wasn't interested in gossip—feeling that most news was gossip anyway. But the photograph was taken at a Democratic party in Manhattan at which Ellie Estevan and a host of other celebrities were present. Albertson Randell was linked arm in arm with Ellie Estevan, on one side, and Katie Babcock, the President of the United States, on the other. All three were smiling gloriously for the world's press photographers.

"I wonder why I hadn't seen this before?" Lanier thought out loud. "It might have helped when I went in looking for Randell."

Christy stood back up. "Well, it hardly matters now, since you did rescue him. Besides, Estevan might only be missing, not necessarily succumbed."

"Yes, but there's a connection here." Then he looked closer at the report. "In fact, there seem to be more connections here than I can figure out."

"What do you mean?"

"Well, it's hard to explain. He did appear anxious to remain, much more so than in ordinary cases." Then Lanier fell into deeper thought, setting down the folio, remembering the blood, remembering Randell...

And the women. "Women seem to play an extraordinary role in his psychological makeup." There was so much he had left out of his report to the President. The particulars, the *bloody* particulars.

He considered the photographs of Ellie Estevan. He had never seen any of her movies, since he rarely had the time to whip into Los Angeles. Since concerts were slowly being phased out by the government, movies were once again becoming quite popular. It seemed that when combined with theater or film, music didn't cater to the effects of Liu Shan's Syndrome.

With popular forms of music practically condemned, movies became the safest form of entertainment. The fantasies were programmed and the music was just dispassionate enough to keep the audiences from slipping. Especially if their attention was spent on someone such as Ms. Estevan. And since Ellie Estevan's career spanned both television and movies, her audience was quite broadly based.

"I take it the scandal sheets don't know about her yet."

"As far as I know," Christy said.

"She certainly is popular enough. I'd guess she's hounded wherever she goes."

Christy nodded in agreement. "Her movies are incredible. People keep going back time and time again. Everyone loves her."

Two things immediately occurred to Lanier as he read. The first was that Ellie Estevan had appeared in one of the country's most libidinous gentleman's magazines—which, upon reflection, was not too unusual for women in the film industry these days. But the other item struck home soundly. Ellie Estevan appeared in the first "particle" motion picture broadcast on television, which ended up salvaging the entire beleagured television industry. Seen in brief five- to fifteen-second clips wedged in between commercials, Ellie Estevan's particle movies had to be watched every night for the bits of action and sparse dialogue that would, over a fifty-two-week period of time, amount to an entire story.

Lanier remembered, years ago, catching a glimpse of a fierce domestic scene on television in an intense ten-second burst right between two commercials. It was the carrot before the horse: he had to watch the next set of commercials to see how the argument resolved itself. To his disappointment, it did not end that night, nor the night after. He watched a week's worth of television to catch the "particles" of the story. He gave up when he considered a whole year of watching television just to catch a few seconds a night of a story.

But the strategy seemed to work for the industry. More people watched television, and more people became enraptured with the charms of Ellie Estevan's fiery eyes and blond-streaked light brown hair. There *was* something strangely compelling about her beauty, but Lanier couldn't quite place his finger on it. He had enough on his mind as it was.

"You said that Perry Eventide and Ms. Estevan had some sort of connection. What was it?"

"Here it is on page five of the report."

He leafed back the sheets.

When it had become clear that the world had a crisis on its hands due to the effects of the Liu Shan Syndrome, Perry Eventide of North Haven Chemicals spent a couple of weeks in the cellar of one of their plants and came up with a formula for Baktropol. It did exactly what was needed to be done to the victims of the Syndrome. It stabilized the sufferer's emotions and cleared his head regarding any lingering emotional problem. The music, whatever it happened to be, no longer had anything to thrive upon, like a parasite deprived of its host.

Overnight, Perry Eventide became a celebrity. North Haven Chemicals owned the patent and Eventide shared little financial reward in the company's success. He wasn't bitter about it, for Perry Eventide, small and unassuming, was an easygoing individual who truly enjoyed going to work among the smells of the Cleveland, Ohio, plant. A bachelor, shy and plain-looking, he swiftly became an "item" for the world press in general and the scandal sheets in particular. He was touted as a trailblazer, a humanitarian, a hero from the mean streets of the petrochemical industry.

But the money came with the fame, and he went on part-time work at North Haven, and eventually had to resign himself to his notoriety. He attended party after party, had meetings with politicians who were eager to be seen in his presence. He breakfasted with other luminaries of the scientific community. He was offered a chair in a research department of one of the best universities in the country.

In some circles it was even being said that Eventide's discovery prevented the rest of the world from going to war with the United States. With industrial pollution from the rich nations increasing unabated, along with the corporate wars being waged in Africa and South America, the United States wasn't gaining any friends. It was given the blame for the whole scheme of things.

When the Syndrome appeared to be the threat it eventually became, something was desperately needed. Virtually all industry and every individual life became unglued. People were disappearing at work; husbands came home to empty households. The sudden discovery of Baktropol was hailed from every corner of the nation as being the panacea the authorities had been searching for.

It was at a Hollywood premiere of Ellie Estevan's latest film, *From Earth's Center*, that Perry Eventide had the pleasure of making her acquaintance. The photograph Lanier held before him told him more than anything the report might have.

"She sure does get around, doesn't she?" He held up a two-column ribbon of newsprint cut from the *Los Angeles Times*. "Doesn't seem like her type, though."

Christy watched Lanier's face for more than a proper and professional interest in the case.

Nothing seemed to be lurking in the shadows.

Lanier plopped the file onto the coffee table and hoisted up his cup of lukewarm tea. "I think the Eventide comes first. He, at least, might have something more to contribute. I'll consider Ms. Estevan after more returns are in." He smiled at the joke.

But there was no joke. Christy momentarily left the room. A tight fist in Lanier's gut told him that he had said the wrong thing. Or possibly the right thing. *Like playing God*, he thought regretfully. Picking and choosing whom to rescue and whom to abandon was really what stalking came down to. Those he decided not to rescue would wander their enclosed worlds forever, unless another Stalker opted for them.

Walkers, they were called. Lanier wanted to help as many people as he could, but time crippled him, as well as mental exhaustion *and* the ever-present need to retain his anonymity. But there constantly hovered a specter of residual guilt when stories grew of mothers committing suicide because no one could search for their children who had succumbed. Husbands going crazy, lives torn in half. The ones who didn't make it out were called Walkers.

They were the accidental inhabitants of someone else's paranoid fantasy, since often the same fantasy would beckon more than just one unfortunate person. Lanier had known one or two in his career, and the other Stalkers reported more. Even in his search for Randell, Lanier hoped that he might find a Walker or two among Randell's dreamlings.

But all those women . . .

At least Lanier could have rescued one or two more in the same sitting. But Randell, unfortunately, had been alone.

So private lives deteriorated, business and industry limped along as best it could. But politics and diplomacy bordered on chaos, and often lapsed into internecine warfare as experts looked for causes and solutions, and lobbied for available funding.

But the biggest agony was music itself.

Music was, and always had been, a vital part of human culture. Folk tunes and whistle-while-you-work melodies were just as important as grand symphonies. The world was slowly being robbed of the emotional release that music continually provided. Music literally saved lives. It made man rocket to euphoric states or plunged him into shallows of despair. Now, music caused terror and instability.

Except to those immune, those who could listen to anything without the fear of succumbing. And there were only eighteen hundred of those.

Ironically, proletarian China suffered as well. For the disease didn't die out by the time it blew over Europe and the Caucasus. Its current mutation guaranteed a long life for the organism. And the Chinese had a tradition of folk music reaching back thousands of years. Millions had disappeared, though the official reports were not saying just how many. It afflicted everyone in ways that Lanier could not bear to consider.

"Let's do the Barber piece in twenty minutes. Shelve the Estevan for the time being. She may be important to the pleasure of many people, but there are priorities," he said, closing the Perry Eventide file.

With a pressurized *whump!* the door to Francis Lanier's workroom closed at Christy's touch. There was silence inside and silence outside. From the music library adjacent to the workroom, she placed herself at the transmission board, staring through the one-way mirror, watching Lanier adjust the equipment on his belt and beneath his priest's collar. Then he seated himself on the floor in his usual half-lotus position, his right foot crossed over his left thigh. Perry Eventide rated an ambulance—in the sense that only senators rate helicopters—and Christy sent out the call to the hospital as Lanier prepared himself.

Lanier, dressed in his usual priest's collar and long black coat, had concealed on his person the usual packet of stimulants and depressants, including sodium pentothal and Baktropol. His Malachi rested under his armpit; three clips hung at his waist. He was prepared for every kind of emergency, and then some. He often felt like a deep-sea diver, he carried so much equipment. But one couldn't be too careful.

He threw back his head and closed his eyes. He started to cleanse his mind, calm his body down. Properly speaking, it was a meditation without a mantra: he listened to the tiny humming in his head, the millions of synapses that vibrated at their own shifting frequencies. And when he was deep enough into a near *samadhi*-state, Christy would begin the music.

Lanier breathed deeply and slowly. His fingers, curled in his palms, twitched. Christy slotted the sonic-wafer of Barber's *Second Essay for Orchestra*, careful not to turn the audio onto the loudspeakers of the library. She still felt shaky at times, especially those times when Francis went under. Like now.

The miniaturized receiver imbedded in Lanier's earlobe softly began transmitting. And Lanier began feeling what it

must've been like for Perry Eventide. *Love*. Troublesome, complex, enchanting. A lost love unlike any that a man had ever
known.

And darkness swelled around him as the vibrations filled
his quiet mind then shimmered down his spinal cord. His skin
tingled. *Letting go, letting go,* he told himself. *Become Perry
Eventide. Search him out.* Breathing in and out. One breath
at a time. Let the darkness fill.

Christy jumped in her chair. The muted *pop!* came as Lanier
vanished from his position on the floor of his workroom. It
seemed unnatural for a living being to do such a thing, and it
always startled her.

The sonic-wafer had run its course.

Dizzy, he dropped to his knees, shaking his head as if he
hadn't gotten enough air. He sat down promptly in the slender,
pale yellow grass and looked around, orienting himself. His
confusions only lasted a few seconds, but when he cleared his
mind, letting the music generate a sense of the vision, he always
knew where he was. And why.

Ascertaining the time of day, he looked up at the sun. But
there was no sun. Instead, a bright strip, extending the length
of the sky, like the surface of a single mirror, glistened brightly.
The sky itself was blue and cloudless, but there was nothing
resembling a sun anywhere in the heavens above him.

At first he thought it was some kind of illusion, but glancing
to either side of him, he observed that the light which draped
the prairie on which he had "landed" seemed just the slightest
bit drab. *Artificial*, he reasoned. *Artificial light*.

He rose slowly, brushing off bits of grass and dirt from his
long coat, staring up at the long track of "sunlight." Ahead of
him sat a low range of sparse hills. Catalpa trees, bent at odd
angles, dotted the countryside.

Then he noticed that, through the haze, the horizon seemed
to curve upward in the soft daylight. He turned around. Behind
him, at a distance of about twenty kilometers, the end of the
world seemed to lift upward into obscurity as well, as if the
earth curved upward rather than down. Yet, he could see a thin
vein of a river, or a stream, bending up with the curve of the
land. The haze of dust or mild pollution made it difficult to
see any further up along the horizon.

The wind riffled his hair, tugging at the folds of his long coat at his feet. He knew then just exactly where he was. He was on the inside surface of an immense O'Neill space cylinder. Only this one seemed infinitely more sophisticated than the two now in existence orbiting the moon's Lagrange points.

It seemed more *real*, much more functional and less barren than the ones men were currently working on in space. The grasses swayed in the slight breeze, and Lanier could make out a flock of blackbirds rushing through a small cluster of sycamores in a wash below him. He grasped a handful of dirt, and not only did its texture seem real, it broke freely and appeared quite healthy in this fragile and highly artificial environment. Up ahead, he noticed deer droppings, and in several spots on the hillside it seemed as if the turf had taken on a bit of overgrazing. *Sheep*, he realized.

Lanier turned his inner ear toward the music, and listened. Yes, he could see it now. He pictured the whole craft spinning in space as graceful as a prima ballerina in a slow pirouette on a stage surrounded by darkness and iridescent faces. The faces were the stars.

He climbed a nearby hill. He couldn't see any cities or prominent structures from where he stood. This strip of the cylinder seemed hilly and rugged. Little could be seen. He snapped out his amplified binoculars. Above him, almost to the zenith, he scanned the terrain overhead for any sign of cities or villages. Eventide was *somewhere*. But Lanier could see nothing but the blurred dreams of lakes and mountains. A puff of green indicated a dense forest. There was nothing resembling a human habitation anywhere. But on the soil beneath his own feet he could see the small crescents of hoofprints. Game trails threaded through the bent grasses.

Where could Eventide be in all of this? It would take him months to explore the inside of the rotating cylinder by foot. There must be hundreds of square kilometers of surface area. Much too much to cover.

Gravely, Lanier realized that Eventide might have created a vacant world. A private solitude given no man, an empty fantasy, a perfect place in which to be alone.

Then an explosion knocked him off his feet, face first into the sod.

"Someone's here," he said sardonically to no one but himself.

The ground shook for a few minutes after the jolt. He jumped up to his feet and began to run toward the "north," where the horizon didn't curve up but stretched forward to the end of the cylinder.

It was rough going across the prairie. Prairie dog towers and snake holes kept appearing, and he kept tripping in them. He topped a small rise and saw beneath him a grove of cottonwoods, their green leaves shuddering in the slight afternoon wind. *Afternoon?* he pondered, realizing that the dimness in the light—perhaps a flexing or angling of the exterior mirrors that provided the light for the cylinder—made it seem like afternoon.

He stopped short of the cottonwoods, breathing heavily. He couldn't possibly be out of shape, but he seemed to be, considering the pain in his lungs, and the giddiness. He bent over. The air was much thinner than it should have been. The ground shuddered once again, but it was something quite different from an earthquake. *A rending, deep and resonant.*

My God, he thought suddenly, *this world is falling apart!* The air was getting thinner because it was leaking out through the walls of the cylinder into outer space! The wind kicked up a fuss through the trees.

This wasn't in the music, he realized. This had something to do with Eventide's mind. Where was he? Lanier dove through the cottonwoods. Just beyond the cottonwood stand he came to a large meadow. He popped his priest's collar and removed his coat. In the center of the meadow, as if fused by lightning, was a flat circle of crystal.

Lanier then recognized what this particular world had come to: the inner surface area was for animal and plant life. The people who maintained the cylinder lived below the surface. This enormous cylinder held wilderness areas, farms, and lakes ranging over hundreds, if not thousands, of kilometers. And this was an entrance to the world below his feet.

He stepped out onto the smooth surface just as another quake shook the ground. This time a slight crack followed the joining of the crystal area to the cottonwoods. It was almost as if he could hear the roots of the trees and grass scream as they were torn apart. But his hearing was beginning to fail. Lack of atmosphere. He felt light-headed.

Standing in the center of the crystal shield, he was jerked

to his knees suddenly as the entire crystal area began lowering. It was an elevator!

He reached for his Malachi, but thought against it. He would wait, for he felt as if Eventide was very near. The music—for he could still hear it clearly—was quite intense. And Eventide must be feeling some sense of danger, because something was conveyed to him in the music that let him know that more than just this world was falling apart.

Another jolt. If there was an explosion, he couldn't hear it. But the elevator stopped, locked between floors in the shaft. He had descended about thirty-five meters. In the glass cylinder of the elevator shaft, he had seen that the previous floors—the inner floors—were empty of life.

He climbed up onto the floor he had just passed. He stood in silence, the floor extending for a great distance before him, filled with fleeing technicians. *Dreamlings*, he realized. And even though the wind rushed about him, everything retained an eerie sense of quiet. He checked his equipment.

His Malachi, suspended underneath his armpit, was set on rapid-fire. But more important to him now was the suit beneath his clothing. It resembled more a scuba diver's outfit than anything else, but it lacked flippers and bulky tanks. He had used it twice before, a long time ago, once in a firestorm in a city that seemed like Berlin, built to the tune of Richard Strauss's tone poem, *Tod und Verklärung*, Death and Transfiguration, and once after that in a bubble dome beneath the Sarasso Sea that had suddenly collapsed in the final sections of Respighi's *Feste Romane*. He had been lucky to survive that one.

And he knew that with the vanishing atmosphere—for that was what the wind was all about—he would probably need it.

The only problem was Eventide. If Perry Eventide perished here, his death would be just as real as if he were on the surface of the earth. Liu Shan's Syndrome was more detrimental than most people who survived it realized. That's why Lanier carried the Malachi. *And* why he wore the suit, which was extremely uncomfortable and restrictive. *Someone* had to survive.

Along either side of the sloping corridor were huge open areas, passageways to rooms that held all sorts of unrecognizable equipment. People spilled from these, and many were screaming. Smoke followed them down the halls.

A man with grease on his face came running out of a side corridor off to Lanier's right, shouting, "It's breaking up! Oh, my God! It's breaking up!" Terrified, his words choked on smoke. He ran past Lanier frantically.

Over a loudspeaker someone shouted, "We have a major breach in Sector B! Breakup in Sector B! This is a condition Red! Evacuate! I repeat, evacuate! Everyone is ordered to the nearest shuttle ports!"

Then came a fiery hiss of static over the loudspeaker, and the voice stopped. The lights began to flicker and dim. Power was draining. And the power, Lanier thought, could either be nuclear or solar—very likely a combination of both. But if it was nuclear, fission or fusion, it could be very messy. Eventide had thought of everything.

But did he think of this? Lanier ducked when sparks showered from a ruptured conduit overhead.

These were the factory decks, the maintenance and reserve quarters. The guts of the cylinder. *But where is Eventide?* Crew members in jerseys of multiple colors scurried to the elevator shafts and stairwells. Some were already in space suits. Eventide would be here if he was aware of the crisis, unless the breakup was intentional, which Lanier doubted.

Then he realized that if this world was created for its solitude and beauty, then Eventide would not be down here in the evacuation bays, but topside on the prairie.

Yet, he wondered, *why the breakup in the first place?* Was Eventide suicidal?

A pang in the music rose in his mind as he turned down a vacant corridor. But what he saw surprised him. Glass splintered from the window casings as the steel of the floors slowly buckled as if in the hands of a titan. These things didn't concern him: the vibrations suddenly, momentarily, phased into a vision of the purest love a man had ever possessed for a woman. Then, Lanier was struck with such profound grief that he knew that Perry Eventide was definitely not down here with the others trying to flee this brittle paradise. He was up on the surface, in love, and unaware, *totally* unaware of the situation.

The lights in the corridor winked out. Screaming poured down the passageway. Another explosion flashed with jagged edges of fire. Its reddish glow seemed to him like a lantern hung on the doorway into Hell itself.

Lanier ran down the hall, passing people, until he found a small workshaft elevator that was not being used for anything.

He lifted the canvas strap that held the vertical doors together. He paused when he noticed that in a recess in the wall hung various sorts of worksuits and maneuvering packs for work outside the cylinder. Piled neatly beneath these items were laminite rescue balls, as they were called, coiled in tight portable cases. They were man-sized balloons in which an astronaut without the benefit of a space suit could sit enclosed, like an embryo, and be towed to safety outside in space for a short time. They had already seen use on a number of occasions, and were the equivalent of life preservers on board a luxury liner.

But there was no luxury here. It was getting harder to breathe by the minute.

Lanier grabbed the small package that contained one of the rescue balls and got into the elevator, punching the vertical button. In the pitch dark, the glow light on his chest illuminated the shaft as the elevator car rose upward on auxiliary power.

He shook his head in amazement. He was always surprised at just how complete were the "worlds" he entered under the Syndrome. He never thought Eventide to be so mentally adept or imaginative. But the music set it up, and Eventide's imagination gave it the sense of reality.

When he broke to the surface, he found himself emerging beside a creekbed that had lost its water into a fissure. Carp and rainbow trout floundered helplessly in the silt and drapes of fallen lilies. The shaft opening was in a little outbuilding structure that decorously blended into the surrounding junipers.

Here on the surface, breathing became exceedingly difficult. The light in the "world" cylinder began to shimmer as the mirrors on the outside of the craft began coming apart. Darkness fell about him in patches, like clouds moving across the face of the sun on a volatile April afternoon. He had to find Eventide quickly.

He turned inward to the music. And again, the vision of love came to him, but only like a flash of summer lightning in a storm that blankets the countryside. The flash vanished and darkness pervaded.

Eventide was definitely near. He could feel it now.

He made sure the Malachi had the anesthetic needles in its

clip instead of the regular bullets he always carried.

He set off parallel to the creekbed and found Eventide within minutes.

Up ahead, on the muddy bank of the creek, he saw Eventide, but he was with someone. The wind was blowing with a near-hurricane force, and Eventide was wrestling with an attractive woman who already wore escape gear. The woman was a dreamling. Lanier couldn't hear them from where he stood, so he shouldered the rescue ball packet and ran toward them in the fierce wind.

The hair of the dreamling was long and shining. Eventide groped desperately for her, virtually oblivious to the conditions of the disintegrating world around him. She fought him off. Lanier couldn't catch a clear glimpse of her face, but assumed that she must have been beautiful.

Eventide screamed above the wind. The woman leaped up the bank in her silver suit.

"Eventide!" Lanier yelled at him. The ground swelled. *Earthquake!*

The woman looked back at him as Lanier climbed a boulder at the side of the creek. The dreamling looked around fearfully. She fled out of sight beyond the rise tuffed with ferns.

"It's her fault!" Eventide groaned as Lanier swept up on him, almost out of breath. Eventide was nearly blue from oxygen deprivation.

The ground tore horribly, and the sound of its wrenching filled Lanier's ears painfully. Given the thinness of the air, the sound of the cylinder pulling itself apart must have been tremendous indeed. Just beneath the ground surface area, the work levels were caving in. Acres of the prairie simply swelled downward, collapsing in the fury of the tremors that shook this fragile world.

Lanier couldn't believe what he was seeing. Huge chunks of land tore themselves up from the surface and floated away as if they were feathers blown about on the wind! Suddenly, Eventide rose, his eyes flaring wildly as he clutched his stomach.

The entire cylinder stopped rotating. Gravity had disappeared.

Lanier leaped, floating toward Perry Eventide, who twirled slowly in the air like a fetus curled up on itself. Eventide was crying hysterically.

"Eventide! I'm a Stalker! You're ill! I can get you out of this!" Just saying those words nearly exhausted him.

But just as he moved for him, darkness filled the entire world within the cylinder. The mirrors outside had shattered, broken into a thousand particles, and light stole from the world.

"Perry!" Lanier shook him, but the sound of his voice seemed strained. The air had thinned drastically. Boulders and sprays of lake water burst all around them.

"Oh, she did this to me," Eventide whimpered, his face smeared with mud and leavings of grass. He coughed violently.

They hadn't drifted too far about the suface when a massive crevasse appeared in the ground. The wind sucked them down into it.

"It's my fault," he moaned. Lanier gripped him with one hand, holding the rescue ball in the other. Things happened too fast for him to reach his Malachi. They would have been dead before the anesthetic took control.

He rolled and tumbled, managing to thrust the rescue ball packet in between his legs. Hastily, he removed a hypo from his medicine pouch. The rest of the contents of the medicine packet spilled out and shot away in the wind. But he held onto the hypo filled with Baktropol.

They tumbled down through the lower layers of the cylinder like debris being sucked down a drain.

Lanier twisted, gripping Eventide, and jabbed the hypodermic into his neck. Eventide doubled up painfully and screamed at the presence of the needle. Letting the hypo go, Lanier reached out desperately for a shorn girder of steel.

Breathing was almost impossible. It was like being at eighteen thousand feet. Lanier's head reeled for lack of oxygen. The few seconds it would take for the Baktropol to take effect were not going to be enough. He moved quickly.

Letting go when he felt himself to be in the best possible position, Lanier burst open the package that contained the aluminum rescue ball. Holding Eventide slackly between his legs, Lanier freed the zipper to the ball and thrust Eventide into it. As he did this, he distended the oxygen tube from the relief packet inside and plunged it into Eventide's gaping mouth. Eventide didn't struggle.

Seconds left. Everything was so incredibly, horribly real!

A long umbilical drifted away from the inflated ball. Lanier caught it and wrapped it quickly around his ankle as he floated.

From his collar, Lanier swiftly ripped open the pouch at the back of his neck and pulled out a plastic hood over his head. From his belt he withdrew a small mouth-filter and oxygen coil. The hood expanded with the flow of oxygen. Lanier whipped on his gloves and tore back the hermetic seal. It wasn't the best space suit in the world, but it would do for the time Eventide spent in this universe. *Hopefully*, he thought, *that will be only seconds.*

They blew into open space.

And like a nightmare, like the final cataclysmic scene from *Götterdämmerung*, the beautiful cylindrical world fell apart. Silently, caterwauling in space.

Lanier gyrated in the quiet of the void. He could see the taillights of various escape vessels fleeing in every direction. In the darkness, he could make out little of the full size of the cylinder, but he could spot the asteroid-sized pieces of the colony drift by. Shards of the mirror system that provided the light for the interior of the cylinder glittered like an incredible flashing constellation.

In the peace of space, Lanier could relax. The music now occupied his complete attention, since the crisis seemed to be over. Yet the music appeared to be waning, the vibrations losing their intensity.

Retrieving the umbilical to the space rescue ball, Lanier drifted with the music as everything began to slowly fade. The stars around him began losing their clarity, began winking out of existence. He drifted toward sleep. Only the sound of his own breathing filled his ears. Everything lost interest for him. Sleep. *Sleep.* He floated.

He woke. Lanier lay sprawled on the shining black floor of his workroom. A few meters away, Perry Eventide lay curled like a baby. The lights suddenly, brightly, snapped on and Christy unlocked the airtight door.

"Fran, are you all right?"

He shook his head, clearing his mind, trying to focus. He zipped off the air-hood. Bitter L.A. atmosphere greeted his lungs. Sweat peppered his forehead.

"Yes, I think so." He turned to Eventide. "I got him, though. It was scary this time. Really scary."

Eventide rolled over with a groan. Christy gasped. The two ambulance attendants, who had been waiting just outside the door, ran in around her.

"What happened to him?" She pointed. Eventide gripped his stomach, rolling over in a pool of blood. He was very pale.

Lanier peeled off his gloves and kneeled beside him. "Nothing," he said to her. "He was all right when I found him. It was rough, but we made it out."

Eventide winced, raising his right hand, which was covered with blood.

"She did this to me," he whispered. The attendants bent over him and lifted him carefully. "Oh, Jesus God," he cried. Blood bubbled at the corners of his mouth.

"He's been knifed," the first attendant said. "Just under the left lung, very deep."

They wheeled him out as fast as they could. The other attendant began working on the wound.

Lanier stood in amazement. *What had happened beside that drained creek?* He tried to recall.

Christy followed the attendants out to the idling ambulance. She frowned, knowing that *this* was the sort of thing that required a helicopter. Not a four-wheeler and a twenty- to thirty-minute ride into civilization.

Perry Eventide was pronounced dead on arrival at St. Luke's General Hospital in Thousand Oaks, owing, in part, to two efficient knife wounds, and another earthquake that broke two freeways strategically in half about eleven-thirty that morning. It took three hours to get Eventide to the hospital, and the ambulance driver perished from smog exposure when millions of automobiles stranded on the freeways in the Valley poured a record amount of pollutants into the air.

That day, three hundred and twelve people died trying to breathe on a hot summer afternoon in the bowl of the San Fernando Valley. Perry Eventide was not mentioned in the *Times* obituary tally.

CHAPTER FIVE

✦◈〰◈✦

The Norfolk Rhapsody No. 1
Ralph Vaughan Williams

The President sat in the morning sunshine that leaned through the bulletproof glass of the Oval Office windows and whimsically considered renaming the office of the Secretary of State to Secretary of Chaos. Floyd Matkin had just been reported "vanished" at the preliminary summit conference in Bonn where the delicate negotiations between Saudi Arabia and Japan were taking place. She wasn't at all pleased with the situation.

War had nearly broken out between the two nations, and as a major ally to both, Katie Babcock didn't want the United States to appear as if it were siding with one nation over the other. The fact that Japan had bombed a major port because the Saudis refused to export what little oil they could spare to Japan caused a great deal of concern among the President, her aides, and Congress. She was having a hard enough time trying to keep the Joint Chiefs from filling the Indian Ocean with every ship the United States owned.

Now, Floyd Matkin, one of the best statesmen this country had ever produced, was gone.

"Rita." Katie stabbed the intercom.

"Yes, Katie, right here."

"Could you bring in the latest score sheet, and tell Ken I want to see him as soon as possible."

"Right."

Rita brought in the list that Katie requested. The Bureau of Statistics daily computed the number of "vanished" individuals at all levels of government employ, including all the major industries. Katie always perused it closely, especially for members of Congress and their staffs.

Floyd's name wasn't on it. *Yet*, she thought dismally. She tossed the sheet onto her desk, annoyed at the sluggishness of the system. She reached over for another cigarette and lit it with a quick, precise motion.

Ken Collins strolled inside the office. His tie loose, he seemed quite relaxed.

"What's up, Katie?"

She pointed to the list in front of her. "Look at this."

"I know. I got the new one this morning."

She stood up. "Well, Floyd isn't on it yet. I suppose it hasn't been confirmed that he's succumbed."

"No, we're waiting on the report. But they think he has gone under from the way the evidence was presented."

"What's the evidence?"

"Well, he went to a reception last night with the Saudi ambassador, and it turned out to be quite a party. A lot of people were there."

"I know. I got wind of it from Rita this morning." She inhaled stiffly on her cigarette.

"And they checked everyone's immunity card, so that they could provide a small orchestra."

"And?"

"As near as anyone can tell, he went outside with a companion and she came back alone. Or that's what they say."

"Wasn't he watched?"

"Hell, yes, he was watched," he said emphatically. "The Swiss and the Germans both had the place cordoned off. We had our own security people and no one could've left without being seen or detected."

"Who was his companion? I'm surprised we don't know

these things." The implication was that "we" ought to know these things. Ken read it in the President's face.

"We don't know who she was. There were a lot of people present who had little or nothing to do with the conference. Mostly friends of friends. You know, a regular bash."

She nodded. "I assume the public doesn't know of this yet. Has it leaked?"

"We're trying to keep the lid on until it can be confirmed. The official word is that he's indisposed. Ill. We think the mission can proceed without him. The two ambassadors and their respective staffs have already met in private, so some of the air's been cleared."

Katie stood in a small cloud of smoke.

"What do you recommend we do about this? You know the public," she asked quite openly.

"Well," Ken rolled up his shirtsleeves, "we have the Undersecretary flying over right now, and we can let him handle our involvement in the negotiations. It's just more important that the ambassadors get together—and be seen together—at the conference. We can stay out of it, which we probably should, given the mess that we left in the Middle East."

"Well, at least too many bombs weren't used then." She walked around the desk. "We can give some of the credit to the Russians for helping with the evacuation. Who needed the Suez Canal anyway?"

Ken thought about Matkin's disappearance. "I've gone ahead and put in a petition for a Stalker since we managed to get the program that the orchestra played. If it's the case that Floyd went under to the orchestra's performance, then we should have no problem. Beyond that, we can only guess what made him vanish."

"OK, Ken," Katie said. "Keep me posted. I have enough to worry about today without this happening to Floyd. Especially now."

Collins smiled, not without affection. "Just leave things to us. We can skim most of the shit off the top for you."

She sat back in the chair behind the great desk.

"So, what's going on out front this morning?" She referred to the three thousand protestors that had assembled at dawn just beyond the front gates. Three thousand in filter-masks.

"It's that nuclear group. They're from Denver protesting the meltdown. It appears that more radioactive debris is entering

the water table in southeastern Colorado, and they think it's
your fault because you won't put your foot down."

Katie stared out the window.

Ken went on. "Then there are a few farmers protesting in
general. Something about the Mississippi spill. That defoliant,
BT-701. They want some heads to roll."

"Shit." She shook her own head, stubbing out her cigarette.
"That was a bad one. I really do sympathize with them. Maybe
I should fly out there and take a look. Talk to some of the
locals. We should run through that emergency relief bill as
soon as we can."

Ken chortled. "If we can get Randell off the floor."

"How long's the filibuster been going?"

"Just two days now, but there's a lot of work to do before
the holidays set in. And they just don't seem anxious to get
any of it done. Particularly Senator Randell."

Katie lit up another cigarette. "Don't worry about Albertson.
One phone call will fix his wagon. I'll see to that. Can't have
that boy ruining things for us."

She fell silent. Ken waited.

"Listen, Ken," she spoke softly. "Those Japanese terrorists
may get their hands on another nuclear device and do something
very stupid again. We all know that. And the Saudis can stran-
gle the Japanese economy. We can't have things like this happening so often. It's a vicious circle. We need Floyd. Do what
you can about finding out just what happened at that party. I
want guest lists, a list of the orchestra members, and any of
the hired help. Run a correlation on all of them through
DataCom as soon as you can. If there are any terrorist connections, I want to know about them. Besides, I have to do
something publicly significant soon if I don't want to get shot
at again."

She didn't laugh, nor did she mean her remark to be funny.
But Ken knew that for as long as she was President, she would
be paying for it. The assassination attempts had become more
and more frequent. The splinter groups and the wackos that
roamed the country swore to see her dead before the year was
out. Her term in office she often saw as a sentence. She had
already racked up more assassination attempts than any President in the history of the nation, a record she wasn't too
particularly proud of.

As Ken turned to go, Katie looked up from her papers. "Hey, is that music out there?" She glanced beyond the door.

"Sure is," he smiled. "It's synthesized music. All the radio stations have it. Two students at Cal Tech tried to commit suicide a couple of weeks ago to computer music, but the Syndrome wasn't triggered. Those two grad students are practically heroes now."

"I wasn't aware of that."

"Unusual, isn't it? But it's better than no music at all." He grinned. "You should listen to the news at night. There are all sorts of things going on in the world."

"Well, I'll be damned," said the President of the United States.

Nebraska, Lanier guessed, gazing appreciatively out over the wide vista of green wheat before him.

He had never known the prairie to be so beautiful before, even back in the real world. The sky blazed the purest blue he had ever seen, as huge rich gray-white cumulus puffed along in the lazy breeze that skudded the tops of the bending wheat. Flowers of a wide range of colors grew at the crowns of the low hills in the distance. And at his feet were hollyhocks and Indian paintbrush, and other flowers for which he had no names. In a distant meadow, dandelions washed in the wind like a wave on a golden sea.

It was a perfect world in which to hide.

Lanier paused, letting the vibrations resonate throughout his body, and the landscape. *Floyd Matkin,* he thought, *there. . . .*

A farmhouse across the field ahead of him was the only human structure nearby. Matkin had to be there. *Why not?* At least it seemed likely. The burdens he carried as the Secretary of State would naturally compel him to seek the security of the pastoral landscapes of middle America. Matkin had grown up in the Midwest, and the Midwest would naturally be a place he might want to return to in times of stress. Times such as these.

A slight chill hovered about Lanier as he walked through the wheat, which was only inches high. He buttoned the wide collar of his long coat, careful to keep the priest's collar in sight for the dreamlings, or anyone else, who might see him.

He strolled through the low wheat toward the farmhouse.

Something's out of whack, he thought suddenly. *Something's wrong....*

An uneasiness crept into his senses. He felt as if he were being watched. But not by Matkin. Lanier was certain of that much. Something else plagued him. He distinctly had the impression that whatever it was that observed him wasn't quite human. Nightmarish. *Alien?* He looked around at the sheer peacefulness of the scenario. He couldn't tell what exactly what bothered him.

He pinched his ear, listening to Vaughan Williams' *Norfolk Rhapsody*, feeling the vibrations ripple through his body.

Then, from behind him came a sound he wasn't at all ready to find out here in the prairie. It sounded like a bass violin being plucked at a great distance: a deep burst, a strong reverberation that faded after a few seconds. He raised his hand to shade out the bright sunshine.

On the horizon, in plain daylight, were five lights of brilliant orange. They moved aloft parallel to the horizon, circling the farmland on which he stood. And they sure as hell looked like spacecraft to him, but nothing like anyone had known on the earth. Whatever they were, they seemed quite intelligent.

That deep, resounding plucking was the only sound they made. Lanier pulsed with adrenalin. *Fear.* This had all the trimmings of a homemade nightmare.

The orange-glowing craft swept behind a hill briefly. But in his sudden paranoia, Lanier felt that a black-clad figure standing in wide, open spaces on the prairie was as conspicuous as a crushed thumb under a ball-peen hammer. How Floyd Matkin got this out of Vaughan Williams' *Rhapsody* baffled him.

He ran for the farmhouse. The orange craft had made a sudden, sweeping turn. A few kilometers off, they were heading directly for the large farmhouse.

Just then, a scream grated forth from the open windows of the farmhouse's second floor. Lanier swiftly leaped the small white picket fence in the front yard. The orange craft had slowed, but were in a direct line to the farmhouse. Whoever screamed upstairs had also seen the strange craft approaching.

Lanier pulled out his Malachi. Another scream pierced the calm that surrounded the farmyard. A cluster of chickens scattered as Lanier ran up to the door.

"Matkin!" he yelled. "Floyd Matkin!" He swung the door open and entered the large living room.

Matkin's voice came down the stairs. *"Jesus! They're coming!"*

Lanier glanced quickly out the back window.

The deep, bass, plucking sound shook the farmhouse. Shutters and walls rattled. What Lanier saw startled him. The five craft were at best two kilometers off. But in the distance, another farmhouse stood against the horizon. The farmhouse seemed to be much larger than this one, and there were a couple of small ranch houses near it. There was also a large barn and two grain silos. Lanier could discern a great deal of farming equipment standing out in the afternoon sun.

As the first of the orange craft swept over the farmhouse and silos, the plucking sound struck again. Lanier watched intensely. The farmhouse suddenly began elongating upward, as if made into taffy, into the bottom of the lead ship. The ship then glowed so brightly that Lanier had to blink to protect his eyes. The farm in the distance was being ingested! The grain silos were then sucked up, stretching into orange columns a hundred meters long. Then up went the farm equipment. The red harvesters became slender, disintegrating crimson streaks, flashing into the bellies of the glowing craft.

Whatever they were, each glowing object absorbed anything that passed beneath it. Anything, that is, that was built by human hands.

And they were heading this way!

"Matkin!" Lanier yelled up the stairs, turning around.

Then he heard a woman's voice. She was speaking softly.

The woman, whoever she was, Lanier realized, could be anyone in this world: a dreamling Matkin's psyche provided as a wife, or a lover for this paradise. He and his companion could be an ordinary farmer and wife out in the gentle Nebraska prairie.

But the screaming. *Why the screams?*

Lanier took the stairs three at a time. "Matkin, I've come to get you out of this!" He gripped the Malachi firmly.

The hallway at the top of the stairs was long, breaking off in either direction of the second floor. At the end of the hallway, off to his left, Lanier glimpsed a quickly fleeing figure as it rounded the corner into another room. His eyes hadn't yet adjusted to the darkness of the second floor.

"Matkin!" He turned in pursuit.

The plucking of the orange craft began phasing into the Vaughan Williams that was playing in Lanier's mind. *This is real!* Lanier thought suddenly. *My God . . . !*

He reached the end of the long hallway and found a second set of stairs leading down the south side of the farmhouse. The figure, clothed in an off-white, almost formal gown—a *bridal* gown?—was striding out across the front lawn. A woman! She leaped a fence like an antelope, never losing her stride or balance.

She had turned around once, but at Lanier's vantage point it was difficult to recognize her. But she was certainly no farmwife. Young and swift, the dreamling vanished over a small hill that led to a creek. Whoever she was, *whatever* she was, she was captivatingly graceful.

With little time to spare, Lanier retreated back down the hall.

"Matkin! Where are you?" He faced a number of closed doors leading into bedrooms and dens. He started trying the doorknobs, running as he did, down the hallway. Each door was locked.

"Oh, my God! Oh!" came Matkin's desperate voice from behind one of the doors.

Lanier lifted a solid boot and caved in the door with a resounding kick.

Matkin lay completely tied up in bed, looking like a moth's cocoon or an Egyptian mummy out of its sarcophagus. He was completely helpless.

"She did this! Stop her!" he said wildly. "It was a game. . . ." Fear flushed his face as the plucking sound increased, almost as if it were immediately overhead.

An orange light suddenly suffused the entire farmhouse.

The building shook with a penetrating thunder. The walls boomed and chairs moved across the floor. It was too late.

Lanier stumbled backward as Matkin started screaming in the vile orange shadows. He scrambled back into the hallway. He didn't have time to anesthetize Matkin because the man was already dissolving in the mist of his tortured screaming. To his horror, Lanier saw one whole end of the room begin to stretch upward in the fluorescent light.

Matkin's mouth elongated fantastically as he was pulled upward in his bindings. Bed, hutch, chairs, nightstand, everything glowed and lifted. Dissolving as they went.

Lanier spun and leaped out of an open window directly behind him, twisting in a flip that he hoped would land him on his feet. He crashed into a large bush just as the huge orange craft mooned directly overhead. The thing had to be about as big as a football field. And the farmhouse was being sucked up beneath it.

Lanier ran off to the side of the house like a wild man, staying fractionally ahead of the dissolving orange light. He had dropped his Malachi in the jump from the window. It was useless now. His heart seemed like it would burst from his chest. He was filled with utter panic.

Behind a large horse chestnut tree, he saw the slanted shelter of a tornado cellar. Without even thinking of what to do, or how to do it, he simply dove into its dark opening as if he were diving into a secluded swimming hole.

He smashed into the wooden stairs leading down to the musky dark of the cellar, rolling off on his right shoulder in a judo fall he had learned years ago in the air force. He crashed into a pile of boxes containing turnips and potatoes. They tumbled around him in the darkness, burying him completely.

And the vibrations shook him to the bones as the five craft drifted overhead, sucking up the farmhouse and everything around it. Pain rocketed throughout Lanier's body, as though he had broken his shoulder.

Yet nothing happened to him.

The slanted shelter of the door to the cellar disappeared, but the stairs remained. Through the potatoes that concealed him, he could see the orange glow recede. Whatever the light touched, it absorbed. He froze with fear, not daring to move.

What a nightmare! he thought. *Who on earth could have gotten this out of Vaughan Williams?*

With the shelter gone, the afternoon light slanted down into the cellar. When the vibrations of the craft could no longer be felt, and the orange glow had gone completely, Lanier rolled over onto a crate of turnips. Painfully, he lifted himself to the stairs. He could no longer hear anything but the *Norfolk Rhapsody* coming from the transceiver in his earlobe.

The ships were gone.

Carefully, he craned his head up out of the cellar. The only thing left standing was the single horse chestnut tree that stood next to the storm cellar. That was it.

Like an incredible vacuum cleaner, the orange spacecraft had scoured the landscape clean of any human presence. All that was left of the large farmhouse was the crater of its basement. Lanier walked over to the hole it had left, and saw pipes spouting jets of water like severed arteries. He could smell gas.

Nothing remained, absolutely nothing. The fence was gone. The tractor was gone. Even the chickens were gone. Not a feather remained behind.

Lanier pushed back a strand of brown hair from his eyes. He stood dumbfounded.

He looked around. The peacefulness at the beginning seemed so out of place here at the end. *Just like the space cylinder breaking up a few weeks ago*, he thought. *It shouldn't have happened*. But it did.

He walked around in the desolation, feeling the empty wind drifting down the fields. He couldn't locate the Malachi where it would have fallen beside the bushes next to the house. It had gone up with all the rest. His shoulder throbbed with pain.

Staring out over the wheat fields, he suddenly recalled the girl who fled. He walked over to where the fence had once reached, and walked beyond to the hill where the dreamling had disappeared. Gaining the top of the hillock, he could see for a great distance. There were no structures of any kind. No farms. No roads. No telephone lines. Just miles of prairie.

The girl was gone. The orange ships were gone. And so was Floyd Matkin, the Secretary of State.

death were of paramount concern to foreign policy decisions. Besides that, with his fractured collarbone, he was laid up for the next two to three weeks.

He could still meditate, and go under any time. But he would carry the pain of the fracture in every world he would enter. The pain would distract him from keeping in harmony with the internal vibrations of that plane, and therefore he had decided to take a short vacation. He would be of no practical use to anyone at all until his collarbone healed. And he wanted to take some time to assess the implications of his recent failures and what they ultimately meant. If anything.

This would give the moving company time to abandon the Malibu ranch for a better, more obscure perch outside of Missoula, Montana.

It seemed that someone had leaked Lanier's name, his profession, and the exact location of his Malibu retreat to the press and the scandal sheets. He became beleagured with pleas from hundreds of desperate individuals who needed his services, services which he simply didn't have the time to provide. Moreover, the Los Angeles pollution index had topped out in recent weeks, and the death rate in southern California had continued to climb because of it. There were more vehicular suicides, more lung cancers, isolated rioting, blackouts and brownouts. And more vanishings.

Los Angeles had rapidly become an unhealthy place in which to live. It didn't take him long to decide that it was time for a change of climate. It took about as long to decide as it took for the doctor to tape up his shoulder, which was about the time it took for the first of the desperate to arrive: Marianne Gleason of Sepulveda drove her propane station wagon onto Lanier's front lawn, barely ahead of a dozen other frantic individuals, demanding that Francis Lanier search for her missing relatives.

Christy had called the doctor's office warning him, and Lanier never returned home. He and Christy met on the way to Washington, D.C., a few days later, in the Denver airport. They left matters in Charlie Gilbert's capable hands regarding the movers and the announcements to the press that claimed Francis Lanier wasn't who they thought he was, and that he was out of town on business anyway. Which was true.

Katie Babcock flowed in from a side door to the office, followed by a cloud of cigarette smoke. She seemed almost military in the three-piece pin-stripe suit she wore. Very sharp and very efficient.

She strode over confidently and reached for Lanier's hand.

"Glad we could meet, Mr. Lanier." When Lanier feinted with his right hand to emphasize its place in the sling, Katie laughed and squeezed his left hand instead.

"Oh, sorry." She pointed. "I heard about your rough landing from Ken. Please have a seat. Does anyone want coffee?" Before anyone could respond, she signaled to the maid who hovered inconspicuously off to one side.

The President stared assuredly into Lanier's calm brown eyes. She noticed immediately the strange sense of centeredness about him, an aura of calmness, as if little in the world disturbed him. It wasn't quite confidence, she decided, it was something else. She found him an unusually attractive man, and perhaps his attractiveness was in some part due to his equilibrium. His self-assuredness, she realized, would be an asset in this world.

This is a very powerful man, she thought. *Watch him closely. He probably has one hell of an organized personal life.*

He sat there, making himself comfortable, breathing easy, calmly while Christy sifted through her materials.

Katie wondered if he was married. She didn't recall reading any mention of it in his file. His eyes were gentle, portraying very little of what worked within his mind. *This man has many secrets,* she decided.

Katie Babcock sat at the wide couch next to the window where Christy sat next to her open briefcase. Lanier himself was seated in a chair at the President's left hand, in full glare of the sunlight. The morning sun, through the smog and residual aeroplankton, cast an amber glow about him.

She lifted his file that Ken had placed on the table in front of them.

"You're an interesting man, Mr. Lanier, with an interesting talent." She opened the file as if Floyd Matkin's death were the farthest thing on her mind. "Tell me, Mr. Lanier, I'm curious. Just how many of you are there? Does anyone know?" Meaning, *We haven't tracked all of you people down yet.*

Lanier read her well. "Please, call me Francis, or Fran." His smile won her immediately. He considered her with such a peaceful expression that his eyes radiated from an inner light that Katie knew she had never seen in any individual before. *Fascinating,* she thought to herself.

But he continued, "Well, no one knows just how many Stalkers there really are. We're all, though, from the same generation and the same part of the country. I've heard that there are about eighteen hundred of us, give or take a few."

Ken Collins closed the wide doors and strolled over to a chair beside Christy, who was busy taking notes.

"This Syndrome is absolutely insane," Katie said to them. "It's a wonder that anyone can get along." She crushed out her cigarette and prepared to light up another. Now she began thinking about Floyd Matkin.

Then she asked him, "But listen, does anyone really know just why you can control the disease and the rest of us can't? I've read the reports, but I don't understand it completely."

Very direct, he thought. *But why not? She's entitled to it.* He shifted uncomfortably in his chair. "Well, I don't know how much you already know, but back in the late eighties, the government found a virus in sheep that was killing off most of the flocks in New Mexico, where I'm from. They developed what they thought was a cure for the disease and sprayed about a million square acres of grazing range. They didn't know if the virus came from something that was indigenous to the plants they ate, or what, but they shot first and asked questions later."

He looked at her evenly to see just how much of this she already knew. "The papers," he continued, "called it an 'outbreak' and wrote the whole business off."

"And what happened after that?"

"It turned out to be a virus that mutated on the chemical the government sprayed. It changed inside the sheep themselves, and when the sheep started surviving the effects of the original virus, the officials thought the crisis was over. My dad's got a whole casebook of clippings."

Katie appeared disappointed. "Is that all that happened?"

"Not quite." Lanier adjusted the sling. "When the virus contacted the chemical, called Lente-89, it apparently thrived and managed to develop the ability to alter a protein bond in the nerve circuits in the spine." Lanier felt funny telling them this. Some of this information the government already knew; and some of it the government didn't want to admit, or recognize.

He continued on. "What the virus did was to lower the level of pure energy that travels to the brain, but only slightly. It caused about two thousand people to become comatose. They were mostly people living on the ranches and the reservations. Their minds emptied, more or less."

"That's terrible," Katie said.

"Well," Lanier said, "it wasn't all that bad. It stopped the sheep from dying, and no human being died because of the changed virus."

"So how did this affect you? Where were you born?"

"In Santa Fe. Dad was a farmer and a mechanic. He got the virus, but Mother didn't. No one knows why. But the army finally said that he must've been out hunting when he contracted it."

Katie smiled at him. "I vaguely remember the incident. I was only a kid then."

"I was born about a year after the spraying, and so were most of the other Stalkers. I suffered some sort of minor genetic damage because of the molecular alteration performed by the original virus my dad carried. Birth defects are often caused by viruses, only mine took thirty years to show itself."

"And that's how you became a Stalker."

"Yes." He glanced around the room. Collins stood impassively, his hands in his pockets.

Until this time, very few people knew much of his personal history. The scandal sheets were digging as deep as possible, but he had burned a lot of bridges long ago. Now, here he was sitting with the President of the United States, having just revealed more about his life than he really intended to. None of the other Stalkers that he knew of—and he only knew about thirty-five of them well—had ever disclosed to the public so much as a fraction of their histories.

Everyone in the world knew that the Stalkers came from the same part of the United States, but no one knew why. *Now*, he thought, *if these people can only keep their mouths shut....*

But in this business, secrets last as long as a plucked rose.

"And then," he gestured with his left hand, "when Liu Shan's Syndrome first appeared in Los Angeles, I was one of the first to go under, and come out. The Syndrome virus is probably very much like the virus that fed off the Lente-89 spray."

Katie was nodding as she leafed through his file, listening. And she was thinking, *If we can duplicate this condition, we might get Congress to rescind the genetic research laws....*

"You went under, then?" she looked up, curious.

"Yes," Lanier said. "It was an emotional thing. I was meditating, and thought that nothing unusual was happening, and just snapped right out of it, willfully, which apparently no one was doing at the time."

"Ken tells me that you're the best. Why is that?"

Lanier suddenly blushed. "Well, I don't know if that's true or not, but I imagine it was because I was meditating for years before this thing struck. I can control my energies better, I guess. I don't know. It's hard to say. The other Stalkers seem to be getting good results as well."

"Well, Fran." She felt very uneasy saying his name. It didn't sound right for this man sitting before her. "I suppose it's caused you a lot of trouble, doing what you do."

He leaned back, careful of his shoulder. "Not yet it hasn't. Well, that's not entirely true. We're moving our operations to Montana, outside of Missoula, on some land I own up there. Someone let word out that I was a Stalker and it had to be someone pretty high up. Anyway, I got swamped with hundreds of people wanting me, and Christy says it got pretty scary for a while there when I didn't return to the ranch."

Christy said nothing, a stern look about her features.

"I can see where a person of your talents would be wanted day and night." She gestured to the small readout that was neatly laid on the corner of the coffee table. She went on.

"We get printouts daily from the Bureau of Statistics on various population profiles, and their rates of vanishings and returns, when they actually do return. Which is rarely. It seems to be getting worse."

Lanier nodded. "That's what I'm told. I don't know the stats myself, but Christy's research keeps me up to date with some of the profiles, at least among the politicians and the military personnel. They seem to require the services of any Stalker the most these days."

"A neurotic bunch," Collins interrupted cheerfully. "There's no telling what they'd do in the real world anyway."

"Don't mind him." She smiled up at Ken. "He doesn't like politics." They laughed.

Katie turned back to Lanier, who was lifting the teacup gingerly with his left hand. "So," she breathed a long sigh. "What can you tell us about Floyd's case that isn't in your report? I get the feeling that you left a few things out."

"The basic details are there," he told her. "There were a few things I couldn't put my finger on, though."

"Go on." She was now very concerned.

He began. "What struck me most about Matkin's case was the contrast between the beginning of the scenario and its end. Did Floyd ever strike you as being unusually neurotic or unhappy? I have to be honest with you in telling you that I don't know much of what's going on, politically, in the country today. I just haven't had the leisure to keep up with things. Particularly private lives. But it seems to me that you would've chosen him for his abilities and strengths. Given the way things are in the world today, I don't think you'd have chosen a person prone to crack easily."

"You're right, of course," Katie told him. "I wouldn't choose someone who couldn't carry the office firmly on his or her shoulders. Christ, the world is falling apart, and the Secretary of State is the one who connects the United States with the rest of the civilized world." She fingered his file. "No, Floyd Matkin I've known for a long time. He was one of my best allies in New York. I just don't understand what happened, or why."

"Was Matkin married?" Lanier asked her.

"No, he wasn't. Divorced, like most of us." She tried to smile, but her eyes betrayed her seriousness.

Lanier turned in his chair, glancing at Christy, who nodded. He frowned slightly. "Well, there has been something on my mind for quite some time now, and I'm not too sure I can verbalize it. But, I believe that something strange is happening, as if the Syndrome itself wasn't bad enough."

"What do you mean?"

"Well, you are acquainted with Albertson Randell. Senator Randell."

She raised her eyebrows. "Yes, I am."

She glanced over at Ken Collins, who shrugged his shoulders. And Katie thought, *This one is really out of touch. . . .*

Lanier fidgeted. "As a Stalker, I rely most upon one's sense of ambience when I go under."

"Ambience?"

"Right. There seems to have been a feeling—an atmosphere, if you will—of romance when I've gone under lately. In the last two important cases I've taken on, a strong sense of yearning had imbued the imagined landscape. This, of course, has a great deal to do with the music itself. But this yearning baffles me."

"What do you mean?"

"People succumb to the Syndrome when things get particularly bad in their lives. The need to escape is with us all. It's a basic defense mechanism. It gets aggravated, as you know, when the Syndrome acts on the music they turn to."

"And?"

"And in these particular instances"—he gestured to Christy for the file—"I had to deal with men of very high importance in our government and industry."

"Well," Katie pointed out, "everyone who goes under is depressed, or at least is supposed to be."

"Most of the time that's true. But these instances involve a woman. Each one of them was desperately in love. And the woman they pursued ultimately killed them, or at least forced them into a situation that killed them." Lanier held the file. "And this has never happened to me before."

He neglected to inform the President of where he had found Senator Randell. He could still smell that river of blood. . . .

"Now it appears," he continued, "that people in science and industry—normal people actually—are suddenly getting unhappy with their personal circumstances and are simply going under the first chance they get. These are just not the kind of individuals that crack. Jet pilots, airline pilots, for example. They're among the most stable individuals that you could find. Christy says that dozens a *week* are vanishing."

"I don't understand. Is this like suicide? Is the disease getting worse?"

"It's something like suicide, but since most people come out of the Syndrome in a few days, or weeks, they're now more willing to escape from the real world than before, even though the planes of vibrations they materialize on could be as deadly as this one, or worse."

Katie sat in a contemplative mood, sucking on her third cigarette.

Christy handed Lanier another list. "Tell her about these."

Lanier picked them up. "Right. We have a listing here already scheduled for possible missions when my collarbone heals. Look." He gave Katie the list. "Aviation people, from pilots to administrators. Military personnel. And scientists. All of a very high caliber, and most of whom either had low Syndrome ratings or were just regular people living regular lives." He shook his head. "The Syndrome is for neurotics and borderline psychotics. Not these people. It's true that the disease is getting stronger, but Baktropol is supposed to keep the symptoms down, especially in normal people."

Katie Babcock scanned the list. "Ken." She addressed her press secretary. "Let's run a check on these people. Run down some personal facts." She turned back to Lanier. "We can probably run a more thorough investigation on these people than you can. Do you think that there is some kind of connection?"

"It's hard to say. But given the fact that these individuals are going under when they shouldn't, and given that the last two cases I've handled I've lost, I'm beginning to feel as if something is happening that shouldn't."

Katie waved her hands about in the air. "Hell, Fran, this whole damn thing shouldn't be happening! We're lucky to have Stalkers in the first place. Listen, do you know that at this moment in history there are more wars taking place on the earth than at any one time? Everything, and I mean *everything*, is falling apart."

He considered her words. "That's what I understand. As I say, I've been out of touch. I do know about the wars, though."

Ken Collins moved across the sunlight, thinking that Katie had better not tell him too much. He tried to get her attention, but decided to keep it to himself. The President of the United States, though, shouldn't disclose sensitive information to an ordinary citizen.

But then he thought, *Just how ordinary could a person with his talent be?*

The President leaned toward Lanier. "This is strictly confidential, you understand, but it's a lot worse than most people imagine." She looked at him very seriously. "The Premier of the Soviet Union and most of his personal cabinet have gone under. They're pleading for Stalkers and we don't have any to spare, but we *have to spare them*. Don't you see? It's détente. I'd like to help them, but I can't. We have our own problems." *And the only edge*, she thought.

"I wasn't aware of this," Lanier admitted.

"And we are getting reports that most of China is now locked in some kind of civil unrest. It could be a civil war. How Japan keeps going is beyond all of the analysts, but our projections indicate that in six years all of Japan will be deserted."

"Deserted?"

"Either killed in rioting or succumbed to the disease. This business between the Saudis and Japan is a joke. It's all on the surface. Floyd and the ambassadors from both countries were doing a song and dance for the whole world. There's no animosity between them. Both nations are close to economic collapse."

Collins sat on the edge of a chair. "And when the Saudis go, what remaining oil they have goes with them."

"Right," Katie echoed. "And this can't go on. We have all the major research centers trying to find a cure for the disease, and now that Perry Eventide is gone, we don't know if anything beyond Baktropol will cure the symptoms."

"No," Lanier responded. "Baktropol will eventually lose its effectiveness. Everyone who uses it will build up a resistance to it, and there's just so much stimulation the human body can take. What we need is a total cure for the disease."

The gravity of the situation began to weigh heavily on Lanier. This was the room, he realized, where decisions concerning billions of people were made. *In conversations just like this* . . .

Curiously, Lanier began wondering what kind of fantastic world a President like Abraham Lincoln would have imagined for himself had he suffered from Liu Shan's Syndrome and heard a Chopin nocturne. Or General Grant. How would people have gotten along in the western territories when the only kind of music was folk tunes?

Everyone needed music to some degree. And few people were tolerating the kinds of music that they were now having to settle with: meaningless concertos by Elliott Carter, computerized sound effects by Milton Babbitt, the stylings of Stockhausen. The romantic composers of the nineteenth century were out.

And, Lanier just then realized, *I'll bet that Tchaikovsky has the Russian Premier in his grasp*.

What music survived was slowly being banned. Radio stations went off the air when only two or three stations per city were actually needed for "news" formats. What else was there? Commercials on television went musicless, jingles forbidden.

Katie crossed her legs, resting her hand on her knee. She flourished a freshly lit cigarette. "But there isn't anything else on Floyd's death you can tell us?"

"No, not a thing. I tried, but the situation was too unreal. The fact that he allowed himself to be tied seemed to indicate to me that he wanted to die. Yet, it was my impression that those orange lights didn't appear until he was firmly bound by that woman, which would have been about the time I came in sight of the farmhouse. Again, that air of romance, that sense of yearning, pervaded everything. She allowed for the whole scenario."

"Who was she?"

"I haven't any idea. I didn't get a glimpse of her face. It doesn't matter. She was a dreamling."

"A what?"

"Oh, that's what we call the people in fantasy worlds. They aren't real to us, but they belong there like furniture to a room. Dreamlings would be like the people you dream about. They aren't real, unlike the Walkers."

"What's a Walker?" She looked at Ken. "This is interesting."

"Well, a Walker is a person who has gone under and just coincidentally landed in a world some other individual has envisioned. It's getting to be quite common now that the disease seems to be becoming more virulent and the vanishings are increasing. It's a very unusual situation. Any kind of programmatic music will have a tendency to allow for the creation of the same kind of world. Take Wagner, for example. No Stalker in his right mind would touch something like the *Ring* cycle. Or even something like Rimsky-Korsakov's *Scheherazade*, or Mussorgsky's *Night on Bald Mountain*. The more programmatic the piece, the more powerful its draw. And a good percentage of the people you would encounter in those worlds would actually be people sharing the same illusion. Walkers."

He seems so calm, Katie looked at him, thinking, *as if this whole phenomenon was like a Sunday picnic*. "This is fascinating, really."

"And there have been occasions where I've shot dreamlings to see if they might be Walkers."

"Shot?"

"Yes, I use a special British Malachi rapid-fire with anesthetic needles that dissolve and congeal the wound. The victims are put to sleep within an average of a minute or longer. It depends on their level of tolerance. The Walkers will simply fade away and return to the real world with me, but the dreamlings will fall down where they're shot and begin sleeping."

Collins checked his watch with a gesture which they all managed to catch.

"I'll leave my report with you," Lanier concluded. "And you're welcome to the list that Christy has drawn up. If you make any connections, please let me know. I'll be out of it for a few weeks, but I'll be returning to my work as soon as I can. Perhaps by then something positive will develop."

The President shook Lanier's free hand. "Something always does. It was a pleasure meeting you, Mr. Lanier." Then she said, "Fran."

Remarkably informal, he suddenly thought. *This woman could be a lawyer, yes. But President? There's more to her than what she gives out. Too bad I didn't vote for her.*

Christy snapped her briefcase shut and followed them out the door. Ken Collins escorted them through the hall. Secret Service men, with oxygen-assisted filter-masks, kept their eyes on both Lanier and Christy. No one but Collins and the President looked at ease.

Lanier turned and addressed the President. "I appreciate some of the information that you've shared with me. Please, if there's anything I can personally do, don't hesitate to contact me."

His eyes glistened as if they were signaling in some unknown cipher. Katie smiled. *Yes*, she thought, *you do have your secrets.* "I'll do what I can."

As they reached the anteroom, Lanier turned to her. "One thing, if you'll pardon my politics, but I'd keep a close eye on Mr. Randell. I don't think he's well. But then, I'm not an expert in these matters. I just thought I'd mention it."

They considered each other briefly.

"I'll do that. Have a nice flight back, Mr. Lanier."

"Fran."

That smile. "Yes, Fran. We'll be in touch."

The door to the small exit hall had been opened. It was something like an airlock, and it had been installed when the pollution and aeroplankton had gotten out of hand some time ago. Christy stood beside the door, buttoning on her filter-mask. Through the windows, they could see the chauffeured limousine waiting at the curb.

She assisted Lanier with his own filter-mask.

Inside the airtight limo, Christy asked him, "What next? You didn't seem eager to tell the President about Ellie Estevan, so you must have a few things on your mind."

He slid the mask up onto his forehead, making sure that the chauffeur couldn't overhear them.

"There's a connection here somewhere, since I haven't lost any patients before this. I don't think it would help having the FBI or the National Security Agency mixing in with this, because I'm not too sure where it leads myself."

They sat in silence as the limousine drove up onto the expressway to the airport. A large bank of smog had enveloped the entire eastern seaboard, and Washington never seemed to escape the vagaries of the weather. Especially man-made weather. Much of the pollution was aeroplankton shells ballooning on their cubic millimeters of hydrogen. He hoped that there would be a flight that could make it out of the city. If the aeroplankton was bad, they'd have to wait.

"I think," Lanier said dreamily, settling into the lushness of the car seat cushion, "that I'll take in a movie or two while I'm recovering. And read a few newspapers and magazines."

"Movie magazines?" Christy queried aside. "Scandal sheets?"

"Something like that."

"I thought so."

On the back of the seat before them was a console that contained a stereo wafer playback system and a radio.

On an impulse, Lanier bent over. "Let's see if this thing works."

There were only five stations on the air, but one station played no news at all, unlike the others. Lanier and Christy looked at each other. The music they heard was electronic.

"Hohvannes," Lanier grinned. "And I'll bet no one will recognize it. The orchestrated version would probably take out half of the city."

The traffic swelled around them. They would make it to the airport before the noon traffic jams and the riot that would later cause several million dollars' worth of damage.

They would hear about it en route to Montana. And they would hear about the homemade Cruise missile that *almost* made it through the White House defenses.

to a small ranch outside of Missoula, Montana. He had been
quite fortunate deciding to abandon Los Angeles when he did.
His meeting with the President had not gone unnoticed by the
media hounds, and the gossip rags and scandal sheets across
the country were rife with speculations, profiles, and political
predictions. He detested the publicity, especially the media's
way of excavating information about him. What they couldn't
find in fact, they conjured as fiction.

But his chief reason for hating the attention was that it could
only interfere with his work. It grieved him to have to be the
one, ultimately, who decided just who was rescued from the
Syndrome and who was not. His only consolation lay in the
fact that there were many other Stalkers across the nation, and
most of them took on charity cases on occasion. And most
were still anonymous.

Yet, as the President had indicated, conditions in the United
States alone had reached such a level of danger that every
available government official and research scientist was needed
to combat the effects of Liu Shan's Syndrome, particularly the
biochemists. The Center for Disease Control in Atlanta had
reported outbreaks of a dozen diseases that hadn't appeared in
America in over eighty years.

So it was extremely important that no one discover that
Francis Lanier had transferred operations to Montana. Government people moved his equipment, people he could trust.
His vast music library, his furniture, his files, everything,
moved by the CIA, no less. Because of his shoulder, though,
he couldn't assist them, and felt, as a consequence, somewhat
helpless for the two weeks it took to move. He could empathize
with that Hollywood Pharaoh. He would feel much better if
there was an island someplace in the South Pacific, or a village
on the coast of Wales where he could send these men for a
few years just to be on the safe side.

He laughed at his own foolishness. He was beginning to
think like some of his patients.

Charlie Gilbert had supervised Lanier's move to Montana,
checking out all the important details of getting his papers in
order and making certain that the whole business was dealt
with inconspicuously. The ranch house that presided over the
forty acres of land in the Bitterroot Valley had only recently
been vacated by a farmer who had lost a wife and a daughter
to the Syndrome. Lanier was sympathetic, and had considered

helping the man as a favor, but Christy's list had grown, and there were priorities. Sadly, there were priorities.

While there was absolutely no question in anyone's mind that Christy was still to stay on as Lanier's aide-de-camp, Charlie Gilbert groaned about it for some time, but not out of disloyalty to Lanier. Charlie had a successful practice in Los Angeles, and had his own roots. They were just harder to pull up than Lanier's.

But Charlie put on his cowboy boots, flew his private jet to Missoula, and spent the day walking downtown in the Indian Summer air while Christy and Lanier spent the day in Washington. It would take a while to establish his own law practice in Missoula, but at least life was slower here, the air much cleaner.

He owed so much to Lanier, and he loved Christy dearly. Back in southern California, life wasn't getting much easier. Mexican terrorists, under the rule of someone named Draco, ruled a third of eastern Los Angeles, and with their stranglehold on the agricultural industry in the San Joaquin Valley there seemed little chance that southern California would return to stability soon.

So Charlie decided to move his practice, and his associates, and live with his wife in Montana. Despite the severe winters, he realized that, with so many people escaping the warmer climates where the aeroplankton throve, real estate swindles would keep him with plenty to do. Crooks were no different in Montana than in Los Angeles.

Charlie had the house divided into two parts. Christy needed a whole office of her own, including the music library and the files and the HomeCom links. Lanier himself didn't take up much space, so Charlie's ideas for the layout of the ranch house suited him. The three of them stayed in a hotel in town until the premises were ready, a hotel known for keeping things quiet.

And Lanier enjoyed waking up in the morning to see the mountains from his rear window, and breathing the fresh, clean air.

His shoulder felt a little too stiff for him to even begin considering a new project, but he and Christy had already scheduled a number of possibilities for the following week. He carefully exercised his shoulder every day, and now it was a question of time before he was ready to proceed. In any case, he was quite familiar with all the profiles that Christy had given him.

Yet he found much that was disquieting about the last several weeks in his life. His meeting with Katie Babcock had given rise to feelings and anxieties he felt he didn't have the strength to carry if they got out of hand. This came from being so much out of touch with the world.

But it isn't every day that a private citizen sits in council with the President of the United States. That meant something. If anything, he was impressed with the fact of the global nature of their troubles.

For the present, though, he took time to relax. Once settled in his ranch house, he spent many hours privately screening Ellie Estevan's films. Although he had the resources for film and video playback in his home, he lacked the adequate facilities for the two holovision films Ellie had made. Nevertheless, he spent many hours viewing the length and breadth of her career. Charlie had procured copies of her films, as well as several of the commercials she had made early in her career. Charlie also had his junior partners compile a rigorous analysis of her history as an actress. It came with items that HomeCom, or private access to DataCom, couldn't provide—publicity photos, clippings from gossip rags, evaluations by studios, and the like.

Ellie Estevan was an intriguing individual to say the least. Her charm seemed to burst from a simple photograph. Her presence onscreen filled theaters across the country, and in Europe, with an aura of overwhelming sexual power that was rarely encountered in any movie star. She was always in demand, and her love life was always a hot item for the scandal sheets.

Yet Lanier noticed that her appeal was particularly apt for the times.

She was still in her twenties, full of energy and spunk. Her soft blue eyes and short curly hair gave her an innocent look, the kind of innocence that the world had lost over the years. She had it. Her smile only hinted at sexuality, but her farm-girl quality made men yearn for her—or someone like her—desperately.

But the roles she took in her movies were anything but innocent. Like many of the female leads in the early years of the cinema, Ellie Estevan played everything from housewife to reformed hooker, from gun moll to Broadway sugarbaby. And these things she did very well. People left theaters shaking, or weeping, oftentimes getting back into line for the late show. Rioting was common at her premieres, particularly in Europe.

Lanier was genuinely surprised—and surprised at his own naiveté—at the stature she held within the industry. For the two years he had been a Stalker, he had had little time for gratuitous pleasures. Movies and holos were ruled out. He had known of Ellie Estevan from what little he had seen of her on television.

Her current film, the highly touted *From Earth's Center*, casts her as an ingenue who destroys the lives of three men— a young lawyer, a writer, and an older businessman who should have known better. The private copy Charlie had acquired for him allowed Lanier to view it objectively, he believed, without the presence of a theater audience. Lanier found it well acted, well written, and tragic.

The music in the movie was totally electronic, and quite listenable, derived from the obscure composition of a man named Fast from the last century. The scenes were staged very carefully, the timing perfect. But one scene in *From Earth's Center* caught his attention.

A close-up shot near the end of the movie had Ellie Estevan as Margo Dalton staring out over the ruins of a fallen space shuttle, on which the multimillionaire businessman had been present. Lanier was startled by the calmness on her face. True, this was Margo Dalton—not Ellie Estevan—a cold-blooded, ambitious woman of twenty-eight. Margo Dalton was calm, heartless, and totally unmoved by the destruction she had wrought.

But Ellie's eyes were exactly like Lanier's. The whole facial expression betrayed her detachment. They were the eyes of the kids he played with when he was young in Santa Fe. And they were quite like the eyes of his benefactor in the mountains south of his hometown. He hadn't seen such serenity in years.

Naturally, on Ellie Estevan, those eyes were compelling and beautiful. Lanier got the impression from the last scene that she in some way had been miscast for the role: she could *act* heartless, but those little-girl eyes seen in real daylight were the eyes of a special person.

Yet he felt that idea wasn't entirely true, either. Ellie Estevan was a gold mine of contradictions. When Margo Dalton turned away from the flaming hulk of the space shuttle, back to her new lover's air car, her demeanor, her physical presence, suggested a calculated energy that could burst with an awesome range of power at any moment, like a cougar's stored magic as it waits in a tree. It was fitting that Ellie Estevan was an actress. Creatively, she would have succeeded at anything she had put her mind to.

There was nothing in Charlie's profiles that could enlighten him on Ellie Estevan's relationship to Perry Eventide. It was just one of those things.

Christy came into the small living room from her office.

"I did it," she merrily announced. "Got you an invite." She folded her arms proudly.

Lanier looked up from the couch and the morning's paper. "Great, when is it?"

"There will be a party at Burton Shaughnessy's mansion near Aspen in a week's time. The weekend coming up, actually. Ellie Estevan will be there, and Burton Shaughnessy is eager to meet you. I guess this is the only benefit from being exposed with the President."

Lanier tossed the paper down. "Luck, I'd say. So Ellie didn't go under, it seems. What did you tell him?"

She smiled. "I told him that now that you have been brought out into the open, you've been considering helping out the movie industry. The city of Los Angeles is practically under siege, but the movie industry survives. He nibbled and bit."

"I'm looking forward to this."

"It's supposed to start sometime Friday, noonish, and he said that it would last the entire weekend."

"Sounds regular for Shaughnessy, if what I've been reading about him is true."

"I think it is," she explained. "There are two or three a year, mostly for political hustling within the industry itself. He's a big wheel. But then again, he probably loves parties."

Lanier got up. "I just hope that there will be others of my kind there." He seemed worried. "I don't know if I'll fit in."

Christy smiled at his shyness. "Listen, accept it. You're high profile now. All the known Stalkers are. There'll be some politicos and government people, writers and producers. Not just movie stars. Most will probably not know you, or care. Not if Ms. Estevan is present."

"Thanks."

"You're welcome," she smirked.

Lanier sank deeper into his bathrobe, grinning. "Why, Christy, do I detect disappointment?"

"Not the slightest," she said feigning indifference, turning back toward the music library.

"Hey, you want to go along? You and Charlie?" He meant it.

She looked back. "No," smiling, "but stay out of trouble. Those bitches can drain a man in nothing flat. All that's left is a shell."

"I've suffered worse, believe me," he said, and he went back to the morning scandal sheet.

Aspen, Colorado, had already settled into the spell of autumn. The heavy snows of winter were a few weeks away, thus the winter tourists were nowhere to be seen. High above him, on the steeply sloping mountains, Lanier could see the aspen leaves turning their beautiful gold as the cold air surrounded them. The skiing afficionados and other seasonal crazies would be arriving in a couple of weeks when the first flake fell and stuck, but for all the white that would soon grace these peaks, Lanier preferred the colors that the fall had brought. *Peaceful*, he thought to himself. *Not austere like the mountains in winter.*

Lanier, so far, had made his journey unnoticed. He had helicoptered from the nearest airport and taken a motel just outside of town. After his dinner, he had taken an idle stroll through the town, past the little "shoppes" on main street, and he was surprised and disappointed at just how much the town had grown since he had last been there, years ago.

Whatever else went wrong with the country, there were still those devotees to summer and winter recreation who could still afford—both financially and spiritually—to come here and play. And play they did. The stores were expensive and quaint, the people outrageously beautiful. Rumors constantly circulated of debauchery and unholy fun. And no one appeared to be over thirty-five, and no one appeared to be in the least bit poor. Aspen hadn't changed in a hundred years.

Christy's map and directions were explicit and detailed. The drive up to Burton Shaughnessy's hideaway didn't take him long. Tucked away behind a wilderness of pines, and partly lodged into the side of the mountain as if a giant woodsman had shoved it in like a logging wedge, the mansion glowed with the party which was already in progress. And, much to Lanier's surprise, there was music pounding out through the encompassing forest.

In front of the mansion was a circular driveway and a wide lawn that boasted several pieces of modern sculpture. Lanier recognized a giant Calder stabile that was also part mobile. Its garish crimson discs turned slowly in the presence of a slight wind. In the driveway itself was an odd mix of vehicles ranging from expensive gassers to steamers like Lanier's own rented Bronco. There was even a very unfashionable army half-track amphibian that was at least a century, and two wars, old. *Americans and their toys*, he thought.

"This should be amusing," he murmured to himself as he walked up the graveled driveway to the front door.

The party was well into third gear, if the din was any reliable indication. The door vibrated from the inside with music and laughter. *At least they're laughing and having a good time*, he thought. The Syndrome would have a field day at a gathering like this if the party chemistry wasn't just right. *Like the Masque of the Red Death*. . . .

Lanier decided not to knock, realizing that this was no formal cocktail party where decorum reigned and etiquette came before all else.

Inside, he encountered a rainbow of luminescent colors. Everyone sported the ornamentation that the fashions of the time demanded. Several people, though, were wearing tuxedos, and one very plastered young lady wore a green khaki jumpsuit and an army helmet with infrared field goggles strapped to the top. African War surplus, he reasoned. She probably owned the half-track outside as well.

Then there were several people in ski bibs; others wore flannel shirts and hiking boots. *Locals, no doubt*, he thought, *prepared for anything*. He felt suddenly obvious, and knew that he wouldn't fit in. But he wasn't dressed any differently than anyone else. No one was looking at him, but he still felt awkward.

A small, brown-eyed, large-breasted girl in farmer's overalls flitted by, holding a large beer mug with a swizzle stick lurching sideways in it.

"Hi," she said cheerfully. "They're in the kitchen mixing

up this stuff, whatever it is." She held up the mug triumphantly. "Go on in and try it. It's great!"

Lanier couldn't ignore her enthusiasm. Besides that, he wanted to introduce himself to his host.

The main room of the mansion, which held the bulk of the party, did not reflect the usual ostentatiousness that most domiciles of the wealthy seemed to require. In fact, Shaughnessy had kept the decor quite simple and utilitarian. This whole floor—and there appeared to be at least three—was totally for socializing. Two fireplaces blazed at opposite ends of the room, and four large wooden beams were exposed along the ceiling. The floor was sunken by about a meter, and cushions lay everywhere. On them were a score of people in various stages of inebriation or hallucination. Whatever these people did for their livelihoods, one thing was certain: all of them were rich. And they showed it very well.

Lanier found the kitchen with no problem. It was the water hole. There was enough movement to the party that he didn't feel out of place, finally realizing that everyone was loose enough to accept a stranger in their midst. In fact, everyone was quite friendly.

Burton Shaughnessy stood in the middle of a chattering group of friends of his, who were mostly young. He held a small, almost petite, glass of the brew that came from a large kettle squatting on the kitchen table. Shaughnessy wore a large tan Stetson and a bolo tie that held the largest single piece of turquoise that Lanier had ever seen. *Here* was the garishness that the mansion lacked. Another piece of turquoise, this one of a pale greenish tint, was on his belt buckle. When Shaughnessy turned around to refill his drink, his belt read "Burt" on the back.

Lanier pondered Shaughnessy's character. *Put him on a horse and we'd see just what kind of cowboy he is. . . .*

Receiving a glass of the compound from a man who seemed, despite his casual dress, to be either part of the staff or the catering service, Lanier looked around the kitchen. Food, in varying states of preparation, lay everywhere. Shaughnessy had apparently hired the United States Army to cater the supply. Perhaps *they* were the ones who came in the half-track. There was so much food that Lanier got the impression Shaughnessy expected more than just a few friends to show up for his party.

The ceiling pounded. From the sounds that were coming

from down the stairs and thundering through the roof, Lanier surmised that there were twice as many people upstairs as there were downstairs. The band was somewhere directly overhead.

Shaughnessy caught Lanier's eye as he stood in the doorway looking lost.

"'Scuse me," he said to his compadres, plowing a meaty hand through the crowd that engulfed him. Shaughnessy was a large man and moved through his guests like an icebreaker.

"Shit, how the hell are you?" He grabbed Lanier's right hand, squeezing it to the bone. "You're Francis Lanier. I recognize you from your picture in the scandals. Glad that you could make it."

"Glad to be here," Lanier smiled, overwhelmed by Shaughnessy's size. He was bigger than Charlie Gilbert.

Shaughnessy clapped a hand to Lanier's shoulder. "Man, this is gonna be *great*!" he bellowed, moving out into the hallway. "We got about a thousand people coming here tonight."

Lanier felt as if he were in the presence of a beached whale. Shaughnessy's girth was absolutely comic and endearing. The man was powerful and friendly.

"What can I call you? Frank? Francis?" He made a funny face, his nose glowing slightly from the alcohol. "Please, God, not 'Francis.' I couldn't live with myself." He laughed uproariously.

Lanier felt as if he'd just been rechristened. "Fran or Frank," he laughed with the man, "will do. Call me anything you want." *What an odd person*, he thought, so he countered with, "What do I call you? *Burton?*"

They grinned like poker players. Shaughnessy snorted. "Hell, just call me Burt. Just about everyone does, except my ex-wives. I won't tell you what they call me."

"I can guess."

The two of them laughed.

Lanier wasn't finding it too difficult to like this man, and he could understand how Burton Shaughnessy survived amid the barracudas of Hollywood and New York. And it wasn't too hard to figure why this man was one of the richest individuals associated with the movie industry.

Of course, as a Stalker, Lanier himself wasn't without means. Shaughnessy seemed to sense this as they stood there talking.

"Well, hey, Frank, tell me about what you do. Sounds incredible to me, since it's never happened to me yet." Shaughnessy took a huge drink, but continued before Lanier could respond. "Of course, I lost my last wife to the disease, and I got a daughter at Syracuse right now I haven't heard from in weeks. But, hell, you know kids. Never stay in touch." He was jolly about everything, it seemed. "I didn't know you people were for real. I guess it's happening to just about everyone these days."

"I'm sorry about your wife."

"Hey, listen pal, she deserved it. She was as crazy as they come." They entered the large main room. "I hear you live up in Malibu Canyon."

"Yes, I did."

"Did? Couldn't take the Canyon crowd, I suppose."

"No, it's not that. It's the only place near Los Angeles I could live. I had to move because of the press exposure when I saw the President." Lanier made it clear in his intonation that the matter was to be dropped.

If Shaughnessy got the signal, he didn't visibly let on.

"Oh, right! I know exactly what you mean. Jesus, I was filming a new holo in this dingy little suburb outside São Paulo, and hundreds of these stupid peasants—and I mean *stupid*— came out of the hills and wanted to be movie stars. I know what you mean. They fucked up everything. I think it was someone from Abraxas Studios who announced that we'd be filming. They've been on my ass for twenty years. We had to move out of town to finish the damn thing."

Lanier nodded, taking a calculated pause to taste the substance in his glass. He would allow a little alcohol tonight. But *only* a little.

"Hey, well, listen, Frank." He patted Lanier on the back. "Why not just mingle around for a while. Get to know some of the folks here. I'll be honking upstairs and down all night long. I do want to sit and talk a bit, though. I gotta go and make sure my ladies can hold up for the night. If they go, I won't have anything to do with myself."

He winked like a uncle.

"No problem." Lanier raised his glass as Shaughnessy weaved down the hallway, his Stetson was like a wild bull above all the heads he passed in the crowd.

Music tumbled down the stairs, pushing ahead of it an attractive blond couple. Lanier recognized the man as a well-known movie actor who owned a ranch in northern Colorado. He was very famous, and now very looped. Lanier began wondering where the actor's wife was, but then tabled his morality, realizing that here in Aspen, one didn't concern oneself with trivialities. The actor seemed better paired with his companion anyway.

Lanier mounted the stairs, rolling back the sleeves of his shirt. He had decided to wear casual dress for the evening, and that meant just shirt, Levi's, and boots. He hated foppery and hated to spend his money on the styles and gimcracks that hung in the windows of the best New York fashion salons. And Shaughnessy wasn't at all offended by such casual dress. Shaughnessy himself looked like a buffoon, Lanier thought to himself, but then again, this is a party, not a fashion show, *or* an inquisition.

But Shaughnessy had style. Lining the walls of the hallway were several valuable paintings. Lanier recognized a Chagall and an Oscar Kokoschka. They were originals. There was also a small Picasso etching, and in the main room was a very large, three-meter square Fritz Scholder original showing an Indian chief reposing serenely with a dog that rested its head in his lap. It was extremely valuable.

Upstairs there was another enormous room, and this one had the band. The band was a small consortium of jazz musicians who had hooked up all of their instruments into a bank of portable synthesizers and mellotrons. The guitar and piano keyboard played their normal chords and notes, but they came out sounding like crystal wind-chimes, or vibrating sheets of tin. Sometimes the sounds reminded him of the vermilion rushing of blood in veins. Lanier closed his eyes, testing the vibrations, testing the presence of possible harmonies on which the Syndrome could feed. He assumed that everyone here was on Baktropol. Its amphetamine quality might account for the high pitch of the party itself.

He soaked up the sound, calming himself inwardly. There was not enough alcohol in his drink to affect his perceptions yet, but he knew that he would have to quit drinking soon.

What he felt he didn't consider too dangerous. Though delightful, the music was unfamiliar enough not to arouse the disease. Whether the people here at the party were fairly normal, or borderline psychoneurotics, he couldn't tell. But the party seemed to be progressing well. He knew that parties were for letting off steam, for raising hell. No one he knew had ever vanished simply by letting his or her emotions reach a peak. But, given how the disease was changing, anything could happen.

It was because he was a Stalker that he felt somewhat apprehensive, despite the festive atmosphere of the party. He, perhaps of them all, knew what the consequences of succumbing would be.

On the other hand, there was no small amount of anxiety in his heart about the possibility of meeting Ellie Estevan. When it turned out that she hadn't originally succumbed weeks ago, but was merely missing on a whirlwind romance, Lanier had come up with a lot of questions and no answers. Mainly he was concerned about just who had requisitioned that she be stalked. Was she playing games with the Stalkers? He didn't know. And meeting her here, with so many different people, he couldn't help being suspicious about the games the rich people play. He knew that he didn't belong here, and he refused to accept the fact that he was someone important.

But Ellie Estevan would fit right in.

Lanier circled the band and found another set of stairs that led up to the roof. The roof of the mansion ran into the mountainside, and a number of people reclined on chairs, crouching on benches at tables, and everyone was eating and drinking heartily. What caught his attention was the generator chugging away off to one side in a clump of low evergreens. A silver tank of propane shone like a landed torpedo in the half-moon's light.

Lanier noticed that Aspen had shut down its electricity after dark, except for the traffic lights and some streetlights. Ever since the dam at Lake Powell had been destroyed by eco-terrorists, most of the four-corners area was without power for occasional periods. The Denver stations had enough drain on their own, providing for a population of twelve million. And every community had to shut down after dark.

The generator would keep the party on its feet for some time to come. Lanier admired Shaughnessy's skill in arranging his life in such a way as to always be able to survive in the highest style. If the whole Aspen area lost its power, Shaughnessy would be able to light up the night as long as his propane held out. Expensive as it was, Shaughnessy, he knew, could easily afford it.

The roof itself was more like a patio. Winter plants of various kinds grew from large pots. The roof was enclosed by a small railing at which people leaned with their drinks. Spaced here and there along the railing were carefully arranged bonsai and occasional pieces of sculpture.

A waiter came up with another tray of drinks. Lanier took one, but swiftly dumped it out into a planter, retaining the ice only. Alcohol had to be kept at a minimum. Tonight was strictly business.

Returning to a bathroom on the second floor, he managed to refill his glass with water, washing out what remained of the booze. He was careful not to offend those who could only have a high time when everyone was drinking.

He decided to avoid the shrill sounds of the jazz band, so he retreated to the first floor where it was much calmer, comparatively speaking. Rounding a corner after pausing for an awkward spell of small talk with a minor actress, he entered the large living room.

And there she was.

Whether Ellie Estevan had been here all the time, or had just arrived, he couldn't tell. But Shaughnessy and a couple of others stood around her, laughing and talking. Ellie Estevan merely looked on passively, smiling when the conversation turned her way. *Those eyes*, he thought as he watched her. Her hair was just a tad longer than it had been in *From Earth's Center*. But it framed that innocent expression, the pale skin of her face. Her eyes were like pools of glacial runoff, reflecting a calm Arctic sky. Not cold, but shimmering and alive. As the cliché goes, she was much more real and attractive than in her movies.

She wore a long coat made of soft leather, quite expensive, and beneath her coat were brown slacks that only hinted at her true form. Her blouse ruffled at her throat, and she wore a small, delicate pair of earrings that dangled like lanterns in the light.

Her smile pulled people in around her, though most everyone at the party was acting cool and detached, as if her presence were nothing to get upset about. He decided then that she had just arrived.

He leaned against the paneled wall and sipped his water and

ice, with its half-moon of lime, and watched.

With a sudden turn of his head, Burton Shaughnessy pointed over to Lanier and gestured. "Hey, Frank. Over here!"

Somewhat embarrassed, Lanier stood away from the wall and tried to ignore the people staring at him. Shaughnessy was laughing. Lanier came over unhurriedly as if Ellie Estevan were just another individual to be introduced at the party.

"Frank, this is Ellie Estevan. I wanted you to meet her." With one large hand, he presented Ms. Estevan. Then he said a curious thing. "She's got your eyes. I'll bet you're brother and sister." He laughed at his joke.

Lanier flushed slightly that the comparison would be such an intimate one. But he thought, *Well, cowboy, you're not a clown after all.*

"Yes," Lanier thought quickly, jumping into the mood of the moment, "we're from the same litter."

That took everyone by surprise. Shaughnessy clapped him on his back like a football coach, laughing.

Ellie Estevan smiled delightfully. She said, "Meow," looking up at Shaughnessy, then over at Lanier.

Jesus, he thought as a wave of electricity circled up his spine like a hawk lifting on a heat thermal, *who is this woman?* That this person had become one of the highest paid, most successful actresses in the movie industry was no mystery at all now. Her eyes seemed to flash across his mind, almost as if he were totally composed of glass.

"Well," Lanier opened, "I *am* glad to meet you. I'm Francis Lanier."

He extended his hand, and when she took it, gently, shaking it, he thought his arm would melt off. "But you can call me Frank, if 'Francis' makes you feel as funny as it does Burt here."

"Glad to meet you," she said somewhat musically as if her words were threaded with notes rather than meaning.

Lanier, not used to socializing, suddenly came up without anything more to say.

But Shaughnessy dove right in. "Well, hey folks, we can talk over dinner. We got some stew and cornbread and some ribs and some other garbage I had 'em make. Let's go on out back." He pointed off to their right, to the side of the house where people were coming in and out with paper plates, foraging beans into their mouths.

They followed Shaughnessy outside.

Lanier had originally planned to avoid the dinner that Shaughnessy was going to provide, so he had eaten in Aspen before coming out. Now he was stuck with the obligation to eat again. He *did* look forward to the conversation. At least the listening part. He wasn't at all adept at small talk; he would have to let things take their natural course. Too, he wasn't the main attraction. Ellie Estevan was here, and it was very apparent that all eyes were on her and no one else.

Off to the side of the mansion was a large lawn that held tables and chairs, and somewhere in the dark were the ruins of a croquet set that someone had taken out earlier in the afternoon when the party was just getting under way. A large bronze sundial brooded at the very center of the lawn. Pine trees enclosed the entire area, and in the chill air the smells of the barbecue rose and drifted sweetly about them like ghosts. Lanier admired Shaughnessy. His imperial style was such that Lanier was convinced that in a former life Shaughnessy must have been a sultan.

They clustered around the long buffet table that was heaped with a pleasant assortment of steaming dishes. Ellie Estevan, he observed casually, moved among everyone quite comfortably, helping herself to the various vegetable dishes. She ate no meat. *Another plus,* Lanier thought. *She knows how to take care of herself.*

He wondered about the food itself. Shaughnessy could easily afford homegrown or pure foods, and as he sampled the baked beans, Lanier made a mental note to ask him about it sometime. Most food was either ersatz or hydroponic. What with chemical sprays, hormones, nutritional additives the government was allowing, it was no wonder to him—or anyone else—that various cancers and protein deficiencies were showing up in the children of this generation, and their parents as well. *But a man's got to eat. . . .*

Following an impulse to stay near Shaughnessy, Lanier moved around the buffet table. He felt it easier to be near someone he knew than to fend his way among the people he knew only by reputation. He didn't want to appear any more awkward than he already did.

But Shaughnessy, attracted to Lanier in his own way—and it could have been the eyes—motioned for Lanier to join him at his side.

A low table had been set up, and around it were eight or so foldup chairs. On the backs of the pale canvas chairs, Shaughnessy had the names of famous Hollywood directors stenciled. Lanier thought it kinky and somewhat indulgent, but a man of Shaughnessy's disposition could do anything he damn well pleased. And besides that, everyone thought that it was cute.

Shaughnessy got SHAUGHNESSY. Ellie Estevan got HITCH-COCK. Lanier got KUROSAWA. The others who had joined them around the table were DE MILLE, HAWKS, HERZOG, OZU, and WERTMULLER.

Like kids sitting in magic chairs at dinner, he thought.

The sweet aromas of the barbecue floated about them. They talked and gossiped. Lanier, for the most part, listened. But so did Ellie Estevan.

With a mouthful of potato salad, Shaughnessy said, "Hey, Frank. Tell us about that thing with the President. That must have been interesting. I've never met her. Met everyone else in the damn world, but not her." He proceeded to chomp busily.

Lanier hovered over an ear of corn, taken off guard.

"Well, we had a conference." He took some time to wipe a touch of butter from his lips with his napkin. "It wasn't anything much. She wanted to meet me and my staff."

Ellie Estevan looked across at him. "That must have been exciting."

Lanier was surprised, but he followed her lead, careful not to betray too much. "Not really. It was just politics, which I try to avoid when and where I can." He grinned at her.

Shaughnessy burst out, "Good man! Good man! They're all a bunch of shysters. Can't run the country for shit."

The tiny freckles beneath Ellie Estevan's eyes stood out in the light of the torches Shaughnessy had the help install that afternoon. *Those eyes. . . .*

"What line of work are you in, Frank? Do you live in Aspen?"

He reddened. He hadn't expected so direct an approach, and now that his profession was supposed to be common knowledge, he felt very uneasy talking about his work.

Again, Shaughnessy to the rescue. "Frank here's a Stalker, believe it or not."

Everyone looked at him suddenly, pleasantly surprised.

"Oh, really?" Ellie said with interest. She seemed taken

somewhat aback. She recovered quickly.

"Yes." He tried to sound noncommittal, evasive, trying to hide his discomfort.

"You must be rich," she said, glowing. Everyone giggled. So did he. She smiled at him playfully.

"I could be richer than I am now," he began, "but most of what I get goes into work for the Syndrome." Then he grinned. "When I do work for the government, though, I really stick it to them. As I said, I hate politics and politicians."

At that moment he noticed something a little unusual. Everyone seemed to be pondering him with an air of respect, something no one else at the table generated. Ellie Estevan surveyed him closely.

"Are you a modern or classical Stalker?" she asked.

Lanier couldn't have been more startled at her question than if she had dropped a rock onto his plate.

"A modern," he said, leaning back in his chair, setting down his fork. "You know about Stalking?"

Shaughnessy and the other guests brightened, looking at one another curiously. "Say," he said, "what's this about modern and classics?"

Now there was a common bond of some kind between Ellie Estevan and Lanier. He folded his arms, considering her.

"It's strange that you should know about it at all. The whole thing is a secret for the most part."

Everyone looked on.

Ellie said, "I met a man from Trinidad, Colorado, when I was filming in England a year ago. He was a classical Stalker working for British Intelligence. He was on loan from the State Department."

Lanier tried to think. *Who could that be?*

"Say, what gives? Fill us in." Shaughnessy was like an eager child listening to a fairy story.

Lanier returned to his plate of beans and ribs, speaking as he ate. "Oh, it's practically nothing. There are just different kinds of Stalkers for different kinds of music. Some specialize in baroque and classical music, and others do jazz and rock and roll for those really far gone. Then there are those like myself who do modern classical music."

Ellie Estevan, spoon in mouth, being playful, said, "That guy I knew was mostly Mozart and early Beethoven. Said he wouldn't touch anything beyond Beethoven's *Second Symphony* or *Fidelio*."

"Opera," Lanier remarked. "He's a brave man."

Shaughnessy asked, "And you do modern music? That's rare, isn't it?"

"No, not really," Lanier began. "Modern music was the best thing when the Syndrome hit because, since the middle of last century, few people became acquainted with what was going on in the world of serious music. Therefore, when the Syndrome struck, the only music that could be tolerated was music no one knew. So most of my patients have gone under at unusual performances of modern music, music that nevertheless hit them the right, or I should say the *wrong*, way."

Ellie seemed to squirm in her chair. "Are you a musician?"

"No. My father was, though. He taught himself piano, and when I was growing up, he used to buy me scads of classical records. Then, over the years my tastes changed and I began to look up obscure composers of modern music and found that a lot of it was actually quite beautiful."

He paused. He hadn't really thought about all of this for years, and wondered what harm it would do if he told them any more. But he knew he had a friend in Shaughnessy. He hoped that the other women assembled around the table wouldn't blab to the scandals. But this business was like politics. Everything was in the public domain.

Ellie Estevan, though, was genuinely intrigued. "So that's where the new movie music has come from. I don't bother myself with these things, you know."

"Right," Lanier said. "And there are hundreds of thousands of recorded and unrecorded pieces of music for concerts and movies, and no one knows about them, virtually. Most of the composers I know about ended up becoming professors of music in universities, since the record companies couldn't make any money off anyone except Tchaikovsky and Beethoven. They just faded away in their tenured positions."

He looked Ellie in the eyes. A slight surge of energy shimmied up his spine. A warm glow radiated beneath his heart, a lightness. The power in her eyes mesmerized him. And he knew that, like so many millions of her rapturous fans, he could very easily fall in love with someone like her. Just for those eyes.

He turned away.

The conversation shifted among the other guests assembled around the table, and Lanier began considering everything the media had said Ellie Estevan was, and put all of those things up against what he could see right before him. Soft chords of a melody began running through his mind as he watched her chat with Shaughnessy or the ladies beside her. They all seemed to be friends. He fell back to a recollection from some time ago. It was the time he had gone under when the Syndrome first struck. There had been a woman quite like Ellie Estevan in his life. She had special eyes and a special way of smiling that made his life all alone a Hell.

A shard of a Shostakovich piece came over the outdoor speakers that led back to the jazz group upstairs. It was a tune, worked into the jazz set, that had haunted him most of his adult life. It returned as they sat around with their coffee and brandy, talking leisurely. Each person around the table, perhaps taken in by Lanier's presence, began to speak openly of his or her own personal exposure to the Syndrome, and those they knew whom it had affected.

Normally he didn't allow his mind to fill with music, to wander where the music cared to go. It helped him order and regulate his emotional life. There was no room for emotional discontinuities, and he had to be discreet. But the music. . . .

Autumn fields. Maple leaves falling in the wind. The light waxing pale toward dusk with the red veins of dying vines streaking up chimneys.

The memory was on him before he could do anything about it.

In one sudden explosion, the chair KUROSAWA crumpled over. Gazing deep into Ellie Estevan's unquenchable eyes, Francis Lanier vanished to the music he hadn't evoked in years.

The party was suddenly over.

CHAPTER EIGHT

❦

Concerto Grosso, for Strings With Piano
Obbligato
Ernest Bloch

"There is something about your mind that keeps you from distinguishing polarities."

Lanier faced the older man.

"I'm thirty-three years old. I've heard all of this before, Two Moons, mostly from you."

The Indian spat into the dust on the porch of his house in downtown Albuquerque, New Mexico, as the first moon of the evening rose in the east. The older man was Navajo, but it was hard to tell from his brand-new Roughout boots with the cocky heels, the well-tailored leather vest he wore, and the light brown cowboy hat perched above a shock of jet-black hair. He even wore glasses that were framed in the latest of contemporary styles. This was no ordinary Indian.

"Listen, Ben," Lanier pleaded, "this is getting out of hand."

His friend smiled up from his whittling stick. A small dog wiggled out from the back of the adobe house that occupied a sizable plot of land in the center of town.

Benjamin Two Moons considered Lanier. "Everyone is responsible, in some discriminate way, for making his own world. You know that."

Lanier stood in the early evening. The walk into town had been long and exhausting. It had given him a great deal of time to think things through.

It didn't bother him that the town surrounding them seemed totally deserted. *This* was an altogether different Albuquerque, New Mexico.

Two Moons had kept it that way.

He continued, "And it's your responsibility to adjust and cope, to accept. A rock in the middle of a creek lets the water go around it or over it. The rock, if it's a good rock, will remained unchanged."

He grinned a row of perfect teeth. Better teeth than Lanier's own. "I know you can do it," he said to Lanier, smiling both wisely and foolishly as if a joke were lurking about somewhere like a banana peel waiting for a foot to come along.

Two Moons stood up and stretched. Lanier heard the Indian's sternum pop. When it did, a spiral of white light burst from his chest.

"Ah," he said, relieved. "That hit the spot." He dusted himself off.

Lanier put his hands into his pockets, feeling clumsy and embarrassed. "Tell me," he asked Two Moons, "did you know something like this was going to happen?"

"Of course. It had to balance itself out. Something had to move you. Nothing remains the same for too long if it isn't supposed to be that way."

Lanier stared at Two Moons in the dark. "And what about you?"

"Well," he laughed, "that's another story entirely."

"Then you see Ellie Estevan as the balancing factor in this particular instance? The evil that opposes the good?"

The Indian stood on one leg and polished a boot on the calf of his other leg. He put his hand on Lanier's shoulder to steady himself.

"That's a bit presumptuous, don't you think?"

"I didn't ask for this. I'm only trying to make sense of it."

"Well, son, whatever stance you take, she is obviously the antithetical force, good *or* evil. It's up to you to decide which."

He righted himself, hitching up his freshly pressed corduroy slacks. "Besides that, Fran," he began earnestly, "you didn't think that this would be a piece of cake, did you?"

Lanier looked partially disgusted. "Hell, no. But I didn't ask for my talent. And neither did you."

"Ah," Two Moons interjected, "but I'm not the one complaining either."

Lanier paced impatiently around in the darkness shrouded about the porch. The first moon had risen quite significantly, moving only slightly to the naked eye.

"Listen, you're an Indian. You've got a *lot* to complain about—or have you forgotten?"

All around them, Albuquerque was completely blacked out. No streetlights were on, no stoplights changed their colors. The buildings themselves resembled the monoliths of a graveyard. They were cenotaphs, for it looked like there were no people here to be mourned.

"Why the emotion all of a sudden?" Two Moons became serious for the first time since Lanier had appeared.

"I don't know." Lanier stirred a toe in the dirt. "It's embarrassing, that's all. This wasn't supposed to happen."

He touched the micro-receiver in his earlobe. It was silent. Then he said, "I'm just getting confused. Maybe I'm having a lapse of conscience."

"Or a nervous breakdown."

"Maybe. I don't know. I thought those things happened to other people, not me. The neurotics."

"It might be more than you suspect." Two Moons pondered Lanier's dour expression. Lanier turned away. Two Moons walked over beside him. "It could be *much* more than you suspect. Life, if anything, is full of surprises."

Farther to the northeast, the second moon reared itself over the mountains like a soiled doubloon. The whole sky took on so much light that it looked almost like dawn. Lanier could see his benefactor clearly in the glow of the two moons to the east of them.

The Indian stepped out onto the sidewalk that led into town. A town that was empty of light and life.

He turned around, facing Lanier, who stood mute and somewhat confused. Two Moons' glasses sparkled in the moonlight.

"But if you're really careful this time," he began encouragingly, "things will turn out much better than you expected. But don't forget"—he waved a nagging finger—"everything must balance out in the universe. Everything. That's Fudd-Smith's Law."

"Who the hell is that?"

Two Moons whistled for the pooch, who came over wagging its tail excitedly.

"Not 'who,' but 'what,'" he said.

"You're not making any sense, Ben."

"Fudd-Smith's Law says that you can't have your cake and eat it too. Which is to say, that everything balances itself out."

"Fudd," Lanier pointed out. "That just sounds stupid."

"Not really." Two Moons scratched the eager dog's ears. "Think about it. 'Fudd' has all sorts of ridiculous connotations, whereas 'Smith' does not. The two belong together because the apparent disharmony calls attention to itself."

Two Moons rose, putting his fists on his hipbones. "Fudd-Smith's Law is merely the moral equivalent of Newton's Third Law of Motion. For every good in the universe, there is an opposite and equal evil."

Lanier frowned. "This is serious. Where'd you pick that up?"

Two Moons laughed. "Look around you! The damn thing is everywhere."

Lanier wasn't satisfied, even if there was a kind of sense to his words.

"Even here?"

"Even here," Two Moons concluded. "Well, the moons are up and I have things to do." He smiled at Lanier. "You can find your way back?"

Lanier smiled, and laughed. "Of course. Don't worry about me."

Two Moons waved and clicked off down the sidewalk. The small dog trailed faithfully behind him.

Well, Lanier thought, *at least I got to see the old guy, even if it wasn't under the most controlled circumstances.*

He regrouped his feelings as though they had been a flock of sparrows scattered before a big wind. Somewhat calmer now, he sat in the rattan chair Two Moons had just recently vacated. He surveyed the world that the Indian had created.

The dust in the air was diffusing the light of the two moons in the east. Two moons. There were no people in this city, red or white. Except that here and there seven women were hiding. They were dreamlings. They allowed Ben Two Moons an in-

teresting pastime in this special world of his. Lanier privately
suspected that the women Two Moons chased after in this
deserted New Mexico town were other Navajo who had the
same talent as he. *Stalkers.* If so, the women could come and
go as they pleased. But some remained, calling down the dark
canyons in their shrill, banshee voices as they would disappear
around the corners.

Lanier smiled at the irony. Even here, he thought, Fudd-
Smith's Law works. Even here in one Indian's perversion of
paradise.

"Well," he addressed no one in particular, "I've got things
to do myself."

Closing his eyes, he reconsidered the penetrating stare of
Ellie Estevan. He found it difficult to fight off the memory of
her face, those eyes and freckles. The vibrations running
through him still persisted.

The sounds of the cicadas in the front lawn soon began to
fade from his conscious mind. He began his mantra. The wind
in the ocotillo that lined the driveway to the adobe house had
ceased to blow. Lanier pushed away all sounds of this world,
and all sounds from within his own mind.

And he found himself standing in five inches of snow in
full daylight in Burton Shaughnessy's side yard where he had
vanished just a short time ago. Just how much time had elapsed
Lanier didn't really know for certain, though he was surprised
that at least a day had gone by. Usually he stayed under for
as long as the music lasted—or resonated in the consciousness—but this was different. He had hoped to return to the
party after he recovered himself from the Shostakovich.

But there was no party. There wasn't even a mansion.

A snowstorm, the first one of the season, had layered the
place with a brownish-white mantle. Burnt timbers, crumpled
foundation stones, and broken chunks of cement lay about the
grounds. An explosion had virtually leveled the house of Burton
Shaughnessy. Snow covered the ruins like a funeral pall.

Beside Lanier were the remains of the picnic area and the
chairs they had sat in. Behind them was the sundial, still erect
and somewhat unscathed. Lanier didn't see any bodies lying
around, and the tire tracks off to one side indicated that the
authorities had been and gone.

How long was *I under?* Sitting on the bronze rim of the sturdy sundial was a small wafer-playback. Lanier plodded through the snow and retrieved the device.

"Hi ya," came Shaughnessy's basso in an oddly cheerful tone. "We had a few interruptions after you left us so rudely." He laughed, and a couple of women could be heard giggling in the background. "Needless to say, we were warned and cleared out. Ellie has informed me that you would return sooner or later and I am informing you that we've moved the party back to my Nacimiento estate in California. We'll be there for a week at least, since I don't have anything else that's pressing. Please come back. Ellie says that you're not supposed to vanish like that, and I'd like to hear all about it. I hope that you're not sick or anything. And I hope that you find this."

The wafer ended and music suddenly broke in. Shaughnessy had used a regular recorded wafer, and the music was Ernest Bloch's wonderful century-old *Concerto Grosso No. 1*. Shaughnessy must have used the first wafer he could find. That he had the *Concerto Grosso* in the first place was simply amazing. Shaughnessy was not so easy to peg as it seemed.

Lanier let it play. The sun was a little too bright for him as its rays reflected off the snow on Shaughnessy's lawn. But the music added to the scene.

Nacimiento? That was above Los Angeles along the coast, safe in the mountains east of San Simeon. Lanier cranked his shoulder around. The pain was still discernible. He wasn't ready yet for real work.

Anything for an excuse.

CHAPTER NINE

✿⊙||⊙✿

Bachianas Brasileiras No. 5
For Voice and Orchestra of Cellos
Heitor Villa-Lobos

Charlie Gilbert wrenched back violently on the controls and the ScatterCat he and Lanier flew lifted and spun like a frenzied moth before a wall of sudden flak over east Los Angeles.

"Damn!" Charlie swore into the pin-mike at his cheek. Lanier could see Charlie's mane of bright red hair through the separated cockpit to his left. Between them, the mid-rotor spun furiously. Charlie commanded the left-hand module of the breakaway VTOL which the government had leased to them earlier that day.

"Where'd Draco get all that equipment?" Charlie wondered, peering below at the camouflaged anti-aircraft guns that lurked between the houses of suburban L.A.

Lanier gripped his own controls in case they had to separate. The flak came from stolen army weaponry. Draco's urban guerrillas were holding much of the city, and fired at anything that flew over chicano territory, particularly the National

Guard. Their VTOL was a civilian ScatterCat, but the guerrillas were trigger-happy.

"Draco's rumored to be quartered in Downey. There's a very large arsenal near there, and they would've had no problem breaking in," Lanier said.

Over the radio, they could hear music.

"Frank?" Charlie asked, listening momentarily to the drowsy, melancholic piece.

"What?" Lanier looked over at him. Charlie pointed a gloved finger at the radio.

"You recognize that?"

The flak sprouted above and around them like black roses. Charlie dipped the ScatterCat to treetop level to avoid it. Most of the artillery wasn't equipped for low-profile fighting. And the VTOL was just fast enough to evade the snipers on the rooftops.

Lanier increased the volume slightly. The music was being broadcast on at least three open commercial stations, stations seized by Draco.

"Yes," he said. "It's a Villa-Lobos piece from last century. How's your Baktropol holding out?" Lanier didn't feel that this was the place to discuss the complexities of Latin American music.

Charlie laughed. "Hell, I'm too busy flying to listen to music and freak out right now." Charlie grinned behind his mike. He was used to this sort of thing, and had gotten his ScatterCat experience during the fall of Johannesburg a number of years ago. And he loved every minute that he was in the air.

But this time, their 'Cat was totally unarmed. Charlie, through Lanier's influence, had gotten clearance to lease the VTOL so that they could get back into the center of Los Angeles. Charlie had left some important microfilm files back in a special place in his suite of offices. They would need something as sleek and versatile as a ScatterCat to get in and out fast enough.

Besides that, Charlie needed the excitement. Montana had already gotten to him.

"Draco's doing it, I suppose," Lanier speculated, "To harass anyone listening in."

They flew under two monstrous expanses of high-tension wires. Lanier gripped his arm-consoles, almost closing his eyes. Charlie was good.

Charlie lifted the 'Cat, spinning off toward the west.

"We're three minutes away. Looks like a mess, doesn't it?"

Lanier looked down below them. Most of the city still functioned, in pockets, like ancient city-states. But many of the neighborhoods smoldered from fires, and barricades were erected on most of the freeway entrances and exits. Very few of the freeways were open, now that Draco had taken over most of Los Angeles. The guerrillas were everywhere, it seemed.

Charlie kept the ScatterCat low.

Lanier listened to the music. He mused out loud. "It's probably Draco's way of getting even. It's quite beautiful." The soprano voice of the singer in the recording filled the narrow spaces of the two modules with a pleasant reverie. Lanier could feel the tensions in his nervous system, and hoped that Charlie wasn't listening to the transmission. He wondered how Charlie and Christy, being so emotionally involved with each other, were able to survive the disease so well. A lot of Baktropol was probably behind their endurance.

"OK," Charlie announced, "we're in for a rough ride. See that?"

Lanier squinted. "Right." They were now over smog-smothered South Gate.

The sky was full of the black clouds of antiaircraft fire. But it was hard to tell if it was the National Guard or Draco's contingent. The fighting in the city was so confusing. Either way, they would have to go through it.

"They're tracking us," Charlie breathed into the microphone. Radar interception indicators blinked before each of them on their individual consoles. "And even if they don't have SAMs, they've got the firepower to bring us down."

Lanier said, "We can go around them."

"I know," Charlie responded. "But we're in a hurry, and, well"—he turned to his right, winking—"this is more fun."

"Right." Lanier smiled back, though not as confidently.

The section of the city before them was almost entirely burned out. An occasional freeway overpass lay crumpled like the broken backbone of a dinosaur. This part of the city was very much a war zone. Large, ugly columns of smoke billowed from buildings and from cracks in gas mains beneath the streets. These latter were on fire. And much of the smoke rising to meet them was from antiaircraft guns.

"Tracking now." Charlie tensed up. The ScatterCat hummed along the tops of the houses.

"Ready," Lanier said, throwing switches. The wheel eased gently into his hands as both modules now went over to manual.

The smoke approached them. The aircraft rocked with punches from the explosions.

"Now!" Charlie shouted, and the ScatterCat pulled apart just before the sky filled with awesome fists of bursting flak. Thunder surrounded them.

In two parts, the ScatterCat went off in either direction and the guerrillas on the ground hesitated for a minute under their nets of camouflage, trying to decide which one to track. A stolen howitzer on the back of a refurbished flatbed swiveled indecisively as Lanier went sharply to the northeast and Charlie banked off toward the west.

Lanier kept low, rounding a hill, and came back into sight. Charlie exited a cloud of smoke, sheared the top of a cyprus tree, and flew ahead of Lanier.

"You OK?" he asked Lanier through the static.

"I'm fine. You want to join up now or keep apart until we pass over Inglewood?"

Charlie banked closer to Lanier's craft. "Let's wing it apart until we get beyond L.A. International. I hear that it's under siege, and we can't afford to get caught in something we can't get ourselves out of. Besides, the Guard is probably shooting at anything within a few klicks of the airport."

"Right."

The two of them raced above the neighborhoods, the abandoned freeways, the supermarkets, and shopping centers. They met no more resistance. Within minutes they had reached the outskirts of Culver City, or what remained of it. The San Diego Freeway was open only to police and military traffic. The caissons rumbled below them.

"OK," Charlie signaled. "I think it's safe now. Let's do it fast."

"Roger."

The ScatterCat quickly joined, in flight, and Lanier relinquished control of the right-hand module to Charlie.

"Perfect," Charlie told him. "Too bad you weren't in Africa. You'd have been better off there than training 'Cat pilots back here."

"I'm not much on warfare," Lanier said. "Never was. I like being safe."

The ScatterCat pulled into the low, dreamy hills that surrounded Beverly Hills. Many of the hills had been scorched with brush fires or mortar fire. Although the Guard had effectively protected this part of the city, mortar shells were often lobbed in from kilometers away at random. The homes of the rich had been among the first targets of Draco's vendetta.

"Damn," Charlie muttered.

They swept over what was left of his offices. A large impact crater occupied half of where the suite of business offices used to be. What was left of the structure listed at an awkward angle, gutted completely by fire.

"So much for that," he said. "I should've had Cradock and Auerbach take those files out first thing. It's my mistake."

Lanier gazed below him. "I wouldn't worry. I imagine most of your clients have already left the city."

"Sure," he said. "But we had information on a lot of local corporations. I was hoping to use some for leverage later on. It was material HomeCom didn't have access to."

"Well, Charlie," Lanier began, "we'll be lucky if we *have* a future later on. Let's get out of here."

"You got it. At least we tried."

The ScatterCat soared off toward the west. Charlie felt it would be infinitely safer if they traveled over the ocean to Shaughnessy's Nacimiento estate. The Coast Guard was informed of their flight plan, and they encountered no resistance once they made their presence clear.

"Are you sure you want to do this?" Charlie asked Lanier when they were well out over the ocean, paralleling the coastline, speeding north-northwest.

Lanier laughed. "Look at this like a little vacation. I'm still curious about Ellie Estevan and Burton Shaughnessy."

"Right."

"No, I mean it."

Charlie, despite his normal extroversion, didn't like parties of the well-to-do. Like Lanier, his own childhood had hovered constantly on the fringe of poverty, and he didn't like associating with people who had been born rich, people who never suffered for economic means.

"You'll like it there. And we won't be long. I want to find

out who hit Shaughnessy's home. There's a lot I don't know."

Charlie grunted. The ScatterCat flew smoothly over the ocean.

"And," he said to Charlie, "we'll impress the hell out of them when you drop the 'Cat onto his lawn."

"I just hope I don't run into any of the honchos I've trounced in court. I've ruined a lot of local media folks. They tend to hold grudges."

Charlie nudged the 'Cat back toward the northeast when the coast near San Simeon appeared. Charlie flicked on the ground control.

"Good," he said. "Shaughnessy's got a directional homer on. We'll find it easily."

The hills around San Simeon were low and brown in the late autumn sunlight. The 'Cat rocked slightly on the updrafts of the shore, now that the sea winds had reversed themselves. The estate came into sight behind a grove of mangificent eucalyptus trees.

This mansion was much more outlandish than Shaughnessy's Colorado hideout, perhaps because this was, after all, California, where things generally tended to be outrageous, if only for the sake of appearances. Two small helicopters and one other private VTOL crouched like sleeping insects on the front lawn of the estate.

"Surprise them, huh?" Charlie said with mock disappointment.

Lanier smiled. "Well then, put it down out in the back. That's where the action is."

Charlie felt happier at this prospect.

He pulled the 'Cat in low over the top of the mansion, causing the pines and eucalyptus to toss wildly beneath the rotors. Women's dresses and carefully coiffed hairdos plunged in the wind. Everyone laughed as the craft settled gracefully at some distance from the empty swimming pool. Leaves from the late-shedding oaks danced in the air all about them.

Lanier popped open the cockpit and climbed out. A number of people rushed over, several of them private guards looking grim and disturbed.

But Shaughnessy was in the midst of the group, and elbowed the riflemen aside.

"Easy, boys!" he said to them. "They're company. How are you, Frank?"

Lanier jumped from the stubby wing of the ScatterCat. He shook Shaughnessy's hand as if neither had seen each other for eons. Both had by now been so impressed with each other's celebrity that a natural alliance had been struck.

"Glad you could get here in one piece," Shaughnessy said over the whine of the rotors winding down.

"So am I."

Charlie clambered down from the other module, and Lanier introduced him to Shaughnessy.

Here, only a few kilometers from the balmy southern California coast, the temperature was quite comfortable. The entire party had been outside all afternoon long, and would still be here far into the night. Lanier, used to this kind of weather, felt that an outdoor party would agree with him. At least, right now he was feeling very much like being at a party. Perhaps it was the excitement over Los Angeles that had drawn him out. He felt like a survivor.

Shaughnessy took an immediate liking to Charlie, perhaps because they were almost the same size.

"You fly that thing well," Shaughnessy said to him, cocktail in hand. They walked back toward the esplanade.

"Thanks. I flew in the war."

"Don't brag," Lanier admonished, smiling. A waiter came out to the poolside with a tray of drinks.

Charlie laughed, taking one up. "It's about the only thing I do really well these days since the practice was shut down."

Shaughnessy's in gear, Lanier thought. *He'll keep Charlie going*.

Shaughnessy said, "I know what you mean. Everyone here had to leave L.A. for one reason or another. Things are mighty hot there right now."

The party at the Nacimiento estate was easily twice as large as the *soirée* in Colorado. More people had flown up from Hollywood or down from San Francisco for the get-together. Lanier recognized many more movie stars and stage actors. Everyone was wearing bright summertime colors.

He ordered a light tea from the waiter. The man waddled away with his empty tray held at his side.

Shaughnessy directed them to a table where the food was set out. Dozens of people clustered about, chatting and laughing. Lanier wasn't taken aback this time at Shaughnessy's style.

Shaughnessy seemed to have a comfortable predilection for largesse, for gatherings where there was a lot of food and a lot of famous, easygoing people to consume it.

"You do this often?" Lanier asked Shaughnessy.

Shaughnessy laughed loudly. "Not as often as I'd like, you can believe me. This is special. Got some politicos here tonight and there's a fund-raiser going on tomorrow night in Sacramento. These happen to be friends of mine."

Charlie mooned over to Lanier's side.

"Shit," Charlie whispered.

"What?" Lanier turned slightly.

Shaughnessy was silent, sipping his drink noisily. He watched both Lanier and Charlie.

"Over there, with those women." Charlie pointed with his drink.

Lanier saw the large form of Senator Albertson Randell laughing among a gathering of ladies. Lanier was surprised this time.

Shaughnessy said to them, "Yep, all sorts come to these gigs of mine. And sometimes they invite their friends." He snorted. His eyes twinkled, as if challenged by Randell's presence. "I don't even get to meet half of them myself." It was almost as if his remarks were meant to understate Randell's appearance at the party. Or, as Lanier thought, it only meant that Shaughnessy wasn't afraid of *any* politico. Even Randell.

Two of the armed guards came up to Burton Shaughnessy.

"Nothing else coming in on radar, Mr. Shaughnessy," one of them said. Both of these individuals looked quite tough. They were mercenaries.

Charlie examined them closely. Belgians. He looked at Lanier, who nodded. The Belgians were among the very best guerrillas in the world. They were excellent fighters and were very loyal.

Shaughnessy put a hand lightly to Lanier's shoulder. "No need to worry about protection while you're here, Frank." He pointed to the men. "I should've had them back at Aspen with me. At least it might have made it harder for the bomber to get through."

"Right," Lanier remembered. "What *did* happen back there?"

Shaughnessy laughed as if this were the kind of thing that happened all the time. "Almost the minute you disappeared, we got an anonymous call saying that there was a bomber in our midst."

"Bomber?" Charlie asked. "I haven't heard of one of those in years."

"Right," Shaughnessy said. "Spontaneous human combustion is rare, but I guess there are enough terminal cases around to volunteer their services to the highest bidder. Anyway, he didn't seem any different from anyone else at the party." He laughed. "We had a *hell* of a time getting everyone out. The guy was drunk and had a magnesium bomb in his stomach. Couldn't put him out, so we let him burn. The whole place went up."

Charlie shook his head. Lanier sipped his tea. Shaughnessy clapped his hand to Lanier's arm. "You know, if Ellie hadn't been there, we'd have thought you were part of it."

"To burn your place down? Ellie?" Lanier was puzzled.

"Well, you did disappear just about the time the call came in. But Ellie cleared things up. She gets around, you know. Defended you gloriously. Besides," Shaughnessy concluded, "I have a lot of enemies. Probably Abraxas Studios did it. Who knows."

"And you believe Ellie?"

"Shit." Shaughnessy grinned. "She could tell me the world was flat and I'd believe her." Everyone laughed.

They walked over to a stand of low bushes where some tables and elegant wrought-iron chairs had been set out. Charlie was still watching Senator Randell move through the partygoers on the veranda.

Shaughnessy caught his expression. "I take it that your politics don't agree with Randell's."

Charlie, who still felt slightly out of place, tried to smile diplomatically. It was, he felt, rather rude to disapprove of the host's choice of guests.

"It's nothing," he declined.

"Sure, it's nothing. It never is. Listen," Shaughnessy confided, "this is California. Randell is out of his element. No one here really likes him except Ellie. We just tolerate him. He's not going to do anything crazy. He wouldn't dare. Not here, anyway."

"Ellie?" Lanier was curious. Two Moons' words still lingered in his mind. There was much he didn't understand, or perhaps didn't want to admit to himself.

"Sure, take a look. She's been around him all night."

Randell was grouped with a small gathering that talked gaily on the covered porch of the mansion. Ellie Estevan was moving casually among them, laughing with the rest. A large yellow rose was in her soft brown hair.

Lanier observed her, even as Charlie Gilbert watched Senator Albertson Randell.

Charlie gestured. "Look at the way he moves through people."

Randell strolled across the porch, cutting through men and women like a jungle-tank through underbrush. It was as if they weren't there at all; as if they were merely ghosts, or fog. Randell had absolutely no sense of other people being in the world.

Charlie said, "The man certainly gets what he wants."

Lanier, slightly piqued by the remark—accidental though it was—saw Ellie Estevan link arms with Randell. Lanier recalled the photographs from the scandal sheets in Christy's file. Randell, being a politico, attracted many of the brahmins in American culture. Naturally, Ellie Estevan would be one of them.

But Lanier didn't like it. Randell used people. He circulated with the rich, the popular, the controversial. He was always onstage, always in the spotlight. It was hard for Lanier to comprehend Randell's place in Ellie Estevan's life. They seemed so damned *comfortable* together.

But when anger began to rise inside of him, Lanier automatically recalled his mantra. *Be the rock in the stream. Let it flow around you.*

Randell moved away from the porch, stepping out into the weak afternoon light. Ellie Estevan was in tow.

Lanier, still holding on to his mantra, pushing out the sounds of the party, saw Randell approach their host. Lanier realized, suddenly, that no one but Charlie Gilbert knew of the fact that Lanier had "stalked" Senator Randell a few months ago.

And if he were lucky, Randell himself wouldn't recall anything of that rescue. Some patients did, some did not. Randell had gone under so resolutely that it was just possible he might not recognize him.

The blood, Lanier recalled. Randell's crazed expression as they ran down the corridors of that incredible world came back to his mind.

"This should be interesting," Charlie said in a low voice to Lanier.

Shaughnessy, suppressing his usual gregariousness, held out his hand to Senator Randell. "Having a good time, Senator?"

Remarkably condescending, Lanier observed, watching Shaughnessy. *This man isn't afraid of anyone. Abraxas Studios or a slightly suspicious senator notwithstanding.*

Randell's thin white hair seemed somewhat yellower in the wan light of the sun. He had a mouth that neither Charlie nor Lanier liked. His upper lip never exposed his teeth. It gave Randell a slight ghoulish character. But when Randell laughed, his mouth changed entirely and became oddly comic.

Randell looked at Charlie and Lanier, even as he shook Shaughnessy's hand. Charlie was right. Lanier noticed how the Senator sized up people immediately. Friend or foe. Ally or commodity.

"Just came out to see what the fuss was. Thought for a moment them damn chicanos had gotten an airplane and were going to strafe this wonderful palace of yours."

Shaughnessy laughed, but this time it rang hollow. He didn't care if Charlie and Lanier knew it was staged. It only mattered that Randell was placated.

"I doubt that Draco would take his guerrillas this far into the wilderness just to bomb a few people. No one here I know is worth the trouble."

Charlie sputtered his drink, and even Ellie laughed. Lanier suppressed a giggle. Randell, slightly woozy on an afternoon of Manhattans, smiled at the apparent joke, missing it entirely.

Lanier turned to Ellie. So far she hadn't acknowledged him. At Shaughnessy's other party she had had her gorgeous eyes constantly on him. Lanier wondered if Ellie was onstage as well.

But Shaughnessy introduced both Charlie and Lanier to Senator Randell, and introduced Charlie to Ms. Estevan, who was charmed to meet him. Only then did she look at Lanier. She gave him an open, enchanting smile.

Randell had apparently failed to recognize Lanier.

Shaughnessy motioned everyone toward the arena of tables and chairs, but Lanier excused himself.

"I'd like to clean up a bit if it's OK."

"By God," Shaughnessy said loudly, returning to normal, "take your time, son. Make yourself right at home. And don't take any shit from my guards." He smiled at one of the Belgians standing next to a large planter. The mercenary nodded flatly.

Shaughnessy's attention was genuine, and Lanier felt much better. Everyone else began sitting around a wide tray of drinks a waiter had just set before them. He wouldn't be missed.

When Lanier turned toward the porch, he was careful to cast his eyes in Ellie Estevan's direction. He stared at her evenly, thinking no thoughts, if anything looking a bit adventurous. He had no other desire than that of speaking to her once again.

One could easily get lost in Shaughnessy's Spanish mansion. Lanier roamed the halls, admiring the tapestries and paintings. The furniture that was not antique was modern and expensive.

He finally found an empty room. It turned out to be a small film library and viewing room. There was a bathroom off to one side, and Lanier stepped into it.

He ran water over his hands and relished its warmth. He wondered where Shaughnessy got the electricity for the mansion. This close to the ocean, wind-generated power would be much more economical than propane. But the mansion was too large for that. In any case, he did appreciate the luxury of warm water. It relaxed him in a way that alcohol might if he had been drinking. He closed his eyes.

"I see you made it back," Ellie said suddenly from the doorway.

Startled, Lanier spun around.

"You shouldn't do things like that," he told her. "It's been a busy afternoon."

"I know," she smiled. "Mr. Gilbert is out there telling war stories. Particularly the one that happened this afternoon. I didn't know that flying was among your talents."

Lanier smiled at her, his heart still racing. In the bright lights of the washroom, Ellie's eyes sparkled intensely. Yet he couldn't tell if she was being anything more than simply coquettish. She looked at him much in the same way he had seen her entertain other people at the party. Especially Randell.

"I learned it during the War."

"Were you in Africa? You seem so young."

"It wasn't that long ago." Now it was his turn to be playful. "You aren't that young yourself." He set aside the towel. "No, I was a trainer in the States. No combat duty. Charlie's the hero in the family."

"Oh? He's a relative?"

"Just an expression. We're almost brothers. He and his wife are my best friends."

They stepped back into the film library. Two sides of the room had ceiling-to-floor shelves that held reels of movie film, and one whole wall was a large, wide screen. There were also two very plush chairs and three long couches in the room. The sounds of the party could be heard through the walls.

"I want to thank you," he said suddenly, "for telling Shaughnessy about what happened."

Ellie pulled out a thin cigarette, rolled in licorice paper, from a box on the table. She lit it elegantly.

"Oh, it was nothing. I just had seen it happen before. Everyone was quite alarmed. I thought it was funny. I told them not to worry about it."

He watched her smoke. She had the elegance and flair of someone who was very definitely at home with herself.

"How is it that you know so much about stalking?"

Ellie was sitting in one of the chairs. She crossed her legs in such a way as to expose herself for a brief instant.

Lanier's mantra jumped back into his consciousness. His body, reflexively, was telling him things his mind refused to face.

But Ellie did seem uncomfortable at the question. Her eyes sparkled, nonetheless. "Oh, I've met a few Stalkers in my time." She held up her cigarette in one hand as if it were a banner of some kind. Smoke trailed away, filling the room with its sweet scent.

She was totally ladylike, refined and casual. She made Lanier feel rather off-kilter. They seemed like opposites. *Fudd-Smith's Law at work*, he thought.

He decided to change the subject.

"I didn't know that you knew Senator Randell so well."

She drew hard on her cigarette, blowing out a long, healthy cloud of smoke before her.

"We're old friends," she said, smiling at him disarmingly, even though she did appear nervous.

Lanier walked around the large library. "I'm not too sure I like Randell."

"I can tell."

Lanier turned and faced her. She was being playful. It was what she did best, apparently.

"No one likes Al, outside his constituency. But he sure is
fun to be around, and he knows a lot of people."

Al? he thought. *Fun?*

He could suddenly see the blood sluicing out of the drains
of Randell's incredible city-within-the-wall onto the lush green
turf. He could still smell it curdling around his feet.

He wondered just then if she knew that Randell had succumbed.

Certainly, she wouldn't know where Randell had gone or
what he had imagined for himself under the disease.

Lanier was quite uncomfortable. He had one kind of knowledge; she, another.

"You know," he began somewhat reluctantly, "I didn't mean
to disappear like that at Burton's party."

Ellie sat smoking thoughtfully. The sunlight that came in
through the window behind her illuminated her entirely. Her
eyes were like pools of stardust.

"I didn't think you did. It *was* rather strange."

Lanier looked at her, considered her ways. "I guess I was
feeling nervous being in the midst of so many . . ."

"So many what?"

"Well, you have to understand that I don't associate with
people in your business."

"Which is what?"

"I meant the movie industry."

She was playing with him. Lanier couldn't tell if he liked
it or not. His body was saying yes while his mind said no.

She said, "Burton knows many kinds of people. Even politicos, even though he hates to admit it." She waved her cigarette in the air, smiling. "We're just folks, as he would say."

Lanier didn't believe for a minute that Ellie Estevan and
Burton Shaughnessy were "just folks." The woman before him
had an incredible aura of well-being. Lanier wasn't in any
position to judge her skill as an actress, but her mere presence
was enough to get her whatever she wanted from this world.

Lanier sat next to her in the other chair. There were so many
questions he felt like asking her. And questions he needed to
ask himself—questions whose answers he might not want to
face.

But being in such physical proximity to her had fired up his
courage. Years ago it had been Marie. Now it was Ellie Estevan, the most engaging woman in the western world. He felt

his skin tingle. A few bars of the Villa-Lobos returned to his mind. A glassy look came into his eyes.

Ellie stubbed out her cigarette. "You aren't going under on me, are you?"

Lanier shook his head, smiling. "No, I was just thinking."

"About what?"

What can you tell a woman like this that won't sound too much like fawning? What can you reveal to a person who's lived as she's lived? The highlands of New Mexico rarely spawn worldly-wise individuals.

"Well, to be honest with you I was just thinking that it's very strange to be here, alone with you."

She sat back, her breasts uplifting slightly, almost imperceptibly so. "Is that so unusual?"

He laughed to relieve the tension. He had nothing to lose. "Of course it is. Up until a few days ago you were someone I read about, or heard about. Not this," and he gestured to her with his hand.

"I'm not unusual, believe me. And besides, you're the Stalker. There are fewer of you people than movie stars."

"But we're accidents."

"I hear that you're the best there is."

Modesty began to cloud his perceptions of her. But he looked up into her calm face, wondering just how approachable she was. Or how approachable *he* was.

"I don't know about that. And I don't know how long it will last. As soon as they find a cure for the Syndrome, I'll be out of a job. It'll be back to real estate or insurance for me. Whereas you'll always be in the movies."

"Until I grow old and ugly," she laughed.

"I can't see you being either. I can see you always being like the way you are, right here in that chair."

He was trembling somewhat and he didn't know why. He still held the Villa-Lobos in his mind. He rose quickly, nervously, and began pacing. She watched him.

"As soon as it gets dark, Charlie and I are going to have to leave," he said out of nowhere.

Ellie parted her legs and got up, walking over to him.

"I don't think you want to go so soon. Charlie can take care of himself. Please stay," she said to him. "I've never really known a Stalker before. At least not one like you."

Bachianas Brasileiras No. 5—the soprano aria drifted

through his mind like the wind across the autumn sky. Dark. Sorrowful.

Then he thought, *Estevan is Spanish.* Ellie came up to him and put her arms around his neck, surrounding him in a soft haze of perfume. Gently she pressed her lips to his.

Then she pulled back, but only slightly.

She said to him in a low, sweet voice, "Don't let any of this fool you." She spoke even as their lips were touching. He held her tight, very tight.

Like a stone in the shallows of a creek, there was nothing that he could do. The rest of the world passed around him on all sides.

Lanier into leaving him alone. Lanier deferred to the man's judgment.

The Pentagon wasn't happy about it, and neither were the scientists at the Doty-Wright National Observatory outside Pine Island, Minnesota.

"There is some talk about suing you," Christy said to him as he read the communiqué.

"I don't think so," he said. "When they think it through they'll realize that Dr. Tyler is expendable. Besides, he wasn't in any sort of danger."

Lanier had never been talked out of returning a patient to the real world, and the incident still sat uneasy with him. But, in the end, it was Lanier's own choice what to do.

He folded his robe over his long legs, putting his feet on the stoneware coffee table.

"But Dr. Tyler did make a curious remark that I neglected to put into my report to the director of the observatory. It was the primary reason I let him stay."

"What was that?"

"Well," he began, "Tyler suggested to me that his world might be better than this one." He had found Dr. Sidney Tyler, an astronomer, ironically dwelling in an incredible underground world, far from the sight of the sun and stars.

Christy silently observed him. "And?"

"I think he's right. Every time I've gone under, I've found that despite all their good intentions to escape, the patients take with them some bugaboo or other, almost in a twinge of guilty conscience."

Christy recalled the occasion she herself went under. "I don't think I did."

"No, that's not true. You were desperately unhappy in that Eden you'd created. You had been crying for hours and it wasn't because you were stuck there. The one chief symptom of the Syndrome is that people go under because they *want* to go under. You could have been eternally happy in that floating garden of yours, but something—perhaps your own guilt—kept you from being happy."

He paused, fingering his freshly shaved chin. "There is always a balancing force." He recalled Two Moons' cryptic remarks. "And the odd thing is that if the fantasy world is a nightmare, like Senator Randell's fabrication, there's usually an element of good backstage somewhere. It all balances out."

"Are you sure? Randell's not the most pleasant person I know."

Lanier smiled through the dark clouds of his mood. "Well, it's either that or it's just my imagination. But Dr. Tyler could be right. His world was remarkably simple. I wish him luck."

They both fell silent for a brief time. Lanier faced the window, which drummed with the cascading rainfall. A fire in the fireplace busily crackled, throwing out a soft light.

From Christy's office, the sound of the readout from HomeCom began rattling impatiently.

"Uh, OK," she said, rising from her chair. "I'd better see who that one is about. I'll be right back."

Lanier watched it rain. The clacking from Christy's office would be another "rush" rescue coming in over the computer, followed by all the details of the patient's disappearance. Lately, he had to resort to encoding the information, since someone had effectively plugged into the satellite relay systems and sabotaged many of the Stalkers.

He had been doing nearly seven retrievals a day, and the list was getting longer. Dr. Tyler wasn't even the most important person he had done recently, but he was trying to get in as many different kinds of retrievals as possible. The strain was beginning to show.

He had been receiving reports daily, through a special linkup with DataCom in Christy's office that was tied in to the Bureau of Statistics and the Pentagon. The information that came in over the screens was worse than the news programs on television and radio reported. It was worse because the information through DataCom was classified and highly accurate.

Most of the major industries in both the United States and Europe were down, yet the ranks of the unemployed were diminishing. The Syndrome took care of that. If it wasn't a new outbreak of typhoid in Southeast Asia, it was the Greenland melt. There had been a horrible nuclear spill in Kuwait that no one could control, and the United Kingdom was torn in a war of secession with Scotland. While there were dozens of skirmishes and revolutions around the world, there were no massive armies in existence. The Syndrome was universal.

There were even rumors circulating that the Russians were helping the Japanese move one of the orbiting mine factories above the moon into a wider orbit so that it could be converted into an interplanetary vehicle. There was talk of moving to

Mars, or even farther out, to Titan, because it was known that the lunar colonists also had the Syndrome bacterium.

And now with the warmer weather, the aeroplankton had become more of a threat than it had ever been at any one time. Aircraft had to keep to the higher altitudes. Aeroplankton choked Brazil. Central Africa had become a stagnant wasteland. The floating organisms completely blocked out any sunlight along the equator. The heat and moisture generated over the smoldering jungles had actually begun to raise the world's overall temperature by one degree. Enough to alter the climate everywhere.

Perhaps that's why it's raining instead of snowing here in Montana, Lanier thought. There was even an item in DataCom that suggested a new ice age in two hundred years if it all kept up.

What concerned Lanier more was the fact that a number of Stalkers were turning up dead, particularly the men and women—like himself—doing high-level work for the government. Two Stalkers, both personal friends of his, had been killed in the Chicago area. One disappeared into Ravel's *Le Tombeau de Couperin* going after the wife of a foreign attaché. The other, a woman, vanished while stalking a corporate head of ITT in Ned Rorem's *Third Symphony*. Neither came out.

Plus, someone had apparently cracked the DataCom channels out of the Pentagon itself, and had begun leaking information about the Stalkers. To Lanier, this was the greatest danger. Experts in the Pentagon had stopped the leaking, but he knew that it was only a matter of time before someone else broke into the channels.

Christy came through the door, holding a long printout. He couldn't read the expression on her face, but it was a cross between confusion and concern.

"What is it?" he asked.

"You'll never guess. In a million years, you'll never guess. But here it is. Verified this time." She walked over and handed him the scroll of computer paper.

He looked at the name, skipping the introductory remarks by the policy investigatory team.

"I don't believe it," he said. He jumped back up to the head of the report and read swiftly. Burton Shaughnessy had made the request.

"Ellie Estevan," Christy murmured, watching Lanier.

Christy had gotten most of the story from Lanier about Burton Shaughnessy's party in the middle of the Colorado woods, and the consequences of Ellie Estevan's stellar presence there. Lanier had been quite open with Christy in relating the tale of his vanishing, and the effect she had on him. Charlie had filled in the rest.

Now this.

Christy stood waiting.

"I can't believe it," Lanier repeated.

He tossed the report onto the coffee table and ran one hand through his hair. "If she went under, that could imply a number of things. One of which is that I could have been completely mistaken about her all this time."

"I don't understand."

"And, it also means," he continued, ignoring her, "that the disease is getting much worse."

Christy picked up the printout. Lanier looked up at her.

"Christy, Ellie Estevan was so centered, so calm. You know what I'm talking about." He rose excitedly. "Her eyes alone revealed it. If she went under, either the disease has gotten out of any possible control, or—" He submerged himself into his thoughts.

"Or?"

"Or something very traumatic struck her, made her vulnerable. And suddenly, too."

"But the Syndrome does that to anyone upset. Why is she so special?"

She realized immediately that it was a stupid question, but Lanier went on. "It happened to me at the party. It just seems impossible that it could happen to her. She seemed so adjusted, immune to practically everything."

Christy watched the moods run across Lanier's face. His expressions shifted as he thought about Ellie Estevan. Christy had never known him to be like this.

He looked to the report that Christy still held.

Christy paced the room nervously, watching Lanier read the report. Lanier looked up, noticing her behavior. It took his mind off Ellie for an instant. He lowered the printout.

"Is there something here I missed?"

She looked at him.

"I don't know if I should tell you this or not. It won't be on the report."

"What won't?"

"I picked up a scandal sheet when I was in town yesterday."

"And?"

"Well, at a Washington rally, Ellie was seen with Senator Randell."

"Again?"

"Yes, but there's more to it than that. There are rumors that he and Mrs. Randell are getting a divorce." She paused. "That Randell and Ellie might get married. In fact, it seems more like fact than rumor, from what I can tell."

Christy sat heavily in one of the chairs.

"It was only a scandal sheet. Perhaps just another rumor, but, Fran, you shouldn't be too surprised."

He stared at her, unbelievingly.

She continued, "It's been in the air for weeks now. You know the kind of lives those people live."

"I didn't know anything about it."

"It's been talked about for some time. It started around the time you went to Shaughnessy's first party. I didn't think of it to tell you. Didn't think it was important. The scandal sheets were full of it."

"But Randell?" The shocks were coming to him one right after the other. Entering a person's Syndrome fantasy was tantamount to entering the patient's unchained libido. Both Randell and Estevan were world-famous. He, an active, influential senator, and she, a talented, beautiful actress, were both powerful individuals in their own ways.

Randell! Thoughts of Albertson Randell's blood-filled world rushed into his mind. Randell was like a dog turned loose in a butcher shop. *And those women . . .*

Lanier could still see them fleeing before Randell in that world. That awful world.

Then he recalled Ellie's eyes in the torchlight at Shaughnessy's party. Or her face in the upstairs window of the Nacimiento estate when he and Charlie climbed into the ScatterCat later that night.

Randell was twice her age. The thought of Randell with Ellie Estevan revolted him. Randell's posturing was so apparent that he couldn't see how Ellie could be attracted to such a man. Like most senators, Lanier thought, Randell was a cutthroat, pure and simple.

But perhaps it wasn't so pure and simple as that. "I just can't believe this," he repeated.

He walked around, perplexed, and partly angry. He scooped up the day's list of projected rescues. It seemed now that people were going under whistling tunes from Bach's cantatas, or singing the Doxology in church. And now there was a considerable amount of evidence to suggest that purely synthesized music, despite its infinite tonal range, was not accomplishing what it was supposed to.

Christy followed him. "What do you think? Do you want to wait to see if she returns on her own, or..."

Lanier thought. "There's a connection here. But some key element is missing. I can see that the disease is getting out of control, that it affects everyone. But Randell..." He tightened the straps of his robe. "I wonder if this has anything to do with his bid for the presidency?"

Christy's eyebrows went up with a surge of surprise.

"Wouldn't hurt his image to have a movie star for a wife. But the election is two years away. And besides that, Babcock and Randell are cronies." Then she smiled cattily and remarked, "And lovers, no doubt."

Damn those scandal sheets! he thought. *What I need are facts, not fictions.*

He stared at her resolutely.

"OK, I'm going in after Ellie." *Privilege of rank.* "When the rest of her profile comes in over the computer, let me see it. We'll just bump back the other runs for today. It won't kill me to work a little overtime." He paused. "And one other thing, look into HomeCom and unscramble some of those 'rumors' of yours. DataCom won't have any of the gossip since the government isn't interested in the personal scandals of movie stars and politicos. Got it?"

"Got it."

"And while I'm gone, I want you to start digging up some facts on Randell. I need more than what we already have on file. Try to expand the security clearance on the use of DataCom. If they don't give it to you, go ahead and buzz the President. She'll give it if I read her right."

Then he said, "Be sure to find out about his 'friends' and some of his connections. Charlie will be over soon, and he'll be handy. He hasn't had much to do since we moved up here.

He'll like the excitement." Then, as an afterthought, he added, "You know, I shouldn't have ever gone after Randell. It was against my better judgment in the first place. I should've let him rot in his bloody paradise."

"You didn't know it was bloody until you got there."

"That's beside the point."

He stalked off toward his room. "And if you run into a snag," he yelled into Christy's office, "lean on Charlie. This is just the sort of thing that turns him on."

Christy gathered the files on her desk. *With Charlie here, things would be fine,* she thought. But at the same time she was feeling uneasy over Francis's anger. *Why anger?*

She held the square sonic-wafer of the piece of music to which Ellie Estevan had succumbed. *Sibelius. Pohjola's Daughter.*

What's going on?

The rain outside thrummed monotonously, dripping from the eaves. The dark gray of the morning light filtered throughout the household. In the living room, she heard the fire jump and spit in the fireplace. She rattled a small plastic box of Baktropol in her other hand. It was the strongest dosage available. She shivered, hoping that it was from the incipient cold. Already, the Baktropol was beginning to wear off. She thought of Charlie.

Strapping the equipment onto his waist and vest, Lanier stood alone in the workroom. He snapped on the priest's collar and adjusted the holster with the Malachi. He thought about Ellie. And the report.

Senator Randell had accompanied her to an elite gathering of movie industry friends and officials where they planned on a private screening of Ellie Estevan's latest movie. The report indicated that everyone had taken substantial dosages of Baktropol, including Ellie. The movie had already been screened at the studio without the music track, and they all had gotten together to view the movie in its totality, with the music fully transcribed.

But it seemed that at the screening a number of drinks were passed around, and some other drugs turned loose. The showing evolved into a minor celebration. When the movie ended, they discovered that Ellie Estevan had vanished in her seat. But everyone was so stoned that it was hours before she was reported missing.

Lanier signaled Christy when he was prepared. The lights

slowly dimmed in the workroom.

The music came to him over the micro-receiver in his ear, and he began his mantra this time. He had some difficulty calming himself down. Images of Randell rose and fell in the troubled music. Images of Ellie in the late afternoon light of Nacimiento began to appear. Autumn was in her eyes.

He fell down a tunnel, a vortex of energy, as the meditation took him deeper into his mind. He synchronized himself with the music, dropping deeper and deeper. And vanished.

Like a soul damned to Hell, he fell into a blistering inferno of towering yellow flames that burst from bubbles on a sea of burning oil.

Hazy and sluggish from the transference, the heat flashed across his face so suddenly that he came to full consciousness within a fraction of a second. He stood on a flat rock that was approximately ten meters across and relatively circular in shape. The rock was an island in an ocean of ugly flame.

He dropped down to his knees, simultaneously whipping off his long coat and priest's collar, a disguise he could afford to do without for the moment. If this was Ellie Estevan's private version of Hell, then the presence of a priest would only make things worse. Much worse. Besides that, it was just too hot to fool with the extra clothing. Such as it was, he could hardly breathe.

The flames geysered about him, falling back, leaving behind clouds of a vile orange vapor that gagged him. From his utility belt, he quickly snapped off the oxygen-assisted filter-mask and drew it over his head.

It took a few precious seconds for him to clear his head of the odors from the sea that surrounded him. It was the odor of burning human flesh, among other unpleasant things. It was a perfect hell of noxious industrial chemicals, pustulant and suffocating. Nowhere was there any sign of life, human or otherwise.

He opened the collar of his tunic as perspiration streamed down his neck and face. The temperature was ghastly; humidity high. It was only marginally livable. *But for how long?* he asked himself, looking around. The rock was too hot to sit on, but his insulated boots kept the heat from scorching his feet. He stood up quickly and tried to see through the bright glare of the fiery ocean and shimmering heat.

Leaving his long coat where it lay, Lanier jumped out across the boiling surface of the sea and landed on another, if somewhat smaller, island-rock. Like a string of carefully sculpted stones in a Japanese Zen garden, the rocks beckoned him out over the seething ocean. He leaped from one rock to another, covering about a hundred meters until he came to an immense rock. The moisture in the air and the sweat of his own body had nearly soaked his uniform through. He knew that he wouldn't be able to take much more of this.

The larger island was, like all the others, completely flat, and was composed of an unidentifiable porous substance. Nothing grew here. Nothing could. He squinted his eyes above the mouthpiece of the filter-mask.

With the flames exploding upward around him, and the fumes wafting in the air, his vision was severely limited. He could see no more than a hundred meters in any one direction. All there seemed to be to this universe was the incredible flaming ocean and the island-rocks that barely protruded from the oily surface. There were no tides, which was just as well.

But, looking upward into the orange sky, Lanier could make out objects—not quite clouds—hovering just out of the range of the flames. They were almost undefined in the shifting waves of heat, but they appeared to bob on the rising and settling currents of hot air from the ocean. Their undersides shimmered with the luminescent explosions that rocketed up at them from the chemical sea.

He couldn't tell for certain what the objects were. The heat obscured his vision. Whatever they were, they were drifting in every direction, at all altitudes, seemingly at the mercy of the thermals.

He pulled out his binoculars.

The objects were actually hemispherical structures, flat on the bottom, and they were lifting and plunging on the heat. Some of the hemispheres were very high in the sky, and others were nearly touching the surface of the flaming ocean.

The sky was filled with the hemispheres. Thousands of them.

And they were very large. Through the binoculars, Lanier estimated that they were about the size of football fields, perhaps even larger. The flat undersides, from what he could tell, were laced with a honeycomb design. Perhaps the honeycombs were used to capture the heat that kept the hemispheres buoyant.

He couldn't understand how such a thing was physically possible. But there they were.

And here I am, he thought, looking around in the heat.

Lowering the binoculars, he closed his eyes, breathing the fresh oxygen from the filter-mask. The rushing flames and the belching oily sea were somewhat distracting, but Lanier focused inwardly onto the vibrations set up by Sibelius's *Pohjola's Daughter* reliably coming through his micro-receiver. Ellie Estevan clearly was not here on one of these isolated islands in this wretched sea. She was inside one of those drifting hemispheres.

The nearest one, too, he surmised. The music had taken a sudden shift.

It may be Hell here below, but the vibrations suggested just the opposite about the hovering structures. Despite the furious, savage inferno of the surface, the feelings emerging from the music suggested that in those drifting hemispheres was a paradise, a place where the inhabitants of this world dwelled securely and comfortably.

The problem he faced was how to get up to one of them.

He knew right away which hemisphere was meant for him. Behind him, coming up slowly at a height of about twenty meters—quite low—was an enormous hemisphere. It seemed almost iridescent, glowing on its own, in the orange and pink sky. And it danced on the heat waves, seeming impossibly delicate and light.

Lanier carried both nylon rope and grappling hooks. Swiftly, he unfastened the rope from the side of the utility belt. The hemisphere was silently coming up upon him, lifting ever so slightly on the heat.

Strapped to Lanier's right leg was a small tube. He pulled it out of its tight holster. The hemisphere would be too high to merely toss the rope upward and hope that the grappling hook would find a hold on the underside of the craft in the mesh of honeycombs. The cylinder he withdrew was a miniaturized launch-tube. Like a mortar, it would be infinitely more accurate than tossing the rope with his arm.

He tucked the grappling hook into the tube, letting the rope itself trail outside at his feet. The large shadow of the hemisphere drifted overhead. It was somewhat intimidating in its immensity, like trying to board a dirigible in midflight. But this thing appeared to weigh several thousand tons. The honey-

comb arrangement on the underside of the hemisphere looked
as if there were places where a hook could easily take hold.

And right in the center of the hemisphere's bottom was a
circular opening. *The entrance? The exit?* He had to find out:
the vibrations were right for this hemisphere, the music very
intense. Ellie Estevan was living in it—somewhere.

He held the tube on his thigh and leaned back. The grappling
hook, followed by the rope snaking upward, burst out in a
muffled explosion. The recoil bruised his leg slightly. But the
hook struck the underside of the honeycombs and fell around
a girder, catching not too far from the circular opening in the
bottom of the hemisphere.

Lanier ran after the rope as it drifted away with the hemisphere. He quickly pulled on his gloves so that he could grip
the nylon rope. And he swung out over the flaming ocean.

The hemisphere, now fully out over the tremendous caldron
of the bubbling sea, lifted suddenly. Lanier began the long
climb, hoping that the moisture in the air wouldn't make the
cord too slippery, and hoping, as well, that his strength would
hold out.

It took him several difficult minutes, most of which were
spent in prayer that the rope would actually hold, as he made
the ascent. The sea below didn't look as if anything could
survive in it for more than a second or two. He decided not
to look down any more than he had to.

The honeycombs of the underside were lined with girders
composed of an albaster-colored material. Perhaps plastic.
Grabbing the lower end of one of the girders, Lanier hoisted
himself up, breathing with great difficulty. The oxygen-assisted
filter-mask could only work efficiently at a normal rate of
respiration. He rested, wrapping himself around a girder.

It was an odd sensation, holding to the underside of the
drifting hemisphere. He felt as if he were beneath a zeppelin
out over the Atlantic. The view, even from fifty meters, and
rising, was spectacular. From here, he could see no end to the
burning sea. The islands stretched for a distance, then faded.
He had landed on an archepelago of some kind, for the ocean
seemed for the most part to be empty of islands or other land
masses. He had been lucky in that respect.

The heat collected by the honeycombs of the hemisphere
was beginning to affect him.

He inched over toward the circular opening, nearly losing

his grip at one point, and pulled himself upward into the hole. There was a small lip, where he sat up, resting. Here, he checked that he hadn't lost any of his equipment in the climb. The Malachi was firmly secured in its holster. The medicine pouch was still strapped to his utility belt. Everything was in place.

The opening in the bottom of the hemisphere appeared to be a well of some kind. Here, the heat wasn't nearly so unbearable as it had been out in the honeycombs. Looking down, he almost felt as if he were a bombardier in an ancient airplane cruising over the ruins of Dresden: the flames beneath him were all that was left of some colossal Armageddon. Hell stretched from horizon to horizon. The heat was making him dream with the music chiming in his ear.

He got up carefully and found a convenient column of iron rungs running up into the hemisphere. So he climbed. He questioned their presence in the well, but dropped it. Everything here was impossible, possessing a logic all its own. And there was no such thing as coincidence anywhere, as Two Moons had once instructed him long ago. Everything served a purpose.

He poised himself for traps, but the climb was only about three meters above the opening. He reached a pressurized door.

Swinging it open, he stepped inside a very small airlock chamber. The door opposite him wouldn't open until he closed the one through which he had just entered. He sealed it, spinning the wheel around. Pressing the button beside the opposite door, a hissing sounded, and the door swung open of its own accord.

Cautiously, he stepped inside.

He recalled Two Moons' statement about the balance in nature. Real or imaginary, there was always an element of good and an element of evil in the world. Pleasure and pain. No one could escape from that one essential fact of human existence. *No one.* And even here, inside the magnificent hemisphere, was the balancing factor. It was the paradise, as Lanier had guessed it would be.

Within the huge structure, the air was cool, moist and somewhat misty. He had halfway expected to see corridors and machines at work once he had penetrated the hemisphere, but upon stepping out of the central core shaft, all he could see was mist and low green shrubbery.

Bushes? Trees? He thought immediately of Perry Eventide's

man-made world, those prairies and forests inside the rotating cylinder in space. But here, there was no apparent source of illumination, for certainly it didn't come from the outside as it did for Eventide's spacebound haven. This was the English moor. Low bushes, short stubby trees, and clover or a soft, green grass lay underfoot. Close by, he could hear the sound of a small creek tumbling over stones.

Considering the sudden change of landscape, considering how it fitted the music in a haunting sort of way, he realized that this pleasant environment completely negated the fact that beyond the walls of the hemisphere was a raging Hell. And at no time did he feel as if he were suspended high over the fiery ocean. Walking away from the core shaft and losing himself to the fog, he could have been anywhere in the English highlands. He removed the filter-mask.

Yet, despite the fact that he couldn't immediately discern the presence of any kind of threat—and perhaps he left it behind him on the islands of the flaming ocean below—he did feel like an intruder.

He pulled out the Malachi and set it on single-shot.

He began walking in a slow spiral outward from the central shaft. The fog was so thick that he couldn't see more than several meters ahead or above him.

This was a place, he thought to himself, where Druids would be lurking around their stone monoliths, holding mysterious rites at dawn. No Greek satyrs and nymphs belonged here; it was too Celtic. There was something identifiably somber about the inside of this particular hemisphere. It occurred to him that if a person were born into one of these worlds, he might not know what was on the outside, if indeed he came to discover that there *was* an outside. If that were the case, then this world might be perfect. *A perfect prison*, he realized.

He came across a stream, somewhat shallow, with small, precisely rounded cobbles. Tiny water-plants sprouted along the sides of the creek, and a turtle the size of a man's fist lounged happily in the reeds. The turf sloped delicately into the creek, and he decided to follow the stream.

He stepped over the creek with the help of a few nicely placed boulders, and suddenly found himself in sight of Ellie Estevan. The music, he realized, had reached a high point. But she hadn't yet seen him.

She was crouching over the stream, dressed in a loose-fitting white saffron cloak and gown. She was drawing a stick through the mud beside the creek, very much lost in a state of profound melancholy.

He holstered the Malachi.

"Ellie," he called, approaching her calmly, wondering if abandoning the priest's collar was a mistake. She was very deeply in the Syndrome.

She looked up at him vacantly. She didn't recognize him at all. He feared that he might frighten her.

"Ellie," he began. "It's me. Francis Lanier. Are you all right?"

She seemed catatonic, confused.

Lanier watched her closely. In her amnesia, she seemed like a different person entirely. Fog drifted around them.

But as soon as he had spoken, something seemed to alter the texture of the world in just the same way that reasoning or speaking in a dream sometimes distorts the dream. He couldn't quite place the feeling, but it reinforced his notion of being an intruder. This was Ellie Estevan's world, not his. He could feel it.

She had forgotten everything. A glazed look spread across her face. Lanier noticed that her hair seemed longer, almost reddish. And she appeared to be much thinner. The folds of her cloak made it hard for him to tell any more of her appearance. She had changed physically as well as emotionally. She was so absorbed by the Syndrome that she had lost all recognition of the world she left behind, nor could she grasp exactly where she was in *this* world.

"Ellie," he started. "I've come to take you home. Everything's going to be all right." He spoke softly, almost as if he were about to utter the words of a fairy tale to a little girl. Ellie turned around, staring at him.

"Do you remember me?" he asked, approaching her. "Do you recall how you got here?"

She rose, slowly, like a ghostly column of smoke.

Like an angel, he thought. *Beautiful, detached, frozen by death and despair.* And it suddenly came to him that this just might be someone else's perverse idea of Heaven and Hell, and not hers. But it was a mechanism that he didn't fully comprehend. He was no psychoanalyst.

She spoke to him, distantly. "These are my sins." She held out the empty palms of her hands. She was crying.

Not her voice, he thought. She spoke as if hypnotized, but he couldn't escape the look of genuine despair and sorrow on her face.

She's in very deep. "Ellie . . ." he coaxed.

He knew that he could grab her and wrestle her down, giving her a shot of Baktropol, and be done with the whole affair. But he also knew from experience that the transition back into the real world was often quite violent. Emotional damage could ensue. He decided to talk her down as best he could.

"Ellie, where are we?"

She didn't move from where she stood. She was like a monument to the dead.

"This is the waiting," she murmured. Her eyes no longer sparkled as he remembered them. It was as if she had already committed herself to the dead. He could sense it in the strains of the music.

"We don't have to wait any longer," he said gently. "We can go back home any time you want. Back to your friends."

She looked at him with her eyes wide, swollen with tears. She opened her mouth, stuttering a cry. "I have no friends. I've killed them all."

He reached into his medicine pouch and pulled out a small bottle. He shook out two tiny pale blue pills. Baktropol.

"Ellie," he started. "It's time to go now. Can you take these for me?"

Automatically, she fingered the two little pills from his outstretched hand. She looked at them as if she didn't understand what they were. It was as if she hadn't seen a pill in her life.

"Go ahead," he said. "Swallow them. They're for you."

She motioned to do so, but just as she did, the earth shuddered. Not shuddered, exactly, but *swelled*, like a ship on an ocean's wave.

The only real earthquake that Lanier had ever been in was one several years ago that had struck Los Angeles. But this was nothing like that quake, nor the rendings of the world that Perry Eventide had manifested. The hemisphere, and the English countryside, tilted horribly, rolling.

The two of them were thrown off balance. The water in the creek leaped up and splashed them, no longer confined to the creekbed. The hemisphere righted itself, or tried to. They fell over like toys.

Then a voice bellowed out through the mist.

"Ellie. Ellie, you are mine. Now and always." It wasn't imploring, or urgent. It was sinisterly confident and demanding. Lanier couldn't identify the voice. It could have been a man's voice or a woman's. The mist and the trees dispersed sound. It came from all around them.

Ellie screamed, sliding into the creek.

Lanier rolled over, grabbing an exposed tree root for support until the ground stopped wobbling. Ellie Estevan twisted across the turf, covered with mud, then rolled with the gyrations of the earth over a small rise, and fell out of sight.

Lanier sat up when the pitch and yaw began to even itself out. The water in the creek trickled back from its unknown source.

He jumped up, leaping the creek, and rushed over the rise.

"Ellie!" he yelled after her. She was running down the opposite side of the small hill, out across the grass into the dense swirling fog.

"Ellie! Stop!" Grimly, he yanked out his Malachi. *Let's do it right this time*.

The other voice boomed overhead.

"Ellie, it's time. Come to me."

The voice was vaguely familiar to him but he wasn't quite sure. He ran after her. The ground still seesawed somewhat, so his shot had to be accurate.

He ran through a thicket of scrub oak and juniper, trying to catch up with her. Thirty meters would do. Beyond that, the Malachi was highly inaccurate.

He stopped and sighted her along the barrel of the Malachi, then fired off a few shots. Tufts of grass ripped up in the spray of the tiny anesthetic needles. He had missed.

She kept on running.

The voice cried, "Ellie . . . Ellie."

Lanier looked around. It was impossible to tell if the voice was created in the hemisphere itself or if it originated within the context of the music.

Suddenly he came to the inside of the hemisphere wall. He should have known that they couldn't run too far unless they ran in circles. This world did have its limits.

She stood alone, facing him, breathing hard, and she was very frightened.

With the nearness of the wall to them, Lanier sensed the

utter artificiality of the world inside this hemisphere. Even the grass beneath their feet seemed thin and pale.

He breathed hard himself, but for different reasons.

He walked over to her, carefully.

"No!" She held out a hand, begging him to stop. "You have nothing to do with this! Leave, now! Please! All the time is up!"

She seemed oddly, and suddenly, lucid to him now.

"Your time..." said the voice out of the fog.

Lanier spun around, Malachi ready, but no one was there. The wall of the hemisphere made the voice seem quite close.

"Listen, Ellie," he began. "Your time isn't up. We can go home now...." The Malachi's handle grew moist in his palm. He hesitated.

"No," the voice asserted. A man's voice. He knew it for sure, now that he could hear it off the solid wall a few meters away. It came from somewhere above them.

"Her home," it continued, "is below. With the damned."

"What?" Lanier looked around. The presence of a third person was very strong, but he couldn't see anyone.

Ellie went pale, her hands to her mouth.

Lanier raised the Malachi, thumbing it onto single-shot. He took aim.

Just as he lifted the rapid-fire pistol, Ellie gasped and seemed to jump a bit in the air from the ground. Then she dropped. A huge piece of the hemisphere in the shape of a hexagon fell out from underneath her.

She dropped from the hemisphere.

"No!" Lanier cried, diving forward, sliding onto his chest in the grass. He grasped the lip of the hexagonal hole.

The heat struck him savagely in the face. Ellie fell, violently twisting like a rag doll as she plummeted three hundred meters into the burning ocean below. She screamed all the way down.

The hemisphere drifted beyond the bursting flames that had engulfed her. Heaven and Hell. One above the other.

Lanier, wretched with grief, pulled himself back. The entire floor of the floating hemisphere was—*had to be*—laced with hexagonal trapdoors. But it didn't matter now.

He knew that he should have shot her. He had waited too long; had underestimated the danger.

He sat up, unmoving. *Like the others*, he thought. *Gone like the others*. He rolled over and slowly got to his feet. The voice overhead was gone, and the fog had gotten thicker; the air somewhat cooler.

Yet the world remained.

"Who are you!" he screamed above the fog.

There was no answer. There was only stillness and fog. He stumbled across the grass and fell to his knees.

CHAPTER ELEVEN

✦⊙⊞⊙✦

New England Triptych
William Schuman

"Wow, it smells like brimstone in here!" Charlie Gilbert proclaimed, removing his raincoat and setting it on the back of a handy chair. His thick red hair, matted with rainwater, gave him the eager look of a mischievous boy, full of pranks.

Francis Lanier, still in his work tunic, still wrapped in his wide utility belt, its holster empty of the abandoned Malachi, sat on the Naugahyde couch with a dour look on his face. Though the air inside the ranch house was relatively cool, Lanier himself sweated unmercifully, his clothing blackened and stained in several spots.

Christy sat across from him. She held a file folder in her hands.

"Hey," Charlie broke in. "Where'd all the dark skies come from, anyway?" He tossed a pouch bulging with papers onto the coffee table.

Lanier looked at his friend.

"I lost Ellie Estevan. She's dead."

Christy had prepared a cup of darjeeling tea upon is arrival. Lanier cradled it on his lap.

"You're joking," Charlie said. "No, I guess you're not." He sat down next to Christy. "What happened? You just got back?"

Lanier slowly explained the circumstances surrounding the attempted rescue, and everything that led up to her death, going into great detail over the flaming ocean and the hemispheres that floated above it. Christy had already recorded his narrative for the report she would compile later that night.

Charlie was horrified. "That's terrible," he whispered. "But whose voice was that speaking to her? Did you recognize it?"

"I don't know whose voice it was," Lanier reflected, "but I thought it sounded familiar."

"A man's voice," Charlie said.

"As far as I could tell. It might have been her subconscious, for all I know." He shook his head.

Christy faced Charlie. "One other thing happened."

"Fran was gone for six hours." This time she was very worried.

Charlie looked across to Lanier. "Is that true? I've been busy all day. I thought you'd gone and come back long ago." He paused, somewhat confused. "But why that long? Surely the music wasn't that long in duration."

"No, it wasn't," Lanier said. "I wasn't gone for six hours *my* time. The whole affair couldn't have lasted more than an hour. I did linger there a while longer, after she fell, but not much. Not six hours."

Charlie exchanged looks with Christy and Lanier. He said, "Is that supposed to happen?"

"No," Lanier said flatly. "No, it's not." He stared down at the floor, lost in his own thoughts.

Christy handed a list to Charlie. "These requests came in while he was under. I have their files in my office. All the research is done. But look." She indicated the list of attached statistics. "The Syndrome has reached its worst point yet. Far beyond what anyone had predicted."

Charlie peeled it back and looked it over seriously.

"I think," he started, "that we're being kept in the dark about most of the situation."

The list bore seven more congressmen, five governors, the heads of two oil companies, and two cabinet members. There was also a presidential aide, Ms. Beverly Silva, reported missing.

"My God," Charlie exclaimed.

Lanier was silent, watching him.

"And these," Christy pointed out, "are just the ones sent here, to Fran. The other Stalkers have similar dockets."

"Can you do all of these people?" Charlie turned to Lanier. "Aren't there other Stalkers who can take off some of your load? There have to be."

Christy paraded around, businesslike, slapping the list with her finger in a frustrated gesture.

"Everyone's overloaded. It's just getting out of hand. And now it seems as if Fran is staying under longer and longer, for some reason none of us knows about. It could be part of a new strain in the disease itself."

Lanier sighed loudly, leaning back and closing his eyes.

"You know," he began distantly, "something's got to break. Losing Eventide was a big blow. He might have been able to come up with a stronger remedy than Baktropol. If only North Haven Chemicals hadn't fired him."

Charlie got up and retrieved his carrying pouch from the table. He stood, rummaging through it as Lanier spoke.

"But Ellie's loss," Lanier continued, "I just can't understand. I could have sworn that she wasn't suicidal. Her eyes . . ." He stared up at the ceiling. "Something made her kill herself. There was something in her makeup that none of us knew about, that allowed for her death. But what was it?"

Charlie held out a small sheaf of papers.

"I think I may have an idea."

Lanier craned over, pouring more gray tea into his cup. "Anything will do. What do you have?" His voice sounded tired, strained.

"Well," Charlie began with a mild touch of flourish, "I set my junior partners to work digging up some facts on Randell that weren't in either DataCom or HomeCom. Mostly stuff through the profession grapevines."

"What did they come up with?"

Charlie passed the forms over to him. "It's all there. Besides being one of the principal congressional trust-busters, he has more fingers in corporations than an octopus has arms."

Lanier leafed through the sheets. "I thought all congressmen by law had to dump their personal funds into blind trusts." He started feeling funny about Senator Randell. He already had an insight into his character that he truly could have lived without.

"Supposedly," Charlie said, smiling wryly. "But given the fact that Randell has 'friends' and that friends often have occasion to talk, it shouldn't be too surprising to see how Randell has maneuvered his congressional activities around his financial interests. And since a separate accounting firm makes his investments under a blind trust, all Randell has to do is indicate where he'd like his money to go, verbally, and no record of it exists. Except..."

Lanier looked up. "Except what?"

"Except that everything that particular firm did for the past five years is in DataCom. The public doesn't have access to it, but Randell does."

Charlie walked around to the side of the couch. "Here." He pointed. "Notice this one."

"North Haven Chemicals," Lanier observed. "That's interesting." He looked up at Charlie. "And I suppose that you've looked into why Eventide was let go."

"What do you take me for?" He smiled broadly. "The Freedom of Information Act can only go so far, legally. We ran into a force-field of inneroffice runarounds. The only thing we got that seemed positive was that Eventide's contract was terminated because of adverse publicity. The higher-ups didn't like the attention. They felt that a biochemist should stick to being a biochemist, not a public figure."

"That's pretty thin," Lanier grunted. "What else? What's this here?"

"Ah." Charlie smiled triumphantly. "This is a reproduction of a list we pulled out of HomeCom, believe it or not. It had to be made public. It's Randell's assets and holdings. At least, these are the ones he filed with the IRS and the Government Accounting Office. Notice his income."

Lanier's eyes widened appreciatively. "*Twelve million? Per annum?*"

Charlie planted his hands in the pockets of his expensive trousers. "He's one very shrewd businessman. I can imagine why he's in politics. And there's no reason why he shouldn't be that rich. Other politicians have come close, if you remember President Bowden. He was loaded."

Lanier examined the papers carefully.

He now understood the importance of Randell's rescue earlier that summer. Randell was a man of influence in most of the major industries and corporations in the country, *and* in Europe. The multinational corporation was one of the most significant legacies of the twentieth century. And Randell had an uncanny understanding of the world economic structure. In times of global catastrophe, Randell was a man to have around. He was something of a financial wizard.

"The bastard's got it coming out of his ears," Charlie Gilbert concluded sardonically. "And it's all legal."

He let Lanier scan the report.

A minute later, he leaned over. "There's a little thing we turned up that you might also be interested in knowing." He referred to another sheet. "Look here. Randell has even got connections in the movie industry as well. You can imagine the money floating around there. He's got interests in production plants, studios, even some law firms. I have some friends in those firms. I made a few phone calls and they confirmed most of what's in HomeCom. They wouldn't comment on what's in DataCom since that's classified. If they did, it'd blow the whistle on them, and probably Randell as well."

Charlie sat back down on the couch. "That's how a man of his stature can manage to meet a movie star like Ellie Estevan and a producer-director like Burton Shaughnessy."

Lanier studied the data closely. "So where's the business about the Saudis? It's not listed here."

Charlie said, "Remember when they got the first workable fusion reactor at Princeton going, and how everyone thought that fusion would take away some of the dependence on Saudi oil?"

"Sure," Lanier said. "And it didn't work out like that, to everyone's surprise."

"Well," Charlie continued, "it seems that Randell's influence in Congress kept the oil flowing and he managed to waggle through those energy laws about limiting the use of fusion."

"Friends with the Saudis," Lanier said in disgust. "At least the Seattle plant was built."

Though Lanier bore no ill will to the Saudi Arabians, he understood, as did everyone, that international politics, especially the Japanese-Saudi War crisis that Floyd Matkin had tried to mediate, constantly orbited around the last of the Saudi oil reserves. But rather than fuel petroleum, it was plastics and medicine the Japanese required. The Seattle fusion plant was the smallest in the world so far, and it was the size of a metropolitan supermarket, and fifty times as heavy: fusion was impractical for running automobiles. So, the Saudis still had their friends in America despite the fact that the Japanese were also the friends of America. And also despite the fact that, by all government projections, the Saudi fields would run dry—completely dry—within a decade or possibly even less.

And on the list at Lanier's knee were two Nobel Prize-winners in physics who had pioneered the microengineering in compacting the new fusion reactors. He looked at the list wondering who came first, the technicians or the politicians.

He hefted the papers Charlie had given him. The key-codes for DataCom cross-references were also provided in case he would want to do any verifying on his own.

"Thanks, Charlie," he said. "You're a good hound dog. I'll look at this much closer when I have the time. When I settle down."

Christy gave him a motherly look. "You aren't coming out of these missions like you used to."

Lanier nodded in agreement, looking as if he had aged ten years in the last few hours.

Christy went on. "Is it affecting you too? Are you losing any ability to go under and come out?"

Lanier shrugged. "I don't know. The disease has gone beyond our expectations. It doesn't even act like a regular disease. But maybe I'm getting more involved, when I shouldn't be." He ran his fingers through his hair. "Perhaps we'd better check up on some of the other Stalkers and see if it's happening to them as well."

Lanier hovered about the living room like the ghost of a fallen warrior, not quite knowing what to do, or feel.

He did feel somewhat foolish falling for a movie star, a person like Ellie Estevan. He had never counted on actually meeting anyone so famous, and then when he did, he hadn't counted on Ellie Estevan's simple reality, her eyes, her charm.

He felt awkward and partially ashamed to admit his emotional indiscretions toward a patient of his, since his previous hesitancies had allowed for more than one death to occur. This time it had been a movie star, someone familiar to millions of people. He shouldn't have allowed her death to happen. He was a professional, a *gifted* professional.

"Listen," he announced to his friends. "I'm going to rest for a day or two. Take things easy." He walked around, not really looking at them as he spoke. "I've got a lot to think about, and I'm tired."

Charlie sat with a long arm about Christy's shoulders.

Lanier continued, "I might need you and your boys to come with me to Washington. I need to talk with the President about the research into the disease. This thing has got to stop. Meanwhile," he looked down at Christy, "let's hold things for a while. You can pick which ones you feel I should do, but leave it for a couple of days. Forward the others to some of the nearest Stalkers. I just need a rest. Time to breathe. Things are just happening too fast."

"You got it, Fran," she said.

Lanier walked back into his own room and closed the door quietly.

Later that night, Charlie drove Christy into Missoula for a leisurely dinner. It was cold. The rains had finally stopped and everything seemed to be holding its breath for winter to arrive. The chinooks, those fronts of pure Arctic air, were coming down across western Canada and the upper Midwest. But given the slight rise in the overall temperature in the world, rain, and not snow, was constantly the result. Already, many of the mountain watersheds suffered. The streets were icy, the air bitter cold to breathe.

They had invited Lanier to tag along, but he declined. He felt like brooding and doing it right. They acquiesced.

After they had left, and Christy had shut down the computers, Lanier dined alone. Normally, during times like these, he would put on a Nielsen symphony, or something by Manuel de Falla, perhaps *Nights in the Gardens of Spain*, for atmosphere. But he decided against that. It might be too dangerous, given his mood.

Instead, he ate in silence.

Although he was restless, he felt that he didn't have the energy to set up the projection equipment in his living room to view the movies he had of Ellie Estevan, for that was the only thing he felt like doing at the moment: retain what of her he could. He couldn't shake the image of her standing alone on the grass of that English moor inside the hemisphere. *Those eyes.* He wanted to be alone, and alone with only her.

But that was impossible, now. So much remained to haunt him. There was so much about her as a person he didn't know, and it was too late to do anything about it.

He let the films lie in their boxes. He thought he'd go ahead and drive into town and see a movie. He fingered his Syndrome immunity card—which every citizen needed now to see any movie—and dropped it into his shirt pocket. It was a false card provided by the government to all Stalkers. It would allow him to appear like an ordinary citizen; help him move through the world like the average Syndrome-ridden individual.

The drive into the heart of Missoula took him past a movie house where they were showing one of Ellie Estevan's earlier films, *Halcyon Days*. Towns such as Missoula always got their movies and holos much later than the rest of the country. In the case of *Halcyon Days*, it was years later.

It was also one of the films that Charlie had provided him with, one which Lanier had seen at least twice already. But two theaters in Missoula were showing Ellie's films, and there was no question that he would see one of them. He decided on *Halcyon Days*.

A line had already begun to form outside of the theater. He hated lines and waiting, but at this time of the night there would be only one showing of *Halcyon Days*. He swung his truck into a side parking-lot, decided to face the waiting anyway.

Stepping out of the truck, he recalled a line from an old Gary Snyder poem that Two Moons had shown him. It described the stars above as being *tough*. *The tough old stars*: above him, the Milky Way flourished in the clear Montana air. There was nothing like it even when he was a kid in New Mexico. The winter constellations of Auriga the Charioteer and Taurus the Bull were climbing up the eastern horizon, and the summer constellations were slowly leaning off toward the west. So long Cygnus. Goodbye Ophiuchus. Scorpio down. Sagittarius dying. It would be December soon. The Pleiades burned anxiously in the east, heralding the oncoming cold of deep winter.

He pulled his cowboy hat down over his eyes and walked up to the tail end of the line.

In the line, waiting for tickets, were ordinary Montana folk. They were mostly logging and ranching types, with a mingling of the university crowd. Everyone, though, certainly dressed western. Lanier felt comfortable with them immediately. There was nothing pretentious about these people. It was far better here than in Los Angeles.

A couple stood before him. The man could have been anyone's Pop, and beside him was Mom. He wore a somber black Stetson with a red and blue feather curving outward from the tooled-leather hatband. She wore tight slacks—perhaps too tight for her age—that still managed to make her look attractive. She snuggled deep inside her sheepskin coat. They both seemed as if they worked hard for a living.

And now, Lanier thought, they've come to see a movie about Hollywood decadence. About easy living and the idle bourgeoisie.

He carefully observed them. How were their lives changed by the world about them? Was this the future they had envisioned years ago when they married, had their children, took on jobs and debts? The most recent brush with aeroplankton was only two weeks ago. Did they work a ranch in the Bitterroot Valley? Did the tractors clog with aeroplankton in their air filters and carburetors? Did their cattle suffocate?

Yes, he thought. Mom and Pop have their problems, like the rest. The wrinkles at the corners of his eyes, the skin of his face like leather, showed Lanier as much. The man could have been his own father, a sheep rancher, cattle rancher, hunter.

A cold wind blew down the street before the theater, brushing them as they waited in line. The streetlights and the theater marquee lights blotted out the stars for the present, as if they were hiding. Yet, he himself was no different, really. He was hiding in Montana, hiding in line with his cowboy hat pulled low as if he were a renegade. He felt only like retreating.

I'm tired, he thought. *I'm tired of everything. I want out.*

Once inside the theater, he lost himself to its almost embryonic comfort. Everyone relaxed in the low lights. And here it was warm.

The crowd was made up primarily of adults, since the movie was rated for only an older crowd. Even so, the film had been highly touted when it first came out. Critics had praised its integrity. Millions, worldwide, stormed to see it as soon as it was available. In Montana, it was pulling in enormous crowds, the same as everywhere else. Lanier was very interested in just how good the movie was to the audience, and he was also curious about its effect. An audience can make a vast difference at any performance. If the chemistry is right, a movie can become an emotional experience simply because of the crowd's participation.

Perhaps it was the lack of an audience when he had his own private screening of her films that made him want to see a movie of hers with a regular audience. He felt that her movies were not any different from any other films that had come out the last few years. They were well produced, slick, and very much in an extravagant mold. But, from his own viewings, they were nothing to rave about, even if Ellie Estevan was very beautiful. *Was . . .*

Lanier glanced around him as the lights suddenly began to dim. *What would they do,* he thought to himself, *if they knew she would be officially reported dead in a few weeks' time, that she died because of the Syndrome? There are many eager and excited faces in the audience. Some of these people have seen this particular film before. They are just regular people: secretaries, insurance salesmen, carpenters, impoverished college students, housewives. How will they react?*

And he sat there, recalling Ellie Estevan's fall through the floor of the hemispherical Eden, the hexagonal trapdoor tumbling beside her as she fell. The heat in his face. The smell. The fog. The cool green grass.

That was real, and *this* is real. A small fist of sadness lodged itself in the center of his chest. *The third chakra,* he thought to himself. *The chakra of love. Just below the heart.*

Suddenly, Lanier stiffened. The curtains parted before the screen, and the music of the film score filled the theater. He recognized it at once. The slow, processional tympani began the theme from William Schuman's *New England Triptych,* and the titles to the film rose majestically on the screen. People shifted, getting settled in their seats. A woman seated in the row just ahead of him shuddered where she sat.

Lanier's eyes went wide with shock. It was as if he were having a sudden heart attack. He gripped the armrests, shaking in a violent seizure.

This is wrong! Something is different!

It was the same opening sequence of the movie that he had seen in his own living room, in the comfort of his own private surroundings, but something had taken over the atmosphere of the film. In this film, music shivered up and down his spine uncontrollably, the seats of the theater themselves vibrated slightly to the tensions the music described. The first scene, as the music continued, took him to the open countryside of Vermont. *Took him there*: as if the whole thing were absolutely, unquestionably real! His heart began beating rapidly.

He was completely entranced, hypnotized. Despite his depression and the knowledge of the death—and the *reality* of the death—of Ellie Estevan, Lanier sat there, fearfully rooted. Mesmerized. He had never seen *this* movie before!

Something was in the actual film itself, mixed in with the soundtrack, and it was being transmitted at a very low level, subliminally. The first character of the film strode into the scene, and as if on cue, the audience began silently weeping, knowing just how tragic the fate of this man would be. Lanier sat wide-eyed, enthralled by the story that was about to unfold before him. His skin tingled with electricity. *The music*...

He got up, forcing himself to turn his back on the effect of the music score. He hastily scrambled up the aisle into the outer lobby. A few disgruntled stares followed him as he burst desperately through the swinging doors.

No one was in the lobby. The ticket taker, the girls at the concession stand, were all inside watching the film. He leaned against the glass counter, breathing rapidly. He shook. The vibrations of the movie could be felt even in here; their effect was diminished somewhat by the walls themselves. He closed his eyes.

All the symptoms of Liu Shan's Syndrome, except milder and much more controlled! Purposely controlled!

Lanier climbed the steps beyond the door with the sign EMPLOYEES ONLY to the projection booth. There, through a tiny glass window, he could see the manager and the projectionist sitting enraptured by the movie. The large first reel slowly rotated above them. They must have seen *Halcyon Days* a hundred times, and yet they looked as if it were their first viewing. Like junkies, they were hooked.

Lanier fought to control the sensations in his spine. There was something in the music, and whatever it was, it was also ingrained onto the actual celluloid itself. Sympathetic harmonic vibrations were being transmitted that coincided with the emotions being displayed by the actors on the screen. *Subconscious manipulation*, he realized, stunned by the discovery.

Lanier stepped back down the stairs, thinking. Movie soundtracks—especially the music chosen for background effect—were always used to coincide with the dramatic elements for the high points in films. It was to anticipate moments at which audience response was to be elevated.

But this was something new, something completely different. There had been many gimmicks to lure audiences into theaters before, but nothing like this. And the audience inside didn't appear to notice the difference. It was the level of Baktropol in their systems. They merely absorbed the situation on the screen as if it were real. As if they were in a dream. It was only because he was a Stalker that he could feel the vibrations so strongly in the first place.

The electricity ran along the nerves in his back and shoulders. He staggered. The vibrations subtly piercing the walls of the lobby told him that the character Ellie Estevan played was now onscreen. The music was hers. It was tormented, stormy. Her drama was about to unfurl itself before the audience like a painter's ready canvas.

It wrenched at him. He ran out of the theater into the night.

It was no wonder the movies of Ellie Estevan were breaking box-office records all around the world. That would account for the crowds, the riots, the people wanting to see them again and again. They were being sucked into the center of the movie's fictional elements by having their very feelings manipulated.

"Where have I been all my life?" he said to the darkness.

Back at his pickup truck in the crowded parking lot, he swung open the door and sat on the cold seat. He switched the engine on, trying at the same time to calm himself. He had to think this through.

The door still open, he looked up into the night sky. He'd left his hat behind in the theater. *To hell with it*, he said to himself.

And above him were the stars. The tough old stars.

"But not tough enough," he said, quickly closing the door and throwing the pickup into gear.

CHAPTER TWELVE

❦

Symphony No. 7
Roy Harris

The pickup slid across the mud and gravel of his driveway, as Lanier pulled in front of his ranch house. He leaped from the side of the vehicle as the front door of the house burst open. Christy ran out while Charlie Gilbert stood alone in the doorway, holding it open to the night air.

"Fran," she met him, speaking urgently. "Oh, I'm glad you're back. Something terrible's happened!"

Lanier waved her aside, almost rudely, looking beyond to Charlie. "No time for that. I just went into town and..."

But he couldn't finish. Christy blurted out: "The President has gone under! Katie..."

Lanier froze. "What?" He looked back up at Charlie.

Charlie stood aside in the door. He said, "It came in over DataCom. We came back and Christy went in to check on something, and it was just arriving."

"And there it was," Christy said, concerned. "And at about

that very minute, Ken Collins, the press secretary, called over the video scrambler.''

Lanier looked at them, unbelieving.

"Where? How did it happen?"

"At a concert at Georgetown University. Tonight, just an hour ago. Ken said that they're keeping everyone mum. The place's shut down tight. But the press will pick up on it real fast. Maybe they have it already.''

"Shit!" Lanier swore suddenly. "What happened? How?"

"No one knows for sure," Christy said. "Collins doesn't even know how such a thing could've happened. All the immunity cards were checked, especially Katie's. They even turned some important people away. Their individual ratings weren't good enough."

Lanier stared darkly at them. Christy had never seen him like this before.

She went on. "Katie was there with Senator Randell, and they . . ."

"Randell?" Lanier, in the center of the living room, still in his coat, spun around. "Randell's in the middle of everything."

"Collins said that the concert was going fine," Charlie related. "Then, *poof!* They went." He waved his huge arms around expressively.

"They?"

"Oh, yeah," Charlie pointed out. "About fifteen people went at exactly the same instant in the performancé." He smiled wryly. "But not Randell. He's still here. He's helping get things organized."

Lanier paced around the living room, his mind completely aswirl.

Christy came back with the printout.

"You know," Lanier began, "tonight something very unusual happened to me."

They watched him. Silence otherwise filled the spaces of the living room. He paced back and forth. He turned to Charlie Gilbert with a fierce look in his eyes.

"Look, Charlie, I want you to get your boys over here pronto."

Surprised, Charlie asked, "Now? What's up?"

"I've just realized a lot of things that didn't seem possible before. Down at the Watson Pueblo Theater they're showing *Halcyon Days*. I want you and your boys to get it for me. I want the actual physical copy of the film. All of the reels. Get a court order or just plain steal it."

"So that's where you went," Christy broke in. "We tried calling you everywhere. We didn't think that . . ."

"I know, I know," he said. "It just came over me to go see her for one last time."

"Ellie?"

"Yes, Ellie." He looked at his watch. "But when it closes tonight"—he looked at Charlie—"*I want that film.*"

He turned to Christy and began removing his jacket. "Then, while I'm gone, I want you to set up the projection equipment we have here."

She gave him an exasperated look, a look that said *It's Friday night, that we need a break.*

"I know it's a hassle, but it'll be worth it, believe me."

Charlie said, "What's this all about?"

Lanier walked over to the door of his workroom. "Well, do you remember years ago—Jesus, I can't recall how long off-hand—but it was before our time, when that technician Lean-der"—he snapped his fingers—"Alex Leander invented a pro-cess of using a set of frequencies in television broadcasting for audience manipulation?"

Charlie said, "Certainly." Christy didn't know what they were talking about. But Charlie continued, "The Leander In-terphase, I think it was called. The casebooks said that the equipment was confiscated and he was going to be brought to trial. Subterfuge, I think. The experts said it was a hoax and Leander disappeared. How long ago was that anyway?"

Lanier said, "Easily twenty years ago. But I think that it has resurfaced again. Get those film canisters from the Watson Pueblo and see for yourselves while I'm gone. If I'm thinking right, you'll be able to use it on any projector. But you'll find that the Leander Interphase is ingrained on the film of *Halcyon Days.* Check it against my copy of the movie. But be careful," he urged. "Don't get caught. I'll be gone for more than six hours this time, if this disease has gotten as bad as we think it has. And I want you guys to be here when I get back."

Christy scurried around in the library for the correct sonic-wafer.

Charlie fretted, watching Lanier change his clothing. "Jesus, I can't believe that the President's gone under. It seems almost impossible."

"Believe it," Lanier said, preoccupied.

Lanier came out of the door, bouncing on one foot, trying to draw up a boot on the other. His long coat dangled like great wings. He fell into a chair.

"Where's the Vice President?" he asked them. "Have the Joint Chiefs been notified?"

Christy answered, "Ken Collins got the word out to everyone necessary after they shut up the theater with everyone in it."

Lanier smiled. "Hostage?"

"That's the word." Charlie gritted his teeth. "Euphemism, more likely."

"But the Vice President."

"Down with the worst case of Cambodian flu on record," Christy informed him. "Appears as if he is the only one with it on the entire east coast."

Lanier sat astonished, fearing the answer to his next question, but knowing that there was now only one answer.

"And the Speaker of the House?"

Charlie and Christy exchanged careful looks. Charlie said, "He appears to be missing."

"Missing." Not a question. A statement.

"That's what I'm told." Charlie looked at his friend; behind his eyes the cogs and gears were clicking into place. Charlie sat back in the chair, somewhat pale.

Lanier stared evenly at them both. The computer printout rattled distantly from Christy's office.

"Then that means no one is at the controls, right?"

Nobody responded. Lanier stood up like an angel of death in his long dark coat. He adjusted the priest's collar. He pulled out his Malachi, cocked it, then put it back into its holster.

"Well, boys and girls, it looks like we have a situation on our hands. Time to go to work."

Sitting in his usual half-lotus position on the cool floor of his workroom, he found it somewhat difficult to calm down. Many things rambled through his mind; many questions, many answers. There was a time in his life when he welcomed the emotional depths that the very best of classical music had to offer. Making love to Erik Satie's *Gymnopédies*. Walking, broke and lonely, through the New Mexico snow with Mahler's *Das Lied von der Erde* going through his mind. But to lose himself, now, to such forces would undermine his whole life, as it had done three years ago with Marie. Now it seemed to be happening once again.

Slow down, cowboy, he thought. *Be dispassionate, act on the knowledge of the last hour, but don't let it act on you.*

Christy dimmed the lights and Lanier fought for his mantra. Images of Ellie Estevan and Albertson Randell shifted across his mind, mixing in with the beautiful music of Roy Harris's neglected *Seventh Symphony*. There came to him memories of Nacimiento, memories of Hell. But he held on to the sound that the mantra generated. His heart slowed. One by one, he let each single thought separate itself and fall away. Memories were turned aside. His breathing was controlled. Only the music itself remained.

Indian Summer. By the way the sunlight seemed tired and drawn, Lanier guessed that here it was near the first of autumn. The air was balmy, the walnut and beech trees still held their leaves. The oaks let their leaves stir in the slight wind that followed him down across the village lane. He could smell hickory on the air.

Appalachia, he guessed. The vibrations were unmistakable. He was back home in some primordial archetype of ancient America. The houses that lined the cobbled street came from a different era, though. He thought that it might be late colonial. Women, bearing baskets of bread and preserves, were stepping from small shops. They wore white bonnets typical of the Puritan mode, their dresses dropping conservatively to their ankles. Someone's chickens were running loose in the middle of the road, and they all scattered as a young man in a buckboard came driving by, their feathers rising like flakes of snow.

The adult men on the sidewalks resembled the Puritan fathers of the country. Lanier almost expected to rub shoulders with Edward Taylor on his way back to his secluded cabin to write another meditational prayer-poem. Or perhaps Cotton Mather, dark and brooding, marching down the street with an air of self-righteousness. Trouble and damnation on his mind.

But this wasn't New England—quite.

Lanier couldn't place the locus of the vibrations, but, given the many shifts of theme in Harris's symphony, it appeared to him that this village was an amalgam of various aspects of early Americana. Not exactly the Plymouth Colony, though William Bradford would be a fitting governor here, and it wasn't quite like the old Virginia plantations; it seemed to be a mixture of all of them. And much more.

Looking up over the tops of the picturesque gabled cottages and log cabins, Lanier was very surprised to see a fantastic tower, constructed of wood, at the far end of the town. It rose forty meters, and was something no early colony would have ever seen, or built.

The tower appeared to be something like a watchtower common along the forts of the western frontier of America. Composed of sturdy logs—possibly cedar and oak—its octagonal pillar lifted above the forest. On the top, a cantilevered command post stood out, balanced on the tall column. There were window slits on all sides, and, for the most part, the whole structure seemed unassailable from the ground.

Just what the tower was for, he had no idea.

As he passed down the street, his coat buttoned tightly over the utility belt and Malachi, no one looked at him curiously. Everyone went about their affairs in a peaceful fashion, ignoring the presence of a priest. And the ominous tower. *Ominous*, he realized, *that's the word for it*. However peaceful these people seemed among themselves, the tower was there for a purpose.

Stepping up onto the wooden plank sidewalk, he tried to relax. A man wearing a wide-brimmed black hat, drawing behind him a reluctant daughter, smiled embarrassedly at him. Lanier nodded and smiled back. He kept on walking. He felt very uneasy.

He knew that of all the patients he had, Katie Babcock was easily the most important. Whatever the reasons for her succumbing, he had to get her out and back into the real world.

Although, he thought idly, *this world isn't all that bad*.

As he walked, he distantly wondered if this village had any kind of threat, such as the British tax laws, or the French massing to the north—or plagues, or Indians. If this was a genuine replica of an early American settlement, then there would have to be a balance somewhere. *Fudd-Smith's Law*. Only a foolish romantic would get consumed in a setting such as this, although Lanier did feel a slight twinge of nostalgia for the life his forefathers led. Perhaps it was the music itself.

He was *sure* it was the music, because life back then was extremely hazardous. Only the most rugged and determined of individuals survived. And Lanier could see it on the faces of these people. He immediately noticed that the women here were not the beautiful, well-fed, beaming beauties of his century. Life here in this world was just as rough and wild as it had been five hundred years ago.

He stopped near a torch-lamppost to survey the community. The vibrations that Katie Babcock gave off were strong at this point, but not nearly as strong as they should be. What he felt was despair, and grief. The music, which was running through his mind at a low pitch, composed the world quite efficiently, and it was Katie's misery that made everything fall suddenly under dark shadows.

Where is she? he wondered, looking around. Back off behind the main street, hoeing a garden? Somewhere churning butter? Is she, perhaps, someone's wife condemned to a life of drudgery?

Just at that point, a deep, resonant clanging came from the tower. A large bell sounded from the top. Everyone in the street suddenly halted where they were and looked toward the tower.

It rang twice, no one moved. Three times, the same.

When it struck a fourth time, the women screamed and scattered up and down the street. Two men beside Lanier ran for the tower so fast and so suddenly that they lost their wide-brimmed black hats. The bell kept sounding.

Lanier, spinning in the maze of panicked settlers, pulled himself aside into a bakery storefront. A young man, dusting his hands of flour, stepped out.

"What's going on?" Lanier addressed him.

The young man, obviously a baker's apprentice, whipped off his apron.

"Four times, that's the signal! It rang four times!" He looked helplessly at Lanier. Terrified, he said, "They're coming!"

He disappeared back into the shop, leaving Lanier out on the sidewalk.

Lanier noticed that some of the people who had fled to their homes were now back out, running down the street toward the tower. Women dragged their children behind them frantically, and the men carried flintlock rifles and bags of shot and silver-gray gunpowder.

The baker's apprentice sped past Lanier carrying a small bundle beneath his arm: loaves of bread wrapped in cloth.

A horse attached to a carriage reared in confusion, throwing the driver to the street. The carriage was loaded with foodstuffs bound for the tower. People were running everywhere.

It's like an air raid, he thought suddenly.

His heart began racing even though he had yet to feel sufficiently threatened. It was Katie Babcock's doing. Lanier had harmonized with the music so well that the apprehensions of the approaching danger were heightened merely because Katie herself was frightened. Wherever she was, she knew what was happening. And it horrified her.

Another young boy ran by. Lanier pulled him over.

"Hey," he said hurriedly. "Who's coming? What's going on?"

The boy jerked his arm free from Lanier's grasp. "Shawnee! There!" He pointed to the sky beyond the tower, then sped off down the avenue.

Lanier looked into the sky.

The sun was bright and pleasantly warm, and the sky itself was a perfect azure, like the inside of a Japanese ceramic bowl. There were no clouds, and it seemed peaceful. He could see nothing.

Lanier reached inside his coat and pulled out the amplified binoculars. Adjusting the power, he scanned the horizon as the colonists scattered around him like a herd of frightened cattle. He tried to ignore them as best he could. After all, he had a Malachi and enough explosives to level the village.

He could spot nothing along the horizon, and nothing beyond the trees behind the community. In every direction he looked, all there was to be seen was bright blue sky and forest.

All directions except one. He looked straight up. Above the village, and particularly high above the tower, Lanier could see tiny, boat-shaped craft descending slowly, as if at the mercy of the wind. They were quite high and moving sluggishly. Not aircraft, not balloons, they were boats.

Indians? Shawnee, did he say? Lanier squinted at them. *What kind of colonial world is this?*

The only thing he could do for the present was to go to the tower with the rest of the townfolk. The overhead boats were only minutes away from the tower. He could see no immediate threat from the craft. But he could be wrong.

Since the villagers might not let him inside the tower—being so obviously an outsider to the community—he decided to do something useful. He leaped out into the street and aided the merchant with the bolting horse. The man was having a difficult time controlling the animal.

An old hand with horses, Lanier ran to the opposite side of the horse and grabbed the reins that fluttered about the huge neck of the beast. He pulled the animal off to one side, facing away from the fleeing villagers, away from the commotion.

"I got him," he said to the merchant, swinging up on the rider's seat. "Here, I'll help you. Let's go!"

The merchant didn't argue, and a temporary look of relief spread to his face. The horse had almost been too much for him to handle on his own.

"But my wife! I've got to get her," he said, running back into his store, which Lanier noticed was a candle shop and waxworks. "Wait here for me!"

Although somewhat apprehensive, he didn't feel the same sense of urgency as the settlers did. His mantra drifted evenly in his mind. Nothing moved him. *Om Mani Padmi Hum . . .*

The man came back out with his wife, a frumpy woman who was as frightened as her husband. She kept squealing, "Jack, oh Jack!" And the merchant kept shoving her toward the carriage where Lanier waited, tugging at the reins, quieting the horse. The animal was still very restless.

Suddenly something struck the carriage solidly with a loud, ugly *thump*! Lanier spun around and saw a massive iron dartlike object imbedded in a flour sack. Another dart fell into the street, followed by another.

The woman shrieked, ridden with hysteria. Jack, the merchant, lifted her bodily into the back of the carriage with the food. She screamed, rolling over in a rustle of petticoats, rumpling like an enormous flower. She came face-to-face with the dart. Seeing it, inches away from her nose, she fainted in a cloud of flour dust.

The darts fell all about the villagers.

Lanier turned the horse around, slapped the reins along its backside.

"Yah! Up there!" And the carriage jerked, taking off down the street.

The merchant, holding on to his hat, looked up. "Damn Shawnee! Look out! Look out! Good God!"

Lanier glanced up when a huge shadow mooned over them. One of the craft was only fifty meters above them, and he could see a number of men—Shawnee presumably—dropping whole racks of the dart objects.

A deadly rain of the sharp, barbed darts plunged right in front of their horse. The darts struck the dusty street, digging in deeply. Two men were felled by them, impaled neatly. One dart caught a woman in the hip, thrusting her to the ground. She uttered no sound, going down instantly dead. Another man, like a pinned insect, vomited blood onto the street, the dart protruding from his stomach.

Lanier gave the merchant the reins. "Here, hold these a minute." And he yanked out his Malachi.

He aimed upward along the port side of the boat-craft. There, several painted faces screamed and howled. The Malachi—set this time on rapid-fire—let out a piercing scream of its own and chewed up the wood railing of the ship. All the heads reared backward with dozens of anesthetic needles stitched across their faces. The boat-craft tilted with the sudden dispersal of weight falling across it.

"Let's go!" he commanded.

The merchant stared at his gun, then at him.

"Move!"

The merchant slapped the reins.

The nearest boat to them was a hundred meters away. But the wind on which it drifted put it between them and the base of the tower. Darts were being freely lobbed from the craft. Arrows hissed downward as well.

Lanier jerked out the empty clip from the Malachi and snapped in a fresh one from his belt. The ship he had just shot at began drifting over the houses behind them. Other Shawnee, outlined in the bright afternoon light, were back again at the railing, leaning over more racks of darts. It took two men to hold a single rack.

The merchant skillfully guided the carriage through the throng of settlers and around the darts that stuck in the street. The other boat-craft between them and the tower had drifted away, out of reach, over a side avenue of small stores.

They came immediately to the base of the wooded tower. The base appeared to be an entire building of itself, low-slung with slanted sides. It looked almost like a blockhouse to Lanier.

And only a woman from the future would know what a blockhouse was for, he realized.

Through the large, out-swung doors, buggies, wagons, and scores of desperate people passed. *An air raid shelter*, he thought.

The carriage wheeled about, and once inside, Lanier could see small balls of fire falling about the rooftops of the village. The boats themselves hadn't touched ground yet, and many of them were still floating high up in the sky. But the settlers could now hear the screams of the Indians quite distinctly. People rushed about.

Lanier looked out through the wide doors. It was almost as if the English and the French and the Dutch had never settled the east coast of America. It was as if these colonists, now in the twenty-first century, had just left a Europe that was for some reason still in the clutches of some leftover, or long-drawn-out medieval era—and the original inhabitants of America, the Indians, had evolved. Their hunting and fighting crafts had progressed a thousandfold. Five centuries is a long time to climb the ladder of technology. Anything was possible, even airborne Shawnee.

Overhead, deep inside the tower, the bell resounded hauntingly, shaking the entire structure. Lanier climbed down from the seat of the carriage. The base of the tower was about the size of an airplane hanger. There was room for hundreds of people, including their horses and wagons. And those hundreds of people were here, now. And everyone was very frightened. They were clearly no match for the Shawnee outside.

Lanier scanned the faces of the women in the crowd, looking for Katie Babcock. The vibrations from the music, which still ran through his mind, told him that she was quite close. But, in the dust and confusion, he couldn't find her in this assembly.

In the very center of the tower base was a spiral staircase. The column of the immense tower began here. Huge beams dug into the earth, and supports ringed the base of the column all the way around it.

Lanier made his way through the men and women to the base of the tower's column. Perhaps he would find the community leaders, and Katie, near the top of the tower. He reasoned that Katie would be one of the leaders here, if not the Mayor herself. It seemed likely.

No one prevented him from mounting the steps and climbing up the inside of the tower. Many men bearing rifles and pouches of gunpowder on slings rushed around him, thundering up the stairs. They were too preoccupied to stop him.

Upon reaching the fourth level of the tower, which he reasoned was probably about halfway to the top, Lanier came to a wide platform where men had gathered around the slits in the tower wall. They were firing their rifles off into the distance. Behind them, their sons were reloading the flintlocks.

Lanier gazed out of one of the window slits. One of the boat-craft had moored to the spire of a distant steeple. Another had drifted down to a large building that appeared to be some sort of community house. Yelling and whooping, the Shawnee descended upon the town. Fires blossomed here and there like wild roses.

Just then, a dark cloud passed above the window, and one of the boat-craft sank slowly within a few meters of the opening. The bottom of the hull was either iron or copper—Lanier wasn't too sure which—and bullets ricocheted off it when the colonists fired at the craft. As soon as the boat lowered further, they could see the Indians.

Screams and yells went up, and grappling hooks went out.

The Shawnee were athletic and tawny. Curiously, their hair was trimmed in Mohawk fashion, and on their faces and bare skulls they wore the ugly streaks of red and purple warpaint. Standing at the rear of the platform, Lanier could see just how determined they were. Tomahawks pinwheeled through the windows. Knives flashed.

He almost wanted the Indians to win this one. But *these* Indians weren't the real American Indians who deserved his compassion.

What a world, he thought, raising his Malachi. The Puritans were poor fighters, poorly organized, and they fired their muzzle-loading rifles all at once in their frenzy. They had to be reloaded by the boys at their backs, and in that brief time the Shawnee were on them.

The Indians leaped from the boat that was now tethered to the tower and scrambled through the windows.

Suddenly they jumped with surprise at the Malachi's staccato growling. Inside the chamber, the Malachi was thunderous—and the Indians either fell from the edge of the boat or they simply fell back out of the windows. The ones who weren't killed in the fall would wake up hours later in the boat with colossal headaches. If they woke up at all.

"Cut those cables!" Lanier yelled, assuming some badly needed authority. *These are weak people, not used to being governed,* he suddenly realized. *Is this how Katie sees herself? Or is this how she sees her people?*

The men stared at him through the dust and smoke that was lanced by shafts of yellow sunlight.

"Do it!" he yelled.

Several dreamlings turned and brought out axes and the cables were severed, the hooks tossed off into space. The Indians slept in the boat-craft, each one with needles sticking in his painted skin.

Lanier spun around and ran back up the staircase.

Within minutes, he reached the command post at the top of the tower. In the center of the room, just above him as he ascended the stairway, was a huge iron bell. He had never seen a bell of this size and wondered briefly how the tower could hold such a thing. It must have weighed tons.

There were also five cannons facing away from the bell. Dust and ash and smoke and utter chaos filled the tower. Dozens of men armed the cannons, dipping long, wadded plungers into their fuming mouths. Each machine took turns firing out the windows, and in the midst of it all was Katie Babcock, shouting down orders, bathed in sweat and smeared with dirt. Tears lined her cheeks.

"Shoot them! Stop them!" she screamed in a broken voice, almost hysterically.

This didn't seem like the President of the United States that Lanier knew. This appeared to be more of the temperment of an ordinary woman caught up in the spell of a crisis that demanded a substantial amount of personal fortitude. Fortitude which she didn't have, at least here.

"*Katie!*" Lanier shouted as soon as he saw her. He stepped up into the room. "Katie! It's me, Fran Lanier!"

Shots from two of the cannons burst around them, deafening everyone. The men suddenly cheered, and through the window before them they could see one of the boat-craft plummeting, split asunder by a well-placed cannonball. The thing dropped like a stone. Whatever was keeping it aloft no longer functioned. The Shawnee fell outward like dolls made of straw.

"Katie!" He grabbed her, shaking her as fiercely as he could.

Wildly, frantically, she looked at him. She seemed about to swoon. Another cannon roared. More men ran up the stairs. They were replacements; some of them were waterboys.

Katie tore herself from Lanier's hold suddenly and staggered, balling her fists into her eyes.

A gentleman came over, very authoritative in a Puritan way, and put his hand to Lanier's shoulder.

"I think you should leave her be," he said firmly, though in a very friendly fashion. "She's been under a great strain lately, and it's enough for us to face the trials that God has seen fit to put upon us." The man's silk shirt was blackened with gunpowder, his wig filthy.

She finally sagged. Lanier reached for her quickly.

"I'm a friend of hers," he told the man. "I'll take care of her."

The gentleman nodded, concerned but conciliatory. He turned back toward the ranks of defenders at the window.

Suddenly, from behind Lanier, he heard a familiar voice.

"Katherine—oh Katherine?"

Lanier turned around and before him stood the tall, impressive figure of Albertson Randell, dressed like a fighting Puritan, his hair all askew and powder stains on his face and ruffled blouse.

"Randell!" Lanier exclaimed.

The man considered Lanier strangely. "Sir?" he asked, rifle in his hand.

"What are you doing here?"

Another cannon exploded, shaking the entire tower.

"I don't know what you mean, sir." A very contrite smile was on Randell's lips. "I am the Governor's husband. Sir Jeffrey Rennel."

Lanier looked at him closely. A dreamling. That's what this was. A dreamling. He should have guessed. He had been so swept up in the turmoil of the scenario that the vision simply startled him for an instant. Randell wasn't anything like a Stalker, and couldn't come to inhabit Katie's world the way he himself could.

But the coincidence!

Lanier couldn't believe his eyes. Albertson Randell. The chaos and heady confusion of the fighting had thrown him. This wasn't Randell. The look on the large man's face told him as much.

They both held Katie in their arms, lowering her to the straw-littered floor of the command post.

Another cannon exploded. The pressure on his ears was enormous. Lanier went deaf for a brief second, still retaining the music and his mantra. He coughed in the smoke. Sound returned slowly. Lanier reached into his vest and pulled out some smelling salts from his medicine pouch.

"These will bring her around," he said to Randell, snapping the vial apart and waving them beneath Katie's nose.

She struggled, thrusting her arms about, trying subconsiously to fend off the noxious odor. She aroused quickly though, recognizing her "husband" and barely recognizing Lanier.

"Katie, are you all right?" Lanier asked. "It's me, Francis Lanier."

She blinked through the smoke. "Francis . . . Francis . . ." It sounded like a question.

Almost as if his part called for it, Rennel/Randell got up and went back to the line of men in order for the two of them to be alone; as if the logic of the scenario required it. It was as if Katie were bringing the fantasy back under her willful control.

"Who . . . ?" she started, still clouded from the noise and fighting.

"We're under siege," Lanier began. "That was your husband. You are the Governor here, not the President. Do you remember being President?"

She sat up. One of her sleeves was torn off at the shoulder.

"Yes, I . . ." She drifted off, her hand to her brow. "Oh, Francis!" Her eyes widened suddenly with recognition. She leaned back, using one arm for support.

"It was too much! Just too much! I couldn't take it . . . back there."

Lanier nodded, understanding. *It's all too much. Wherever you go, wherever you are. . . .*

She grabbed his arm. "It was beyond my control, everything!"

Lanier watched her as her mind slowly became clearer, her thinking more resolute. Katie Babcock was, by degrees, becoming Katie Babcock, the President of the United States, again. She climbed up to her feet.

She continued, "The diseases, the corporate wars, the chicano guerrilla taking over southern California. I can't stand it anymore!"

Not quite Katie Babcock, yet, he thought, watching her. *But almost. The human being inside of her is back, but the warlord is still missing.* Here, in this twenty-first-century colonial world, the passive, feminine characteristics of Katie Babcock had taken over. Katie Babcock was one of the strongest, most aggressive corporate lawyers that had ever stalked Wall Street, and she had been a very tough senator. It wasn't in her basic constitution to become so weak.

But, in this fabrication—this ostensibly serene and rural setting—she had allowed herself to become more yielding, gentle. Perhaps it was a manifestation of something; some previous state that she had lost or sacrificed when she began moving up through the political circles of New York and Washington: something she desperately wanted back.

Here, in this world, she got it. And she got the flying Shawnee. That was the balance. The weak with the strong. The gentle with the terrifying.

And Randell—or Rennel, he wondered. *What was that all about? Did she dream him up too? Or is Randell more of a natural element to her psyche than anyone knows?*

But it all balanced out, in this world, *and* in the one she had abandoned.

Another cannon exploded. More of this and Lanier would lose his hearing. And he would have to retain the music as best he could if he were to get them both out of there alive.

He approached her gently. "Katie . . . we have to get you back. Something terrible is happening and we need your help." He looked at her sincerely.

"*I* need your help, Katie."

She shook her head, quite lucid now. "No," she stated, her mind made up. "I won't go back. I don't *want* to go back. The country's falling, Francis. Don't you understand? The population is diminishing because of the Syndrome. Industry has collapsed and the Congress wants me to declare martial law. And the goddamn aeroplankton . . . ." Again, she shook her head vigorously. "I just can't stand it anymore. I didn't bargain for this."

Smoke drifted around them, mixed in with the frantic cries and yells of the colonial defenders. Gunfire cracked. Men fell backward, pierced with long arrows.

Then the tower shook, but not from cannon fire.

The Shawnee had breached the tower, and one of their boats had lodged on the very top of the command post.

On long, braided ropes of hemp, they suddenly swung inside, swarming over the smoldering cannon snouts and the men at the windows. They came in from all of the surrounding windows, and the colonists fell to fighting hand-to-hand.

The Shawnee wore swords in leather sheaths strapped to their backs, and these were quickly drawn.

The settlers inside the command post didn't stand a chance with the short swords drawn against them. The Indians began mowing the men down like blades of sawgrass in a field.

Lanier grabbed Katie around the shoulders and rushed to an opposite wall, away from the savages. There, with his back against the wall, Lanier raised the Malachi and fanned the whole inside of the command post, defenders included, with a lightning burst of anesthetic needles. He shot the ones closest to him first, and quickly jerked out the empty clip. In the confusion, he snapped in another clip and shot down all the rest.

Within seconds, the whole floor of the tower command post was piled with sleeping combatants with the exception of Katie Babcock and himself. Even the dreamling, Rennel/Randell, slept soundly.

"A bit extreme, mind you," he said. "But it does tend to do the trick."

Then he saw a peculiar thing, something he'd been waiting to see happen for a while now. A few of the bodies, among both the colonists and the sleeping Shawnee, began to fade right before their eyes.

"Look." He pointed. "They were Walkers. I told you about them, remember? They were real people."

Five individuals disappeared, and headed back, sound asleep, to the real world. But that meant, he suddenly realized, that this world was constituted of slightly more than just the pure elements that Katie Babcock, in her neurotic fantasy over the Harris symphony, had dreamed up.

For it occurred to him then that there might not be any way to tell who was real here and who was not. Theoretically speaking, you could have a world composed entirely of Walkers and not dreamlings. *But,* he thought, *who'd want a world like this one?*

Suddenly he smelled fire.

From down the well of the staircase that threaded up the center of the tall tower, Lanier heard screaming.

"Oh, my God," Katie gasped. "They've set fire to the tower! They made it below to the village!"

Lanier ran to the window. The whole town, with a good part of the forest surrounding it, was broiling in smoke and flame.

Curiously, off in the distance, where he hadn't taken the time to originally observe, were other wooden defense towers in towns several kilometers away. Two of them were also aflame.

It's a war, he realized. A coordinated effort to destroy the colonists. If Katie stayed, she wouldn't have a chance, even if they did manage to push back the Shawnee and rebuild the community. The Indians far outstripped the settlers in both technology and hostility.

Katie stood apart, frozen with fear. The screams got louder, the smoke thicker. It was happening too fast!

The tower rocked again. A boat drifted by and the Shawnee catapulted a firebrand into the midst of the sleeping dreamlings.

Lanier backed off, pushing Katie aside. The firebrand burst into several pieces and the smell of burning flesh filled the chamber.

If he shot her now with an anesthetic needle, it would require time for the drug to take effect. *She could die in that time*, he thought. *Especially here, in this fire.*

"We have to get out of here," he said. They had to find a place where he could withdraw her from the fantasy as peacefully as possible.

And that might not be possible, he suddenly realized.

Lanier looked out the window and saw that one of the boatcraft was still tethered to the top of the command post by a number of dangling grappling hooks. It was empty, having formerly held the troop of Shawnee that had invaded the tower, who were now fast asleep and burning to death.

Lanier pulled out a grappling hook of his own, this one made of textured steel alloy and not the crude iron the Shawnee used, and tossed it out on a long nylon rope. The hook attached itself to one of the suspended ropes. Lanier reeled his nylon rope in, with the floating boat.

Craft were still descending from the clear sky, and below

him the streets of the colonial village teemed with hundreds of Indians who were looting and burning at random.

"Here!" he yelled back at Katie. "Let's get in."

She stepped back into the smoke, now quite frightened and reluctant.

"Let's go!" He gestured frantically, trying to hold the boat to the burning tower. Flames had appeared in the stairwell. The smoke was so thick that it hurt his eyes.

Hell, he said to himself. *I'm not losing this one!*

He pulled out the Malachi and dropped the President of the United States with a single burst. The needle caught her squarely in the stomach. She fell onto a pile of fallen colonists.

He yanked on the rope, then let go of it, hoping that the boat would drift closer to the tower before bobbing away on the wind. He ran over to Katie and scooped her up into his arms.

At the window, the edge of the craft drifted up to the wide sill, and Lanier tossed her like a sack of potatoes into the bottom of the boat. He thought for a minute the boat would capsize with the sudden weight thrown into it, but it righted itself easily.

He mounted the window ledge, flames at his back, and leaped out over the few meters that separated the tower from the boat-craft. Quickly, he disengaged the lines and the boat began drifting away on the currents of air heated by the flaming tower.

He rolled over and the craft hovered gently. It moved off from the tower and the colonists trapped inside. He watched as Katie slowly faded back into the real world. If he hadn't known her as the President of the United States, the woman disappearing before his eyes would have looked exactly like a Pilgrim woman in her apron and wide, cumbersome dress. Every feminine feature of hers was disguised under layers of powder-stained cloth. *Governor*, he thought. Even here, despite her weakness and sensitivity, she still had a predilection for power.

Slowly, he calmed himself.

But in the back of his mind he knew that the people in the tower were dying, and some of those people were Walkers, not dreamlings. Those screams he'd heard: some of them were quite real. They were back there dying a real death.

Roy Harris's *Seventh Symphony* played on. Even if this

CHAPTER THIRTEEN

✦⦿❦⦿✦

The Unanswered Question
Charles Ives

Lanier regained consciousness in a dark room full of bodies that were sprawled in various awkward positions. Next to him, Katie Babcock wheezed in her drugged sleep.

A light burst in upon him, and Christy stood in the doorway.

"You're back!" she said excitedly and somewhat relieved. She yelled over her shoulder, "Charlie, they're back! A whole bunch of them, too."

Daylight? Lanier looked through squinted eyes beyond Christy to the bright light filtering in from the front room.

"Is that daylight?" he asked.

"Yes," she replied, smiling. "You've been gone for twelve hours, now." She checked her watch.

Relieved and worried at the same time, she wrung her hands nervously, standing before the sleeping bodies.

"Twelve hours?" Lanier asked, trying to rearrange his senses. He nudged Katie Babcock. "Twelve hours. It's certainly getting worse. I was only gone for an hour at the most. At least we got her back."

Charlie loomed in the doorway, eclipsing the sunlight to the workroom. "May not do any good, though."

Lanier slowly got to his feet, smelling of gunpowder and burnt wood. "Why's that?"

Charlie and Christy exchanged pained looks.

"Randell's taken over, more or less," Charlie reported.

Lanier detached his priest's collar. "Randell?" He was too exhausted to be surprised.

Charlie began, "The Vice President finally slid into a coma early this morning, and the new riots in Los Angeles and Chicago caused him to vote himself into power, at least until Katie returns. Half of Congress itself is gone, vanished, and General Carey and the Joint Chiefs backed the referendum." He paused briefly, almost as if trying to catch his breath.

Just twelve hours, Lanier thought ironically.

"And," Charlie continued, "he declared martial law, just to hold things down. So far, no one's objected too strenuously. On the other hand, no one knows if anyone *has* objected, since Randell now controls the media and all forms of communication."

Lanier couldn't believe what he was hearing. For an instant, he wondered if he had, in fact, returned to the real world. This seemed like a nightmarish facsimile. He drew a dirty hand over his forehead.

He paced around the sleeping forms at his feet, feeling uncomfortable. His clothing was soaked with sweat and his mind was still unsettled. He felt as if the dirt and filth of the entire world were upon him.

"But," Charlie began eagerly, brightening, "we did look at the film. You were right."

Lanier faced him. "What did I tell you? They're different."

"I'll say they're different! We had to exchange your copies for the ones down at the Watson Pueblo, but the difference is astonishing. The films are heavily ingrained with the Leander Interphase, or something very similar to it, and the studio that rents them out obviously knows what they're doing. They're mesmerizing."

From behind them, Lanier heard someone stir. It was the President.

"Do any of them need any medical attention?" Christy asked, looking down at them. "Is Katie OK?"

"I think so," Lanier said. "Those guys," pointing at the

be able to get at me. I would be trapped in whatever place I was."

Her eyes glowed. Lanier did see. Perhaps had seen all along.

Christy came back into the living room with a tray of coffee cups and a pot of coffee and said, "But we had an extra copy of the wafer pressed just in case, and that case turned up. They think that Charlie and I just live here now."

Lanier nodded. Everything made sense in its own perverted way.

"So they think you might still make an appearance," Charlie concluded. "That's why they have the helicopter out. They'll probably visit us again soon, though. Randell's too cagey."

Charlie drew the curtains closed.

They all began eating the club sandwiches Christy had prepared. Lanier questioned them both.

"So what did the two of you come up with? Things should be fairly obvious to you by now."

They looked at each other. Katie ate in silence, her eyes focused intently on Lanier.

As if it would help him explain things, Charlie began rolling up the long sleeves of his cowboy shirt. He snapped the pearl studs of his cuffs and slowly peeled them back onto his forearms.

"Well, it looks like this. Randell has been manipulating events all along. It's my guess that he was the one who leaked your identity and your Malibu home to the press. I can't prove that, but he's the only one who could, really. And he's the only one who might want to."

Katie watched. There was a vengeful, dangerous look in her eyes. Her personal power was returning from the shock of the Syndrome. She was, after all, the President of the United States. It would be best to wait things out. These were true allies, she realized. *That asshole Albertson ...*

Charlie continued. "Through DataCom—before Randell halted the information flow for security reasons—we found out that a great deal of Randell's personal fortune comes through the movie studios he owns. All of this wasn't ever made public, so we dug deeper. One of the studios he owns is the White Condor." He looked evenly at Lanier. "It's the one that Ellie Estevan had her contract with. And it's safe to assume that all the prints of her films come out of the factory ingrained with the Leander Interphase process. How he got hold of it is still a mystery to us, but he's old enough to have been in a position, politically, to look into it. He was twenty-nine when Leander disappeared."

"Leander process?" Katie asked with a mouthful of tuna sandwich. She was famished. "What the hell's that? What are you talking about?"

Lanier turned toward her on the couch.

"Well, last night I drove into Missoula to see one of Ellie Estevan's movies, called *Halcyon Days*. You may have heard of it. Anyway, I had already seen it privately in my own home some time ago. But the prints the studios so graciously gave Charlie were just ordinary celluloid prints."

"So? What's this about the Leander process?"

"I'm getting to that. Years ago, many years ago actually, Alex Leander, a technician working out of MIT, invented a means whereby a person could manipulate the emotional responses of an audience through certain high frequencies mixed in with the voicetrack or soundtrack of a film or video tape. You wouldn't even notice what was happening to you. But you'd find yourself responding very enthusiastically to the movie you were viewing or the speech you were listening to on television. You'd laugh louder at a television comedy, or cry harder at a drama, whether or not the acting or the direction or film editing provoked it. Originally, I understand, he pioneered the process for use in video only, and not the movies."

"Right," Charlie agreed. "Then they arrested him and the government confiscated the works. What they told the public was that the whole business was a mistake, a hoax, that no one should pay any attention to it."

Lanier continued. "So, I drove into town to see Ellie's movie, and I could feel the vibrations that were coming from the film score, even though no one else in the theater could. I imagine they just thought they were seeing a very powerful movie."

"What a weapon," Katie said firmly. She now understood many things she hadn't previously.

"I need a cigarette," she commanded.

They all looked at each other, embarrassed. No cigarettes. She brooded, thinking that it was a nasty habit anyway.

"It does explain a lot of things, but not everything," Lanier started.

"Like what?" Katie asked.

Lanier turned inward for a brief instant, recalling Ellie's special eyes, the innocence of her face. He was glad he had abandoned the Watson Pueblo Theater when he did. He couldn't have survived *Halcyon Days*. He knew what followed in the film. And he knew what followed in the real world.

Lanier moved close to Katie where they sat on the couch. "Katie, what was between Senator Randell and yourself? I'm sorry to get personal with you, but this has gone beyond the boundaries of our private lives."

At first she felt uncomfortable, but then she realized that he was right. For all his political naiveté, he was right. *He's a good old boy*, she thought.

"We've had an affair, off and on, for the last ten years."

Charlie Gilbert and Christy looked on, awed.

"That's right," Katie continued. "It would've ruined us both, ruined our careers, but it just went on and on. I'm surprised that it stayed out of the scandal sheets for as long as it did. I guess we were lucky."

"Or careful," Lanier remarked.

She lost herself to her own musings. "I wonder," she said, "what it was that Albertson put in my drink."

"What?" Lanier asked, puzzled. "What drink?"

"At the concert, just before it began, we all had drinks with the new symphony director and his staff. I'll bet Albertson put something in my drink, that bastard. He wanted me out of the way."

Fire sparkled in her eyes.

Lanier was somewhat taken by this woman at his side. She was *the* power in the United States, and it showed in her character. It was in her eyes, her face. She was used to power, and understood what it made people do.

"So, with the millions—perhaps billions—he is raking in from the world movie industry with this stolen process, as President, or acting President, Albertson Randell is the most powerful man in the world," Lanier said.

"Well." Katie stood up imperially, resolute. "I'll put an end to this nonsense once and for all."

"No," Lanier said.

They looked at him. Katie stood still.

"Not just yet. There are more unanswered questions facing us besides what Randell is going to do now that he is on the throne."

Katie watched him. *This is a Stalker speaking*, she realized. His face was dirty and lined with exhaustion. He looked as if he'd just walked out of the mouth of Hell. *But those eyes* . . .

He continued. "Have any of you wondered why the Syndrome is mutating so rapidly, and why North Haven Chemicals—or any other pharmaceutical corporation—hasn't come up with a cure?"

They were silent. Charlie, though, was nodding, following Lanier's reasoning.

Then Katie said to them, "Maybe there *is* a cure."

"Exactly," Lanier said. "Or Albertson Randell would've gone under once again. He's not stable at all. It's my guess that Perry Eventide was the one to stumble onto it. Baktropol is the first step. A cure couldn't have been too far beyond that. Listen." He gestured emphatically. "If they can now cure most forms of cancer, it shouldn't be too difficult to find a cure for a bacterium."

"Now, Fran, wait a minute," Charlie pointed out. "Medicine is a bit more complicated than that. If the Chinese couldn't come up with a cure for the Syndrome, why do you think we could?"

"Because all events point to it. In the first place, Atlanta and the Center for Disease Control are still intact. Their facilities are just as good as those at North Haven Chemicals. And second, that insurrection they're having now in China has brought all science and technology to a standstill." He paused, gesturing with a small wedge of a club sandwich. "No, what I mean is this. DataCom shows that Randell is a silent partner in North Haven Chemicals. Though he's not allowed to overtly support any legislation in their favor, he's nonetheless interested in the company's financial success. He could easily, though surreptitiously, divert funds or information from Atlanta to North Haven. And, if you recall, the company owns the worldwide distributing franchise on Baktropol, *and* the sole rights to its manufacture."

"He has the world by the balls, so to speak." Katie remarked.

"You could say so, yes." Lanier looked at her.

Katie sat back. "Then he simply used a dose of something that counteracted the Baktropol I had taken earlier. He would have access to a number of drugs like that. It could've been anything."

"It has even occurred to me," Lanier then said, "that they

might be in some way responsible for the mutations of the Syndrome, but that would be nearly impossible to prove, even if North Haven did have the facilities for controlled recombinant DNA experiments. The disease, after all, is global."

"So now," Charlie interrupted, "Randell and his group will give everyone the cure, right?"

Katie glared at him. "Of course not. He'd be stupid to. That's what will keep everyone in line. As long as they have a cure for the Syndrome, or a stronger preventative, they'll keep it to themselves with everyone hanging on. As long as Albertson keeps everyone believing that the nation is suffering from a crisis, the people will willingly play into his hands."

Everyone was silent for a few minutes.

Lanier peeked through the curtains. He couldn't see the helicopter. Only the early winter light was falling on the Bitterroot Mountains. The whole thing seemed like an extended nightmare, almost like one of the worlds into which a patient might have fallen. Except *he* was the patient.

He went into the other room to change his clothes.

Essentially, he wanted to be alone for a few minutes to think about what was going on around him. The eyes of Ellie Estevan still haunted him, now that he had the President's rescue behind him. *Those incredible eyes, that smile.*

He had told himself—almost as many times as he had repeated his own mantra—that he would never again fall for a woman. At least, not in the way he had for Marie back in Los Angeles years ago. Now, everything was being mixed together, his personal life with his public duties and knowledge. *Everything is connected*, as Two Moons once said.

And now Randell was out to make sure that he was dead or effectively out of the way. He realized that reinstating Katie Babcock to the presidency was only a matter of a phone call to Ken Collins and the Pentagon. *That* was no problem.

But the weight of the national circumstances bore on him as if he had suddenly become an unwitting beast on a treadmill: each time he returned to the real world, things were worse off than they had been. Aeroplankton. Wars. World temperature rising. Disease. Diminishing resources.

He recalled the remark of the astronomer he had not brought back a few weeks ago. *Maybe his world was best. . . .*

He pulled off his tunic. He looked at himself in the mirror. *You're getting old, cowboy. Old.* He always thought that getting old would never become a problem, that there'd always be someone to help him out.

But not Marie. Not Ellie Estevan.

At that moment, Lanier suddenly recalled what Charlie had just said only a few moments previously. That Randell owned the studios that Ellie had worked for.

He ran into the living room.

"Charlie," he said, shirtless and excited. "Christy, listen. Did they identify Floyd Matkin's escort at that party during the summit?"

Charlie set down his coffee cup. "Yes, they did. I thought you knew."

"Who was it?"

Christy looked at him. Charlie spoke. "Ellie Estevan. She was all over Europe at the time. Wasn't it in the report?"

"*Jesus*," Lanier swore. "It all makes sense now—God, does it make sense!"

"What are you talking about?" Charlie asked.

Katie Babcock watched.

Lanier ran back into Christy's office. He punched on the light. They followed him inside.

"How much of the national data base has Randell shut down?"

Christy said, "Anything pertaining to national security, which means DataCom. That would include industry, transportation, all of the utilities, and all of the access to communication information."

"But not business. Not HomeCom channels."

"Of course not. He'd be crazy to debilitate the country's source of income. There may be martial law, but people are still going to have to go to work."

Lanier smiled thinly. There was no mirth to his smile.

"Good," he said, sitting at the console. Thumbing it on, he keyed in his own private code for access to HomeCom.

"What are you doing?" Charlie asked.

"There are a few things we never found out about just why Eventide and Matkin died."

Katie Babcock leaned through Christy and Charlie, glancing over Lanier's bare shoulders. "What do you have in mind?"

"Well, I've assumed all along that they perished through some sort of death wish of their own. But there was always a dreamling present."

"A woman," Christy added.

"That's right. I never thought about it until now, but it just seems too coincidental for Matkin and Eventide to die in the same way, especially given their real-world associations."

Charlie said, "But they didn't die in the same way. At least, not according to your reports."

"Yes, they did, because the same individual was present."

"A dreamling?"

"That's enough to go on." He looked up at Charlie. "Did you ever see any of her movies?"

"Whose movies?"

"Ellie Estevan's."

"Once, some time ago. Years ago, in fact."

"Do you remember her eyes? What they looked like? Or better yet, remember Shaughnessy's party?"

Charlie looked at him curiously. Lanier turned back to the waiting console. He punched in a code for open access to insurance records. Insurance records and credit files would still be open to all of the proper sources. Since Lanier had the facilities for such data retrieval—being a Stalker—he had the proper codes.

He punched a cross-reference to Ellie Estevan.

"There." He pointed as the lines began drawing themselves out across the screen.

"Ellie Estevan," Katie read for them, her hand on the back of Lanier's chair. "Married to Michael Estevan." The screen read off the dates of the marriage and then the date of the divorce a year later.

"No." Lanier lifted a finger to the screen. "This is what I'm after."

Katie Babcock read, "Ellie Estevan, born Elizabeth Jinn, New York City." The date of birth was three years after Lanier's own birth date.

"I don't understand," Katie began. "What's important about that?"

Lanier said, "Well, she may have been born in New York, but look where her father was born."

The cross-reference to Elizabeth Jinn Estevan's father read, "Durango, Colorado."

Lanier took a deep breath.

"When Ellie was first reported vanished back during the summer, I read her portfolio, saw where she was born and thought nothing about it. But it's not Ellie who's important, it's her parents."

"Oh, Fran," Christy suddenly said. "She's a Stalker."

Everything came back to him. The girl leaving Perry Eventide wounded beside the drained creek in the disintegrating cylindrical world. The girl fleeing the farmhouse on the prairie that the orange spacecraft consumed. He should have known. But there was no way that he could have.

Lanier was silent. *Those eyes.* Burton Shaughnessy even noticed the similarity. He felt so commonly stupid not to have guessed.

"Yes," he whispered. "Her parents lived in the area and would've been naturally exposed to the same chemical. The cases got fewer and fewer as the years went by, but," he nodded his head, his heart racing, "yes, she was a Stalker."

He clenched his fists, staring at the words on the mute console.

"I still don't understand," Katie told him.

Lanier turned from the console and walked through the hallway, into the living room, nearly in a daze.

He spoke. "Randell owns White Condor Studios, if not outright, then indirectly. He nevertheless runs it through his influence. Randell also has enemies, both political and financial. It seems so simple now."

Charlie sadly added everything together. "Randell," he began, "through the Leander Interphase, built Ellie Estevan's career, made her into an international star, far beyond anything she could've amounted to on her own."

"He *owned* her," Lanier said not looking at them.

Charlie went on. "Even though she would've had an independent contract, such was his influence that she couldn't refuse. She could get more money and better parts through White Condor and the Interphase."

Then Katie said, "And he had her escort his enemies..."

"And stalked them when they went under since she was immune," Lanier concluded.

There's the balance, he realized. *For every good force, there is an opposite and equal bad force.* In this world and all of the others, Fudd-Smith's Law was hard at work.

"So she had to do it," he told them. "It wasn't her nature, but she had to do it. Her career was too far along. And that's what killed her."

"What?" Katie was confused.

"Just before you went under, Ellie Estevan herself vanished.
I went in after her, and she died. I failed to rescue her."

"That voice you said . . ." Christy began.

"Randell," Lanier affirmed. "Or merely her own conscience
acting. Her own guilty conscience."

Lanier dropped heavily onto the couch. He shut his eyes,
hoping that the world itself would vanish, go away and leave
him alone.

Just then, one of the Shawnee walked out into the living
room from where Lanier had left them sleeping. He was rubbing
the small needle wounds in his neck and on his chest.

He startled everyone. Everyone but Lanier. The Indian
leaned in the doorway, livid in the red warpaint on his torso.

"Ow," he said expressively, blinking and staggering.

Behind him, the other Shawnee, quite passive now, appeared. Katie stepped back, hiding behind Charlie. The nightmare world was still too close for her.

Christy walked over to the first Shawnee. "Here," she said
comfortingly. "Let me help you."

"Thanks," the Indian said politely.

The other Shawnee shook his head as if trying to dislodge
the quagmire that the drug induced.

"Please sit down," Christy offered the two men.

The first Indian was a tall, very thin man, and very tanned,
though it was hard to tell through the makeup and paint. The
other was not nearly so tall, and he wore less paint. Their
narrow manes of hair made them look very frightening to everyone in the room.

Christy poured coffee and indicated the tray of sandwiches.

"Oh, Christ," the first one said, digging in. "Thanks,
thanks . . ."

Lanier, as if in a trance, leaned over, looking quizzically
at each of them, thinking.

The second Indian asked, "Where are we?"

"Near Missoula, Montana," Lanier informed him. "I'm
Francis Lanier, a Stalker. These are my friends," and he indicated Christy, who stood before them, and Charlie, who
stood off to one side. "And this," Lanier indicated Katie Babcock, "is the President of the United States, whom I'm sure
you recognize." There was a touch of irony in his voice. But
the men missed it.

They stopped wolfing down the sandwiches, somewhat shocked by Lanier's assertion. But beneath the grime and smoke stains, they could see that Francis Lanier was right. This was, indeed, Ms. Katie Babcock.

They seemed to recollect immediately where they had just come from.

"Were you in the tower?" the second Shawnee asked. He wore a jaunty blue feather hanging from his right ear.

"Yes, I was," she told them. "You were trying to kill me."

They seemed confused. They looked at each other.

"It's . . . it's so strange," the first man started. "It was like a dream. We were just fighting. We had to . . ." He looked at his companion. Only their Mohawk haircuts made him look like Indians. Their mannerisms spoke otherwise.

"I didn't even know you," the second Indian said to the first. "I thought I was the only one there."

"There are three more asleep in the other room, in case you didn't see them," Lanier informed the two men.

"What are your names?" Christy asked.

"I'm Tom Dunlap," the first Indian said, now no longer an Indian. "Montana did you say? I'm from Cincinnati."

The other looked at them almost as if they were all crazy. "I'm Wallace Frazier. Jesus Christ, is this for real? I'm supposed to be in Houston." And they could now discern a slight east Texas drawl.

Like the millions of voices Lanier frequently heard chattering between the planes of existence, a million thoughts raced through his mind. *Ellie Estevan. Albertson Randell. The Leander Interphase.*

Then he thought of the astronomer who refused to return to the world he came from. *You're right, doctor,* he suddenly realized. *So right . . .*

"What *is* all of this?" Wallace Frazier, the man from Houston, asked.

"This," Lanier said to them, "is one of the best things that could have ever happened to us."

CHAPTER FOURTEEN

⋘◉◉◉⋙

Fanfare for the Common Man
Aaron Copland

In Los Angeles, most of the San Fernando Valley was in flames.

Salvos from the tightly organized urban guerrillas went off sporadically as National Guard troops flew over in helicopters trying to cordon off the pockets of civil unrest. When they weren't doing that, they were either dropping in food and supplies to the millions of trapped citizens or trying to effect an evacuation toward the Mojave Desert. The fire and smoke and smog filled the valley with a fetid bubble of amber light.

No law was in existence, even martial law. The state government in Sacramento was helpless in maintaining any kind of order. When the Mexican nationals flooded in to help Draco scour out the barrios of enraged chicanos, there was nothing that the Governor could do to stop them. Phone lines were cut. Those that remained were effectively scrambled. Radio was the only reliable form of communication left. And with the government in Washington in its own state of confusion, the local citizens wondered whom they were fighting for, or against. No one had any idea when the fighting would stop, for it seemed to be going on continuously, with no end near.

The security guard at White Condor Studios didn't care one way or another. Hyped up on Baktropol-9, he listened to the pirate radio station play its subversive music. It was classical music, but he didn't mind. It sounded rather pleasant, in fact. *Copland* . . .

Wearing his oxygen-assisted filter-mask, the security guard slowly paced the cement steps of the processing plant that still, in all the civil disorder, functioned. It ran twenty-four hours of the day, every day of the year.

He looked up. It was common to see the crimson running lights of the attack helicopters of the Army National Guard flash overhead, moving off behind the hills into the valley below, ferrying the reinforcements and equipment. All citizens were off the streets by sundown, and the choppers made him think back to the African War: gunfire in the streets, mortar explosions blossoming suddenly in the avenues, rockets launched by renegade urban freedom fighters. Chaos was everywhere.

Here, though, he knew he was safe. The plant was remote, innocuous, and impenetrable. Who would want to lay siege to a fortresslike brick and stone building? He thought that being a cop was much better than being on active duty in the Guard, particularly because of the fracas below in the hills.

It was almost like watching a war movie. The tiny radio and wafer playback dangled by its black cord from a hook inside the glass booth by the door. Listening to the music, he watched his city burn. It was either under attack by its own citizens or being besieged by an overly equipped and poorly organized National Guard. *The bombs bursting. The rockets' red glare* . . .

He shuddered, relieved knowing that in his own neighborhood life was still somewhat tranquil. And tomorrow was his day off. He made a mental note to catch Senator Randell's emergency State of the Nation speech tomorrow morning. There had been rumors circulating of some severe changes in Washington. There were rumors of a new President; rumors that Katie Babcock was missing, or assassinated, or that she had resigned. There was talk of suicide in high places. No one knew for certain, but everything was to be answered tomorrow by Senator Albertson Randell in a press conference that was to be broadcast worldwide.

He knew that something was up. But he didn't know what. No one did.

Lost in his thoughts, the lone security guard stood in a cone of diffused light before the only entrance to the film processing plant. He was thinking of the trucks that would be coming later that night for the latest prints of the movies, and he didn't notice the shadowed form of a man approach him from the side of the building. He hadn't seen anyone in hours, and his attention had lapsed as the night wore on.

The guard stepped out along the large cement steps to stretch himself just in time to see a fire engine scream down the street, waving its spectacular red and yellow lights in every direction.

The tall, shadowy form came up behind the guard just as the fire trucks passed by.

"One move, clown, and you're dead," the shadow said firmly through the filter of his filter-mask.

The guard jerked around to see a man—face concealed by a wide-brimmed slouch hat and filter-mask—who wore a long black coat that dropped all the way to his ankles. He held a vicious-looking machine pistol in his gloved hand.

"Just stay where you are," Lanier told the guard.

Lanier stepped quickly to the light, then tugged the security guard over to the glass booth, out of the reach of the light. Lanier yanked out the man's automatic and thrust him against the wall. He snapped down the radio from its perch and crushed it under his boot heel.

"What the hell is this?" The guard didn't know at first whether to giggle or to start shaking with terror. This man, he felt, whoever he was, wasn't one of those damn chicanos. *Some stupid punk, probably*.

The guard stared at him through the lenses of his filter-mask.

Lanier touched his right ear with a finger and a thumb. He spoke. "I got him. Come on down."

"What's going on? Who are you? You'll never..."

The guard felt foolish asking him questions. He was the one who should be providing the answers, with his gun. But the intruder had removed that possibility. *A robbery?* The guard knew that robberies were common in the film industry, particularly for its industrial secrets. That's why the security was so tight. *But*, he thought, *he'll never get through the front door....*

Lanier was strangely easy with the guard.

"Just stay out of sight," he told the man, "and no one will hurt you." Lanier was smiling mischievously behind the mouth-piece of his filter-mask. His goggled eyes made him resemble a creature out of Hell itself. The guard began quaking.

Suddenly, from overhead beyond the factory in the night sky, the guard heard a terrific roar. A VTOL, very military and very fast, came swooping like a gigantic predatory bird out of nowhere. It made a tumultuous landing on the street in front of White Condor Studios. Leaves, paper, and other debris scattered in all directions in the yellow light cast down by the streetlights. The craft bore the Seal of the President of the United States.

This isn't the National Guard, the security man realized, frightened. *Something is going on....*

A door on the side of the aircraft hurriedly cranked open and a dozen soldiers thundered out. They were Marine Rangers, hand-picked African War veterans for the President's own private squad.

After the troops swarmed out of the VTOL, whose engines were screeching down to a lower whine, a man with a briefcase came down the steps, followed by three U.S. Army officers. All were wearing oxygen-assisted filter-masks. Although the man with the briefcase was unarmed, the officers were not.

One of the Rangers ran up to Lanier, ahead of the three army officials.

"We're ready, sir," he said sternly behind his filter-mask.

The security guard began sweating. Lanier dragged him out from the shadows. Two other VTOLs dropped out of the sky. These were transports: more soldiers were inside.

"Now listen to me," Lanier said to the security guard. "We've shut down all communications within a two-mile radius of these studios. We've also jammed the airwaves, cut all cables. No calls can come in or go out. You're going to let us inside very peacefully and very willingly, or we'll blow the whole front side of the building down into Pasadena. The decision is yours."

The guard was staring into the eyes behind Lanier's goggles. Brown, flecked with dancing lights: calm, sure, powerful. He *would* blow the building if he had to. And perhaps with him in it.

From the two VTOLs that had just landed, infantry soldiers

were disgorged. A battery of guns from the VTOLs trained themselves on the building.

The security guard nervously stepped over to the glass booth and pressed several buttons and punched in computer lock codes. Ten automatic rifles and a number of handguns were trained on him.

The steel doors hummed apart and the assault troops rushed inside. Lanier followed them up the steps. He gestured to the three United States Army officers. They ran up to him, almost grateful for some action. Lanier pulled out the map.

"This is where the computer said it should be, Colonel. It's probably well guarded, or it just might be so inconspicuous that it could be out in the open. In either case"—he stared through the goggles of his filter-mask—"be careful. If they destroy it before we can get to it, the whole operation is off."

The Colonel nodded, pulling down his radio helmet. "That's what we're here for. Don't worry about a thing."

Lanier pulled the guard after him. He signaled two Rangers over, said to them: "This man is yours. He moves, give him a haircut."

Standing in the open door, Lanier waved to the presidential VTOL and the man with the briefcase at the base of the stepladder. A small group alighted from the aircraft. Meanwhile, soldiers stationed themselves about the grounds, running off into the darkness, digging in behind trees.

A man—a large man—with a full head of red hair came up to Lanier, drawing behind him a diminutive blonde. Both wore filter-masks, and they both intimidated the security guard who stood with his back against the wall, flanked by the two husky soldiers.

And behind everyone else came a slender woman and the man who carried the briefcase. They, too, wore filter-masks against the rank Los Angeles air.

The security guard was startled. It was the President. *Jesus Christ!* he thought.

Lanier held his Malachi, now loaded with a clip of bullets and not the harmless anesthetic needles.

"No funny stuff, bucko," he said. He tore off the guard's mask.

The President came up the steps to the studio, followed by Ken Collins. Charlie Gilbert and Christy let them pass inside.

Katie turned to Lanier.

"We've got to pull this off quickly. Albertson may or may not get wind of this, but I want this thing done right. He's got enough on his mind if he's taking over the country tomorrow."

Eyes of steel. The guard stared at Katie, uncomprehending as to what was happening. Everyone was ignoring him but the two guards, one on either side of him.

"We don't want him doing anything stupid," Katie concluded.

"He's already done a few stupid things," Lanier said underneath his filter-mask. "But we won't quibble."

Katie turned to the soldiers. "We start taking prisoners with this one here. Let's get inside and get this thing over with."

She looked back at Lanier.

"I hope that you're right about this," the President said, removing her filter-mask, now that they had entered the building. She immediately lit up a cigarette to calm her nerves.

"So do I," Lanier told her as they walked. He pulled off his filter-mask.

The air inside the factory was sweet and pure. It was completely filtered and processed.

"It'd better work," Lanier then said, as they walked briskly down the corridor. "But I don't see any reason why it shouldn't."

The President turned. Thirty soldiers had followed them into a large reception hall. She pointed to the lone security guard.

"Keep him here. The rest of you, fan out. You've got your instructions."

The warlord, Lanier thought.

Ahead of them, where the assault troops had penetrated, a small amount of turmoil and racket greeted them as they walked toward the main processing areas. They followed the map Lanier held.

The building was immense. More than a hundred people worked in the manufacturing studio at any one time. And most of the plant was underground. Above ground, it functioned like a fortress.

But Katie had managed to dig up the blueprints to the place through a special presidential code into DataCom, and with the help of Ken Collins, who was pleased and surprised at her return, they managed to keep the entire process a secret.

The Rangers had surprised most of the guards at the various check stations along the way. Those they couldn't take by surprise, they took by force. And the in-house camera surveillance system was no good without the security personnel to back it up. No hidden alarms were tripped.

The soldiers, followed by Lanier and the President, went down a flight of stairs into the first lower level of the plant where they came to the main processing room. Here, movie film was developed and duplicated. The Rangers had by now lined up the factory personnel against one wall.

The President walked into their midst with such an air of authority that everyone's eyes followed her. The lab personnel along the wall couldn't have been more surprised to see her. The Rangers bursting in with their filter-masks on and automatic rifles held out were a hard act to follow. But follow it she did.

Katie Babcock addressed them. "I don't want to hurt anybody. You probably aren't aware of it, but what you are doing is illegal. It's part of a conspiracy."

They looked at one another, their hands still in the air.

The President continued: "And if you *do* know it's illegal, it doesn't really matter. You won't be hurt by these gentlemen, but I'm afraid that you will be spending the night and most of tomorrow in this building."

Lanier marveled at the control she had over the situation. He knew that without her support in this matter, he wouldn't be able to accomplish what he had to do. Only the President could have gotten the plans to the building, being the only one to know the correct codes to DataCom at the Pentagon. And only the President could drum up the muscle to effect the break-in without tipping off either Albertson Randell or the Joint Chiefs.

The President of the United States turned to Lanier.

"You know where it is?"

"I wouldn't recognize it if I saw it, but the equipment is surely here." He gestured around him. "In this room somewhere."

He faced the line of workers. "Look," he announced. "You can lower your hands. If you cooperate, no one will be bothered. Now, who among you is the boss?"

A man wearing a stringy, loose tie and an open black vest stepped out of the line, rather belligerently.

"I am. I'm in charge here. What's this all about?"

Lanier motioned him over. "This is an official board of

inquiry by the President of the United States. We're here to either bust heads or make use of the Leander Interphase Translator. We want you to show us where it is, and we want you to show us *now*."

"I don't know what you're talking about," the small man said innocently.

Ken Collins came over and fingered the man. "Look. We know what's going on, and we want the Leander Translator or you're all going to jail. All the films that come out of this place are ingrained with it, and we can prove it. Give it to us or you'll never see the light of day again."

The crew boss suddenly didn't look innocent anymore. Everyone could read it in his eyes.

"I don't know of any..."

Lanier grabbed him and lifted him off the ground by the collar. He threw him against a desk. No one moved to stop him, not the Colonel, not the President.

"Listen, asshole—we'll tear the whole goddamn building down to find it. We know it's here and we've come to get it! You're bucking up against the United States Government. Give us what we want," and he pulled out the Malachi and stuck it in the man's mouth, "or I'll fill your teeth with lead."

The little man squirmed along the top of the desk, turning the color of mushrooms. He said, "OK, OK!", his lips trembling on the mouth of the Malachi. Perspiration dotted his forehead.

He looked back to the other employees in the factory for moral support. *Any* kind of support. They were wide-eyed and just as pale, empty of the will to resist.

Then a soldier ran into the room. He said, "Colonel Johannsen, we've shut down the entire factory. The place is surrounded and all the roads are blocked off. Lieutenants Moore and Melser are on the roof in a ScatterCat. We're secure."

"Good work," the Colonel said. The soldier disappeared back into the outer hall.

Everyone turned back to the little man. The weight of the moment settled about his shoulders. He seemed about to crumple.

"This way," he finally told them. He led everyone down a corridor.

The soldiers continued to hold the workers against the wall. Colonel Johannsen stepped back, allowing everyone to file into the hallway.

"In here," the crew boss said, pointing to a door with a "No Admittance" sign on it. The door was locked with an electronic combination lock.

"Go ahead. Open it," Lanier ordered the man.

"I don't have the combination," he said meekly. "The guy who has it won't be in until the morning."

Lanier turned to the Colonel, who had been carefully watching the proceedings.

"Colonel, you have someone to pick this lock for us? I'd rather not blow it open."

The Colonel nodded. He turned behind him. "Callahan! Over here!"

Callahan shouldered his rifle and ran into the hallway, threading his way through everybody.

"Yes, sir!"

"Can you get through this?"

Callahan walked among them like a kid spying a new toy at the toy store. Nothing mattered but the lock.

"Yes, sir. It's simple."

Ignoring everyone, he set his rifle against the wall. He pulled his pack from his back and laid its contents out on the floor.

He lifted a small gray box, which he put up against the combination lock.

Within seconds the combination appeared in bright red letters on the small screen of the box. He turned to the President.

"We're lucky this time," he said. "It could've just as easily been a voice-coded lock, but it wasn't." He smiled at her.

The door clicked open. Callahan stood up and let them pass inside.

The room was small, containing a complex array of equipment. Screens and computers lined one wall. The computer was presently inoperative. The main object of attention, though, occupied one whole wall opposite the computer. It was a movie screen. And just before the screen was a single-body contour couch. A compact machine stood at the left hand side of the couch, and from it led wires that were attached to a headband and two wrist bands.

Lanier gazed at the small machine. "That's it exactly."

The President turned to him. "How does it work?"

Charlie walked around the couch. Lanier faced him. "You know anything about this?"

Charlie nodded. "It's quite simple to operate."

Everyone looked at the Leander Translator as if it had been

a cobra, for they knew what it could do.

Charlie said, "It's an awesome weapon. I imagine that the Pentagon would want such a thing under wraps."

"Colonel." Katie turned to the officer, who stood in the doorway. "What do you think?"

The Colonel nodded. "I'm not aware that such a device ever came to our attention."

Charlie said, "It figures."

"So how does it work?"

Charlie pointed to the couch. "Someone, and it really could be just about anyone, lies on that couch and watches the film in question. The film"—he turned around, pointing to the projection booth—"comes from there." He looked back again at Lanier.

Lanier stood at the machine.

Charlie continued: "The individual's emotional responses are then recorded through the Interphase Translator, mastered onto the celluloid, and then the vibrations go out with the soundtrack when it's run through an ordinary projector."

Lanier was lost in thought. He turned to Katie. "It's my guess that the last person who sat here was Ellie Estevan. An actress with her personal power could invoke the proper emotional responses. It would be easy for her." He paused slightly. Everyone watched him. He continued. "Then, whoever controlled the process could magnify the emotional intensity of any given scene. Ten times or a thousand. What I encountered at the Watson Pueblo Theater was tremendous. The vibrations were subtle yet overpowering."

Christy had found the projection room door. They turned around when she switched on the lights. She found the microphone. The projection room was entirely soundproofed.

"OK in here," she said behind the window of the booth.

Ken Collins was beside her with his briefcase.

Katie turned back to Lanier, worried. "And can you do it with a recording as well?"

"Yes," Lanier told her. "It can be done on any recorded medium. What Randell has here is a perfect method to gauge and control the emotional states of anyone within reach of radio, television, or the movies. In this case, he's used it to amass a fortune through the movie industry—and he's kept the process totally secret. So, with the Syndrome bacterium causing so much personal disorder in the lives of people all over the world, who wouldn't want to go to the movies to bury his or her troubles?"

"Incredible!" Katie exclaimed. "I just can't understand how a thing like this works."

"Well," he said, "apparently it does. Randell had to be careful with the Interphase ingraining. I suspect that he kept the vibrations at a very low level. He couldn't have his audiences vanishing where they sat. First, that would attract suspicion. Second, he would stand to lose millions of dollars from his main source of income. No, he's not stupid at all."

Lanier turned to the crew boss. "Show us how it works and set it up." He faced the soldiers. "The rest of you can get out now. I'll need absolute quiet."

The small man hastened over to the machine, busying himself with the dials.

Everyone vacated the room but the President and Charlie Gilbert. Collins and Christy looked on from the windows of the projection booth.

"Where's the film you want to show?" the crew boss asked Lanier.

"Not film, but sonic-wafer." Lanier removed his long coat, keeping the shoulder holster and Malachi in place.

"What?"

Christy waved from the booth. Between her slender fingers she held the centimeter-square sonic-wafer. She slotted it into the console.

"We're using a sonic-wafer," Lanier told the little man. "We're going to ingrain my Interphase responses onto a recording."

The man looked at Lanier as if he were insane.

Lanier continued: "So you'll have to set the machine for the adjustment."

He lay down on the couch.

Quite reluctantly the crew boss attached the leads to Lanier's wrists. Then he rubbed some petroleum jelly on his temples for the headband contact points.

"Listen, you," Christy said to the crew boss through the microphone. "I've got the switchover down. Turn the machine there all the way up." She was adjusting a dial before her.

The boss looked at her, halting. He said, "Are you crazy? Do you know what that'll do?"

Christy smiled, settling back in the swivel chair at the board.

But Lanier wasn't smiling now. No one said anything.

"Go ahead," he told the man. "Do as you're told."

"Francis..." Katie started.

"Yes?"

"Are you sure this'll work?"

Lanier craned his eyes upward from the couch, looking at her. *The President of the United States*, he thought.

"There's no reason why not. I suspect that no one has tried the Leander Interphase at full capacity. No doubt they kept the intensity down when Ellie sat here recording her own responses. But still, they wouldn't have known."

Katie looked concerned.

"Collins?" Lanier spoke loud enough for Ken to hear through the microphone in the booth.

He leaned over Christy's shoulder into the board mike. "Yes, Francis."

"Don't screw up. Make several recordings. If Randell stops you, make sure that Colonel Johannsen has a copy. I don't want to spend the rest of my life alone."

And he meant it. No one knew what he was feeling. No one knew how close he had come to giving up. But the fragments of hope had been cast about him like broken bits of a china teacup. Slowly, though, the pieces had begun to fit. *Everything is connected*, as Two Moons often said.

Everything.

"Count on it," Collins reassured him.

"One other thing," Lanier told him. "And this includes you too, Christy. Turn off the audio in the booth. Watch the meters to see that the entire piece is played through. But I don't want anyone listening. If I understand things right, the Interphase is extremely powerful. Got it?"

"Got it," and she dimmed the lights.

"OK, I'm set." He turned to Katie Babcock and Charlie. "You two better get out now." He smiled. "And take care of yourselves."

She inhaled weakly. "Fran..."

Charlie held her arm. "It'll be all right. You'll see." He turned to the crew boss, who had completed the operation. "Let's go into the booth, friend. You've got a few more things to do."

And they left Lanier alone, with his thoughts, in the dark.

CHAPTER FIFTEEN

✦❦✦

Tintagel, Symphonic Poem
Sir Arnold Bax

That night in Lanier's Montana ranch house, they had all realized that the situation before them had reached crisis proportions. And they realized that its resolution went beyond the simple arrest and exposure of Albertson Randell. The deaths of Perry Eventide and Floyd Matkin proved as much. His arrest could not in itself undo everything he had caused, either directly or indirectly. Lanier had Ellie Estevan to think about. Someone had to pay for her destruction, somehow.

Moreover, they knew that if someone as stable as the President of the United States could succumb, then the political and environmental circumstances that prompted her disappearance were absolutely beyond anyone's capacity to deal with. That Senator Randell wanted the presidency only showed his overall irresponsibility. They realized that the man was clearly insane.

He only wanted to be on top, another King Croesus, the most powerful man in the world. He apparently had found a cure for Liu Shan's Syndrome, kept it to himself and his allies, and planned on keeping it out of the reach of the rest of the nation. And the world.

They had no proof before them, but it made sense.

And, in the time that Francis Lanier had journeyed to retrieve the President from the flying Shawnee, Charlie and Christy Gilbert had pieced most of it together. Lanier, torn by the unexpected death of Ellie Estevan, had figured out what they had missed.

And more, much more.

If it hadn't have been for his urge to drive into town to see *Halcyon Days*, he might not have stumbled onto their only workable solution. All the loose ends had suddenly, clearly, come together. Everything made sense, finally.

It wasn't enough to put Albertson Randell out of business. As they knew, there was no real incriminating association to be made between himself and the deaths of Eventide, Matkin, and Ellie Estevan. There was no way they could concretely demonstrate that Randell had intentionally authorized the use of the Leander Interphase Translator at the White Condor Studios. And it could have been pure coincidence that the Vice President was genuinely ill, sleeping in a coma, and that the Speaker of the House was missing or succumbed. And it could have been someone else who put a neutralizer in Katie Babcock's drink, making her succumb to Liu Shan's Syndrome.

Randell, of course, would make an apologetic show of bowing out gracefully when Katie and Ken Collins stomped into the worldwide telecast that Randell had scheduled for the next day. Everyone would be surprised and overjoyed that the President was back, and healthy. And Senator Randell would insist that he had to take firm measures while she was gone. He would be happy to step aside. He would be contrite. He would be humble.

But that wouldn't do, Lanier realized. All the problems that Katie Babcock faced—that they *all* ultimately faced—would still be with them. Some were surmountable. Most of them not.

And Lanier had hit on the solution by looking into the startled faces of the two air-marauding Indians and the other surviving Walkers who came out into the living room later that night with headaches and sore spots where the anesthetic needles were delicately dissolving into their skins.

"What if," Lanier had asked them excitedly, "there were

a world, a fabrication, that was composed of Walkers only? Or real people and not dreamlings? What if everyone could enter the *same* world when they succumbed to Liu Shan's Syndrome?"

They looked at him as if he had been driven over the edge by the crisis and the death of Ellie Estevan. He even looked older to them.

But it did make sense.

And so he found himself alone, lying on the contoured couch, wired in to the Leander Interphase Translator. *Alone*. Everyone was in the projection booth, staring into the darkness of the chamber before them.

In the few minutes left to Lanier before Christy engaged the sonic-wafer, the crew boss attended to the proper adjustment of the volume and intensity. Colonel Johannsen stood at his side with the business end of a .45 automatic aimed at his ribs.

Alone. Lanier could hear only the sound of his own breathing. Christy then engaged the sonic-wafer, and Lanier made a concerted effort to calm his mind like he never had before.

Tintagel. It was a symphonic poem he had heard only once before in his life. It was by Sir Arnold Trevor Bax, who died in the middle of the last century. The piece was obscure enough that if anyone heard *Tintagel* they would have no previous emotional ties to the work. It would make Lanier's task easier, make the transition much smoother than it would normally have been.

Tintagel . . .

And he thought. And he felt. He fell into the vibrations with the full force of his psyche. The emotion surged up through the shields of his consciousness. *Ellie. Marie*. The multitude of feelings poured out through the Leander Interphase Translator, following the beautiful strains of *Tintagel*, and were in turn transcribed onto the sonic-wafer slotted before Christy in the projection booth.

And as *Tintagel* played and translated Lanier's pitched emotional responses onto the sonic-wafer, he thought about that world. *Tintagel!*

It would be empty of people. The skies would be clean, free of pollutants, the winds would blow clear, and trees would grow where trees hadn't grown in decades. Oceans would be full of the lost herds of whales, and aeroplankton would only be a memory.

An untouched world. An untapped world, the riches of the earth buried and just waiting to be used, all over again. *This time in the right way...*

The music would allow for that world. It would be a tranquil world, and Lanier, with his mind and imagination, built that world. There would be cities, empty and waiting. As he floated in the music, he let the vibrations take their own course. And the music: he could see it before him.

The cities were smaller, more efficient. Everywhere. There would be fewer people to inhabit them. There would be fewer roads, fewer markings upon the land. Everything in proper order. Harmonious, like the music.

And, for the first time in years, he longed for such serenity, such pastoral beauty, just like the worlds he had entered for Matkin and Eventide. Even Ellie Estevan within her hemisphere almost had it right. They knew what it took to bring them to peace. For the point was, why stay in the worst of all possible worlds? *Why?*

So, Lanier yearned to make the world complete. He yearned for perfect clouds of silver and white up against a bright blue sky. He yearned for the stars to be uncluttered by smoke and haze. No more radioactive wastes buried in salt domes or in storage vaults. No more mutant diseases like the bacterium that caused the Syndrome itself. It would be a new world entirely. And it would be built from scratch.

His emotions peaked. His heart beat in time to the music. For the first time in years, he wanted things to be perfect.

And he succumbed to *Tintagel*.

And dropped onto the grassy slope of the hill behind his small ranch in Montana. Broad afternoon. December. The air was crystal clear and snow lay in patches on the ground, absolutely white and pure. He could feel the calmness. He could feel the world empty of the people yet to come. Missoula, just kilometers down the road, was smaller, and waiting patiently.

And, moreover, he couldn't hear the music—*Tintagel*—any longer. The music had vanished along with the former world. His heart raced with keen excitement. He had made it! He no longer had the disease, no longer had to sustain his mantra, no longer needed the music.

This world was now the real world.

A cold wind brushed up against him, and he realized that he was without his coat. He had come into this world as he had left the other one. He ran down to his ranch. Autumn and winter were his favorite seasons; seasons not of death, but of survival. They were seasons he had missed living in Los Angeles selling his worthless pieces of real estate, seasons he often felt gave meaning to his life.

But that was in another world, many years ago.

And, he realized, this would be a good year. If Collins pulls it off. A good year for everyone involved.

At eight o'clock, Eastern Standard Time, the reporters of the remaining news agencies and newspapers waited that morning for Senator Albertson Randell, acting President, to enter the White House press room. Cameras and sound equipment had already been set up by the technical staff, and everyone waited tensely, mulling over among themselves the various rumors that had brought them there.

In the director's booth at the rear of the large room, a handful of men, wearing headsets and speaking in low voices, coordinated the proceedings, counting down the seconds to go before air time. The news conference was being telecast around the globe. And where video didn't reach, radio did. Randell had seen to it that the satellite connections were functioning well; at least as best they could under the circumstances.

The statistical projections for the press conference audience held that over three hundred million people had direct access to television facilities, not including radio. Since most businesses and industries were temporarily at a standstill, the experts couldn't predict just how many people would be watching. As it was, many cities in both America and Europe were without electricity: some were on fire. Mexico City was a nuclear holocaust. Its war with Venezuela was over. Tokyo was gone. Peking smoldered in its ruins. Moscow was incommunicado.

But the rest of the world waited for Albertson Randell's announcement.

Five minutes before press time, Ken Collins and Colonel David Johannsen, along with several members of the Secret Service, loyal CIA, and a number of armed military personnel, strode down the hall briskly toward the control booth.

The soldiers dropped back in pairs behind them, taking up key positions in the White House corridors. Since Ken Collins was still the presidential press secretary, everyone let him pass.

He entered the control booth, quietly. The director turned around and smiled. "Well, hey, Ken! Good to see you back!"

Collins held the door open for the head of the Secret Service to climb through.

The director nodded a greeting to him. "Mr. Rushton, come on in." He had been working all morning long with most of the White House technical staff, but hadn't expected the head of the Secret Service himself to show up.

"How are things going, Bob?" Collins asked the director with his most congenial smile.

"Great. We've five minutes to show time. We missed you here. The last couple of days have been like a Chinese fire drill. No one knew what was up. Things are quieter now." He smiled at everyone from his swivel chair.

"Well," Ken began softly, "there's been a slight change in plans."

"OK. What's the scoop?"

Ken said, "While the conference is going on, I want you to run the video and run this over the audio."

He held out a small sonic-wafer. "We want you to cut out the sound transmission of the press conference as soon as Randell goes on and play this instead."

The director looked at the sonic-wafer of *Tintagel*, confused. "I don't understand. This isn't in the . . ." and he began leafing back his program notes on his clipboard.

"Do it," Rushton ordered. Two Secret Service men pulled out their service revolvers and held them on the director.

"What's going on?"

Collins was careful. He had known Robert Dobbins as the director and coordinator for all White House media facilities for a number of years. As press secretary, he had worked with Dobbins closely. They were slightly more than acquaintances or business partners.

Collins looked out of the beveled windows of the control booth down into the press room to make sure no one on the outside saw what was going on on the inside.

"Now, take it easy, Bob," he said. "This is all on the up and up. Believe me. The President wants it. In fact, ordered it," he smiled. "Ordered it herself."

"Katie . . . ?"

One of the assistant coordinators beside Bob Dobbins, wearing a set of earphones and a pin-mike, said, "Thirty seconds, please. Standby."

No one else moved. The assistant looked sheepishly over at the director. The Secret Service men held their guns low, out of sight.

Collins handed Dobbins the wafer. Rushton looked on.

"The President?" Dobbins asked, puzzled. "She's all right? It says here that . . ." He had the text of Randell's startling announcement before him. "But I don't understand."

"You don't have to," Rushton said. "It's all been taken care of. Just play it over the audio. And don't let those inside hear it either."

"Ten seconds. Cue camera one."

The director turned to the microphone. The assistant counted down the seconds. Bob Dobbins switched it on.

"Ladies and Gentlemen—the President of the United States."

The Seal of the President filled the television screens on the console before them. Albertson Randell came out from behind the curtains at stage left and stood before the gathered news-people. He dwarfed the podium that had originally been con-structed for the smaller Katie Babcock. He kept the podium for effect.

Dobbins then took the sonic-wafer from Ken's outstretched palm and slotted it into the board, throwing three switches as he did. He glanced back at Collins, questioningly, and Ken stared at him, nodding. The only people who heard what Al-bertson Randell had to say were the press audience. *Tintagel* began playing back through the earphones of the technicians at the control booth. It was on audio as well, so Ken and the Secret Service agents could hear it.

"Now—" Bob Dobbins squared off. "Mind telling me what this is all about?" He pointed to the sonic-wafer of *Tintagel*.

Collins ignored him for a moment, watching instead how the press corps was taking Randell's announcement. Everyone inside the press room began looking at one another, amazed and perplexed. Randell had just announced that he was assum-ing the presidency. Permanently.

"Yes," Ken said, hearing the opening chords of *Tintagel* flood the control booth. The emotional patterns of Francis Lan-ier were imprinted on the recording so strongly that everyone was beginning to become overwhelmed by the music. Baktropol couldn't prevent anything from happening now. The Leander Interphase ingraining would nullify any preventative except a downright cure.

Suddenly one of the Secret Service men vanished with a resounding *pop!* Bob Dobbins swung around. Rushton only stared, knowingly. Then he himself vanished. The last expression in his eyes was not one of recognition, but one of mesmerization. The music enthralled them all. The Interphase, ingrained at its most intense level, was working.

Collins said to the director, fighting the music for a few minutes more, "I want this on constant broadcast. Put it on automatic. Can you do it?"

Bob Dobbins' eyes glazed.

"Bob!"

He snapped out of it. "Yes, sure. But why?"

Dobbins' assistant controller suddenly vanished, his headset dropping to the chair cushion.

"We're moving," Ken said with a smile.

"I don't understand . . ." but Dobbins shut down the console anyway, switching over to automatic replay. "We're on for as long as you like."

Good, Collins thought. *It'll be up to NASA to hold on to the transmission after the wafer stops playing here.*

He knew that the satellites would broadcast the piece for as long as possible all around the world, wherever radios and televisions were picking up Albertson Randell's historic takeover of the United States.

The reporters began to panic. Soldiers—the new White House elite guard—ran into the room. Collins watched impassively. His skin was beginning to tingle. His spine shuddered with what seemed to be a thousand watts of electricity.

Bob Dobbins, staring wide-eyed, suddenly vanished.

Ken let go of himself, falling into the music. It would be several minutes before someone realized what was going on in the control booth. But that's all the time it would take. By then, millions would be gone. *Transferred.*

And he vanished on the spot. The control room stood empty as the sonic-wafer, locked into the repeat position, played on and on.

Lanier, wrapped in his Arctic parka, stood beside an old cane chair on his front porch. The lights in the surrounding

Bitterroot Valley were, one by one, winking on. As were those in Missoula.

They're arriving, he thought. *They're coming home.*

Christy's voice came from the living room through the door. "Fran, it's the President. She's on the horn."

He slowly turned around and came in from outdoors.

On the videophone, Katie Babcock's face, haloed in the usual aura of cigarette smoke, came smiling through.

"So," she said. "How's it feel to be unemployed?"

He smiled thinly, relieved. No one suffered from Liu Shan's Syndrome anymore. And no one needed to fear music because of it.

"It feels fine, Katie."

She grinned. "We've got some more reports for you."

"Let's hear them."

She reached beside her, drawing up a few sheets of printout. She almost resembled a newscaster, and had been collecting reports all day long such as it was.

"Our projections show that we can retrieve just under one billion of the world's population." She beamed as she spoke. "It turns out that much of South America and the Orient, despite their own troubles, were tuned in. We don't think Africa caught the broadcast, but there might be isolated pockets that'll show up later. We're getting an excellent response from all the major Indian reservations, particularly the Navajo and Hopi. I guess all they do is watch television or listen to the radio anyway. And one other thing happened."

"What's that?"

"You have this thing for buffalo?"

"Not particularly. Why?"

"It seems as if South Dakota, Wyoming, and parts of Nebraska are covered with buffalo."

Lanier laughed. "Good. Let's give them back to the Indians."

Katie was pleased. "But," she began, "some parts of the country are completely uninhabited. Did you do it on purpose?"

Lanier squinted into the videophone. "No. Not at all. I tried to make it so that anyone who heard the music would return to their same region. Why? What's missing?"

She consulted another sheet of computer paper. "We're missing most of the southeast; Los Angeles and all of southern California are also gone. There's an enormous bay where L.A. used to be. We think that you must've feared the big quake due the area, and dreamed one in. In any case, that part of the country must have been completely cut off by the fighting by the time we got out of there and this morning when we set things up in Washington." She shook her head. "And it's too bad."

Lanier was saddened. He had a number of acquaintances who apparently wouldn't be coming here.

Katie went on: "Ken has given me some further projections. In about two days' time, the influx will decrease rapidly. There will be fewer and fewer people to man the transmissions, the radio stations, and the like. In about five days, all those who're going to come will be here." She sat back, tossing the papers before her. "And no more Albertson Randell."

The Iron Lady, he thought. *The warlord. Chew 'em up and spit 'em out.*

But it was as he suspected. The only people who would remain were those who had no access to media, and those who had the cure. They would be trapped back there. With a significant portion of the earth's population now gone, the rest of civilization wouldn't be able to hold up. Even without the transfer, Lanier knew that civilization wouldn't have lasted more than a few years anyway.

"We have a whole new world to explore and rebuild," Katie Babcock said softly over the videophone. "If our economy can recover and reorganize in time, we'll be the first to start things right."

Lanier looked at her. "That was the agreement. This is our only chance not to screw things up." He thought of the clean rivers now running through Ohio, the clear sky over London, and the open-pit mines that had only forests and fields above them. *That's the way it should be.*

"And it seems," she concluded, "that you gave us another fusion facility in upstate New York. That makes three now."

Lanier nodded, not really knowing the full scope of his changes.

"Well, Katie, keep me posted," he told her. "I'm taking a few years off for a vacation to see just what I've done."

"Take as many as you want," she said. "And . . . Fran?"

"Yes?"

"Stay in touch." Her image faded. Her smile was the last to go.

Christy and Charlie were poking at the chips in a fire they

had started in the fireplace, and everything surrounded them with an air of coziness that neither had known for some time.

Christy stood up. "Oh, Fran. This is the best thing to happen."

Lanier tried to smile, but felt drawn inside.

She went on: "I only wish that . . ."

Lanier gently waved her off, smiling. "We have enough wishes for now. Most are working out."

Charlie and Christy looked at him. Charlie said, "Why not stay inside tonight? Relax."

Lanier lifted up the hood of his parka.

"No, Charlie. I'm fine. I just need to walk a few things off tonight. I'll be gone a while."

"Well, we'll be here when you get back," Christy said.

Lanier smiled at his friends. "That's the best news yet."

CHAPTER SIXTEEN

⚜

Coda

He stepped back out onto the porch.

The sunset on this, the first day of their world, had been glorious. And now the stars shimmered and twinkled as if the night sky had been raked with a billion bits of shattered glass. It was pure, intense, and brilliant. As he walked out onto the dirt road before his house, the stars were so bright that they cast shadows all around him. He almost wished that Charlie and Christy were out here to share it with him. But they had each other inside beside the fire. . . .

As he stood there on the country lane, far from the golden glow of the curtained living room window, he wondered about the balance. *Fudd-Smith's Law.* Good old Two Moons. You can't have your cake and eat it too.

Even here it works. He looked up at the street sign that used to say LYNCH LANE and DALLAS ROAD, that now read in this new world, BABA AVENUE and WITSCHEL WAY. Even among the changes, the balance had to be struck. Even here, on this small corner of the world.

He stood in the darkness and starlight thinking of Ellie Estevan, thinking of her death, the sacrifice. It made all things equal. *But,* he wondered, *was it too much—or was it merely enough?*

He didn't know. There were no more questions. There were no more answers. And this was what he had to accept. And accept it he did.

Digging his hands deeper into the pockets of his parka, he walked on down the road under the tough old stars.